Having My Baby

Theresa Ragan

ISBN: 1477501932
ISBN-13: 978-1477501931

DEDICATION

For Jesse, Joey, Morgan and Brittany.
I am the luckiest mom in the world.

ACKNOWLEDGMENTS

Editor: Cathy Katz

Proofreader: Faith @ The Atwater Group

Beta Readers: Janet Katz, Sally Chamberlain, Brittany Ragan

CHAPTER 1

Derrick Baylor left his mom, dad, and siblings in the backyard and headed inside his parents' house. All he wanted was a couple of ibuprofen and a few minutes to himself, but the moment he walked through the side door, what he got instead was a high-pitched shrill that pierced his skull and made him forget all about the pain in his right knee.

Bypassing the kitchen, he made his way toward the noise, favoring his bad leg now that no one could see him. He'd been tackled by the best in the NFL: Hawk, Sims, and Lawson. A little knee injury wasn't going to take him out of the upcoming season.

The awful sound was coming from his old bedroom. He opened the door, frowning when he saw a portable crib in the middle of the room, the room he planned to sleep in tonight. He leaned over the crib. The baby looked fine: No horrible smells. Nobody bothering it.

He'd been thinking about babies a lot lately, he realized, as he watched the squirming infant. And when he thought about babies he also thought about love and marriage and Maggie. He would be thirty soon. Women weren't the only ones with a biological clock ticking away like a time bomb.

As he watched the baby, he found himself hoping his tiny niece would stop crying. Not because the sound bothered him, but because it scared him. *Was she in pain?*

At closer view, he realized babies were, indeed, sort of scary. They were fragile and wiggly. Hopefully somebody would come to the rescue. If he picked the kid up, he might accidentally hurt her. Footballs he could handle—babies, not so much.

"Wahhhhhhhhh."

Damn.

Besides wanting the ibuprofen, he'd come inside to get away from his adopted brother and supposed friend, Aaron, and Aaron's new fiancée, Maggie: the girl Derrick was supposed to marry someday—not Aaron. Maggie had lived across the street when he was growing up. Maggie was his neighbor, his girl, his future wife—not Aaron's.

He had learned recently that Aaron and Maggie were planning to be married before a Justice of the Peace, sooner rather than later. Apparently, they had recently moved in together too.

Derrick thought he could handle this little party his mother threw together in celebration of Aaron and Maggie's engagement, but he was wrong. Seeing them together made him tense, made him feel things he didn't want to feel.

"Wahhh. Wahhhhhhhh."

Garrett, his second brother to marry so far, was the first to have a baby. Garrett was making them all look bad, making it appear as if finding a soul mate was easy. Finding a soul mate was like looking for a lost diamond on a twenty-mile stretch of crowded beach. Impossible.

Many of his friends thought they had found "their other half" and now they were divorced.

The baby continued to cry. Her name was Bailey. It could have been worse. His brother and sister-in-law could have named her Apple or Saturn. Bailey was lying on her stomach but that didn't seem to affect her vocal cords. "There, there," Derrick said as he reached inside the crib and lamely patted her back.

She cried harder.

"A screecher, huh?" he said as he leaned forward and looked her over, trying to figure out how he was going to pick her up. He was number five of ten kids. He'd held his share of babies before, but mostly when he was younger. He was out of practice, that's all.

The baby's head was the size of a large peach or maybe a really small melon. It even had light fuzz on the top of its skull. He touched the top of Bailey's head, felt a divot, and yanked his hand back.

Her screaming increased an octave.

"I was only trying to make you feel better." He sighed. "But don't worry, I get it…you're a girl and that's what girls do best…they make lots of noise."

"Very funny," a female voice said from the doorway.

He looked over his shoulder, surprised to see Maggie standing there watching him with those big blue eyes of hers. Her arms were crossed in front of her, her blonde hair all shiny and soft around the top of her shoulders. He'd been avoiding her all day. And now he knew why. Looking at her made his gut twist and his heart ache.

"She won't stop crying," he said to get his mind on other things. "What's wrong with her?"

Maggie's smile made it all the way to her eyes.

"Did you try changing her diaper?" she asked.

"Now who's the funny one?"

Maggie moved to his side, leaned over the side of the crib and picked Bailey up as if she wasn't as fragile as she looked.

"Kris asked me to check on her. Do you want to hold her?"

He took a step back. "Do bears like to dance?"

"I'm sure they do," she said with a smile.

"Bears do not like to dance," he informed her. "They like to eat people."

"Fine," she said as she took the baby to the changing table. "Bears like to eat people. Are you going to help me change her, or are you going to go back to sulking instead of celebrating like everybody else?"

"I think I'll go back to sulking, thanks." He watched Maggie for a moment, remembering the good times they shared when they were kids. He and his brothers used to play flag football in the street with Maggie. She was one of the boys back then. It was hard to wrap his mind around the idea that Aaron had gone and proposed to her after they had all vowed to keep away.

Vows did not have an expiration date. Nobody could have Maggie—it was only fair.

Back then, every male within a five-mile radius had a crush on Maggie.

Derrick knew he should let it go. He was an adult, all grown up. He should be happy for his friend and adopted brother, but he wasn't. He felt betrayed. Derrick headed for the door, but he wasn't quick enough. Mom showed up and stopped him before he could escape.

"There you are," Mom said. Her gaze swept past him and zeroed in on the baby. "Oh, there's my precious itty bitty baby girl. How is she?"

"She's just like her aunts," Derrick said. "She's a crybaby."

Mom laughed and then reached out toward the baby before she realized her hands were full. "Here," she said, handing Derrick a stack of mail as she passed by.

"What's this?"

"Every time you move, your mail slowly trickles back here."

Derrick shuffled through the pile of mail.

"There's a letter from CryoCorp that came in the mail months ago," Mom said. "I thought they had the wrong address, so I wrote 'return to sender' and put the envelope back in the mailbox, but the letter came back the other day."

"What is CryoCorp?" Maggie asked.

Derrick found the envelope, put the rest of the mail to the side, and opened the letter. He was too busy reading to answer Maggie's question.

Dear Mr. Baylor,

As you know, CryoCorp is a leading provider of human semen…

Yeah, he knew that, but that didn't stop his heart from skipping a beat.

Our staff is made up of professionals eager to help our clients achieve realistic family goals through an excellent semen selection and confidential, personal counseling.

I know. I know. He skimmed to the last paragraph as he wondered why CryoCorp would contact him after all these years. His semen couldn't possibly still be usable, could it? Besides, years ago he had sent a letter asking to be removed as a donor. Going to CryoCorp was a stupid move on his part, something he'd done for the money before thinking things through.

Here at CryoCorp we strive to enable recipients to attain their goals. Therefore, we would like to thank you for your donation and for helping to make dreams come true.

Making dreams come true? His heart rate kicked up another notch as he read back over part of the text.

The recipient of your sperm has met all required standards.

"This is ridiculous," he said aloud. "Years ago I sent CryoCorp a letter telling them to remove me from their donor list. I even sent their money back."

His mother was too busy with the baby to notice the panic in his voice, but Maggie didn't miss a beat. She was at his side before he could curse under his breath again. She took the letter from him and when she finished reading it, she pinned him with a look he couldn't decipher. "You donated your sperm?"

He nodded, but he didn't appreciate the accusing look in her eyes: as if he'd given something away that didn't belong to him. "Do you have a problem with that?"

She opened her mouth, closed it, then opened it again. "Of course not," she said. "But obviously *you* do. Did you donate your sperm to CryoCorp, or not?"

"Maybe."

She huffed, sending wisps of blonde hair flying about.

"Mom," she said over her shoulder. "Would you help me get a straight answer out of him?"

Derrick frowned. "Since when do you call my mom, Mom?"

"Since forever," she said, clearly angry with him now.

Their gazes locked and some sort of weird staring war ensued until he purposely let his gaze fall downward, past her small upturned nose and onward to her perfectly formed lips. He'd kissed those lips before. Long before any stupid vows were made, he had kissed her. But it was their last shared kiss he remembered now. He'd never forget that kiss for as long as he lived.

His mother, baby in hand, must have picked up on the tension in the room because suddenly she stepped between them. "Don't do this, Derrick."

He raised a hand in frustration. "What did I do this time?"

"You're creating drama again," his younger brother, Jake, said from the doorway.

Derrick looked over at the door and glared at Jake. "Who asked you?"

"I've been standing here long enough to see that you're up to your old tricks. Maggie belongs to Aaron, your friend and mine…our brother. Remember him? They're engaged and this is an engagement party. Maggie picked Aaron, not you. Get over it."

"Stop it," Maggie said. She held up the letter from CryoCorp. "Derrick has a problem."

"Tell us something we don't know," Jake added in a lazy drawl.

"Now, Jake. That's enough," Mom said, prompting Derrick to smirk at his brother. A childish reaction he'd admit, but one he chose to blame on the fact that he was back home with all of his siblings, not to mention Maggie and Aaron, all under the same roof, everybody pretending to be perfectly fine with the way things turned out. He never should have come.

"What does the letter say?" Mom asked.

Maggie looked at Derrick. "Mind if I read this aloud?"

"Be my guest." Growing up with a big family in a small house meant there was no such thing as privacy. No reason to try and keep secrets when he knew full well they'd all find out what was going on sooner or later.

"It appears," Maggie said, "that years ago Derrick donated sperm. Apparently that sperm has been chosen by recipient 3516A."

Jake snorted. "No kidding. How long does sperm last?"

"There's no expiration on frozen sperm," Maggie said as she skimmed the contents of the letter for a second time.

Derrick's jaw dropped.

Jake laughed.

"I went to CryoCorp before I was drafted by the Los Angeles Condors," Derrick explained. "I was in desperate need of cash. I also sold my blood back then."

"Why didn't you come to us for help?" Mom asked.

"You and Dad had financial problems of your own at the time and don't forget you always had a zillion kids running around here."

"What made you change your mind about CryoCorp?" Maggie asked.

Derrick remembered perfectly well his reasons for changing his mind, but didn't feel the need to tell everyone that he thought about his future a lot. The thought of having biological children out there who didn't know him hadn't felt right. He had come to the conclusion that if he ever had children of his own, he wanted to be a part of their lives. Nothing against families who needed donors; without sperm donors, many couples would never realize their dream of having a family. For Derrick, though, it just wasn't something he was ready to do. "I changed my mind," he finally said, "that's all."

"Do you have a copy of the letter you sent CryoCorp asking to be removed from their donor program?" Maggie asked.

"I don't know." Derrick thought of all the boxes piled in his garage at his home in Malibu an hour away. The chances of finding a copy of the letter were one in a million. The computer he'd originally used was long gone.

"If you have proof that you sent the letter," Maggie went on, "we have options."

"*We* do?"

She nodded.

Derrick had only seen Maggie on a few occasions since she left for college. He'd heard through the grapevine that she'd decided to go to law school, but he hadn't been able to imagine it. Maggie used to be a goofball, the kind of girl who climbed trees and rolled in the mud. She didn't have a serious bone in her body. But watching her now—back straight, eyes unblinking, serious voice—she had *lawyer* written all over her.

"I'll call CryoCorp first thing in the morning," Maggie said. "I'll tell them we have a copy of the letter you sent and that we insist they cease and desist from any further use of your sperm." She chewed on her bottom lip. "The only problem," she added, "will be if 3516A has already become impregnated."

Jake chuckled and before Derrick could usher him out of the room and really give his brother something to laugh about, Aaron and three more of Derrick's siblings squeezed into the bedroom to see what all the excitement was about.

Aaron came through the door first. His hand slid around Maggie's waist in a protective gesture as he turned to Derrick. "What's going on?"

"Looks like we might have another baby to add to the chaos," Jake said.

Derrick's dad, Phil, was the last one to push his way through the door. "Who's having a baby?"

Phil looked Maggie up and down, prompting Maggie to raise her hands in surrender. "It's not me," she said as she handed him the letter. "It's Derrick."

They all hovered around Phil as he read the letter aloud. After he finished, it was blessedly quiet for a minute.

And then the teasing began in earnest. And the baby began to cry. And a fierce pain shot up from Derrick's knee, making him realize that if he didn't get out of here soon, he was going to suffocate.

CHAPTER 2

Three Months Later

Across the street from Chandler Park in downtown Burbank, Derrick sat in his BMW and watched for any sign of a pregnant woman. He opened the window. A cool end-of-May breeze carried in the scent of newly cut grass.

With the help of a private investigator, he'd finally dug up information on 3516A, also known as Jill Garrison. He didn't have a picture of the woman, but he knew Jill Garrison was five foot four, with brown hair and green eyes, and weighed in at 120 pounds.

CryoCorp had told Maggie that they had no record of the letter Derrick had sent asking to be removed as a donor and therefore, CryoCorp refused to dole out any information regarding their client, 3516A. If it hadn't been for the investigator he hired, Derrick wouldn't be here now watching three women run after too many children to count.

After arriving at Jill Garrison's apartment this morning, it only took a few minutes to learn from a neighbor that she was at Chandler Park helping a friend with a birthday party.

Maggie had advised Derrick to stay away from the woman. There were legalities to sort out, she'd said, but Derrick didn't listen. He still didn't know whether or not 3516A, aka Jill Garrison, had become impregnated, and he wasn't going to be able to sleep until he knew the truth.

Derrick kept his gaze on the closest woman. She was blowing bubbles and making the kids laugh. They all ran after her, trying to catch the bubbles in their hands. Tall and slender, wearing a red jumpsuit, her long red hair glistened in the sun. The woman in red was not only too tall to be Jill, she was not a brunette and she wasn't pregnant.

A few feet away from the bubble blower, another woman entertained the kids by playing red light, green light.

Derrick lifted his Ray-Bans for a better look: brown-hair with lots of untamed curls and long legs—much too tall to be Jill Garrison.

The third and last woman was the lady in blue: blue T-shirt, blue tennis shoes, and a blue floppy hat that covered her face and hair. She was reading a book to a couple of younger children and it was impossible to tell the color of her hair or how tall she was until one of the kids began crying, forcing the lady in blue into action.

He squinted into the sun. The lady in blue had black hair—no, make that brown. She wore a pair of white short shorts. He guessed her height to be five-foot-four.

Bingo.

She was petite and definitely *not* pregnant.

Tension left his shoulders and neck. He could breathe again. Life was good.

Children's laughter lifted his spirits as he laid his head back on the headrest, slid on his sunglasses, and shut his eyes. Just the idea of becoming a father made him feel claustrophobic, not because he didn't want a child but because he wasn't ready. Guys needed to be prepared for this sort of thing. Besides, he preferred to have a child the traditional way—after he married the mother of his child. He chuckled to himself at the realization that he'd resorted to spying.

What the hell was he thinking? What would he have done if he'd run into a pregnant Jill Garrison. Ha! Maggie was right. He never should have come.

A couple of *rap tap taps* on the passenger window got his attention. He sat up. A glimpse into the rearview mirror revealed a police car parked behind him. An officer leaned low and tapped on his passenger window again.

Derrick pushed the button on the side of his door and the window slid downward. "How can I help you, officer?"

"Please step out of the vehicle, sir."

Confused, Derrick did as the officer asked. He then stepped around the front of the car and onto the sidewalk. Two women stood behind the officer. It was the bubble blower and another woman he hadn't noticed before. Her brown hair was tied back in a ponytail and her back was to him. The two women huddled together and whispered so he couldn't hear what they were saying.

Derrick slid off his Ray-Bans, hooked them on the front of his shirt, and waited for the officer to finish scribbling on his notepad.

This time when the officer looked at him, his jaw dropped. The officer pointed his pencil at him. "You're Derrick Baylor, quarterback for the Los Angeles Condors."

"That's right." Derrick offered his hand. "What can I do for you?"

"Officer Matt Coyle," the officer said as he pumped Derrick's hand. "I'd appreciate it if I could get your autograph. My sons are big fans."

"Not a problem."

"Officer, please!" the redhead interrupted.

Give the lady in red a devil's fork, Derrick thought, and the picture would be complete.

Officer Coyle cleared his throat. "These ladies," he said gesturing toward the women, "noticed you've been parked here for quite some time. Frankly, they were concerned about the children's safety."

The bubble blower turned toward Derrick, plunked both hands on her hips and looked him square in the eye, clearly *not* impressed by his celebrity status. The other woman merely threw a worried glance over her shoulder, which told him she was the guilty party, the one who had called the cops.

Derrick stepped past the officer and toward the ladies. "I'm sorry. I should have made my introductions sooner."

The redhead narrowed her eyes. If looks could kill, Derrick would have fell over and died right there on the sidewalk.

"I came here looking for Jill Garrison," Derrick said.

The brown-haired woman turned about, her eyes wide. "I'm Jill," she said.

She stood at about five foot four. Brown hair. Green eyes. "Holy shit."

Her eyes narrowed. "Pardon me?"

"Holy shit," he said again, slower this time as his gaze fixated on her enlarged belly.

Bubble Blower grabbed her friend's arm as if pulling her out of harm's way. "Officer," she said. "Mind giving us a little help here?"

"Mr. Baylor," the officer said, "have you ever met either of these women?"

Derrick's mind was numb, but somehow he managed to say, "No. Never."

"You're making the ladies nervous, and truthfully, you've got me wondering too—what is your business with this woman?"

Derrick pried his gaze from the woman's stomach and raised his eyes to Jill's. "She's having my baby."

Jill Garrison dropped her hands to her belly. "Excuse me?"

"You're having my baby," he said again and yet he wasn't really sure if he'd said anything at all. A foggy mind and thick tongue weren't helping matters. For months now he'd wondered if there was a woman out there somewhere who was pregnant with his baby. One day he'd feel excited by the thought and the next day he'd feel nothing but dread. His emotions had been running high. At the moment he didn't know what to think or what to feel, but that didn't stop his heart from thumping hard against his chest.

The officer scratched his jaw. "I thought you said you'd never met the woman."

"That's right. I haven't."

"Then how could she be having your baby?"

"It's a long story."

"I have time," the officer said as he tucked his notebook away. "How about you ladies?"

Bubble Blower crossed her arms and tapped her foot. "Definitely."

Derrick couldn't keep his eyes off the woman named Jill.

Could she truly be carrying his baby?

Judging by the terrified look in her eyes, she could be. She looked regal in appearance: flawless skin, every hair in place, chin tilted upward, stiff and unbending. His gaze lowered to her ring finger. Nothing there. She wasn't married, which he figured was a good thing—one less person to deal with.

Derrick shifted his weight from his bad leg to his good leg and started at the beginning. "About six years ago I became a donor to a company called CryoCorp. Eighteen months later, I sent them a letter asking them to remove me as a potential client. Three months ago I received a letter from CryoCorp telling me recipient 3516A, aka Jill Garrison, had selected me as a donor. And here I am."

Jill Garrison's face paled and her legs wobbled. The woman was going down. Derrick leapt forward and caught her in his arms before she hit the ground. He held her limp body, glad to see she was still breathing.

"Officer!" Bubble Blower cried out, clearly appalled by the sight of him holding her friend. "Do something."

Officer Coyle headed for his vehicle.

Across the street, the long-legged woman and the lady in blue rounded up the kids. Derrick had an audience.

"Stay calm everyone," Officer Coyle said. "There's an ambulance on the way."

"Hey, Hollywood!" one of the older kids shouted to Derrick. "Can I get your autograph?"

The lady in the floppy hat quickly ushered the kids toward the picnic bench where the balloons swayed to and fro.

A sharp pain shot up from Derrick's knee. Jill Garrison's full weight was not helping matters. He headed for his car. Bubble Blower followed close behind, stabbing a sharp fingernail into his back. "What do you think you're doing?"

"If you could open the back door," Derrick said, "I'll lay your friend on the backseat."

"Oh, no you don't. You could be another Ted Bundy for all I know."

"My name is Derrick Baylor. I play for the Los Angeles Condors. The officer and the kid across the street can vouch for me, or would you rather hold her yourself?" He turned toward her, but she raised her hands in protest and then rushed to open the car door.

Derrick set his bum knee on the floor between the back and front seats and laid her down on the seat without any jarring movements. As he tried to pull his arm out from beneath Jill Garrison's head, she reached out for him, curling her arms around his neck.

~~~

Jill released a contented sigh. Thomas had come for her. He was holding her in his arms, making her feel as if she was floating in air as he carried her over the threshold. Thomas leaned over and set her on the bed. Afraid he might leave too soon, she reached for him and wrapped her arms around his neck.

Then she kissed him.

Thomas seemed tentative at first. His mouth felt firmer and hotter than she remembered, bordering on dangerous as he finally seemed to let himself go, enjoying the moment. The kiss was thrilling and she didn't want it to end, but he pulled away. "Thomas," she said. "Don't go." But it was too late. Everything ended too soon when it came to Thomas. *Everything.*

Jill's eyes fluttered open and her breathing hitched upon seeing a gorgeous man hovering over her.

It definitely wasn't Thomas.

It took her a moment to remember that it was the same man who'd proclaimed to be the father of her baby. The man held her head in the palm of his hand. The top of her pregnant belly brushed against his hard abs. "You're not Thomas."

A devilish smiled played on his lips. "Can't say that I am."

"Tell me I didn't just kiss you." But she knew she had. His eyes...the answer was in his eyes. And her lips—the unfamiliar taste of him still lingered on her lips.

"The ambulance is on the way," he told her.

Anxiety set in as she recalled blacking out and falling. "Is the baby all right?"

"I think so. I saw you fading fast and managed to catch you before you fell on the sidewalk and hurt yourself or the baby."

Sandy poked her head inside the open door. "What's going on in there? What is he doing to you?"

"It's okay," Jill told her friend. "We're just talking."

The man named Derrick started to back away, but Jill grabbed his arm. "Before I passed out, why did you say I was having your baby?"

"Because it's the truth."

She waved Sandy away, and her friend disappeared, but not before letting out a disgusted huff.

"I hate to disappoint you," Jill told the man, "but you're definitely not the father of my baby."

"How can you be sure?"

"CryoCorp has their donors fill out extensive amounts of paperwork." She should know. She'd spent the past eight months memorizing every word her baby's donor had written about himself. "The father of my baby has blue eyes. He's a few inches taller than you, and he went to—"

He winced.

"What? What did you do?"

"I sort of lied."

"Nobody can sort of lie. You either lied or you didn't."

"You're right. I lied," he said. "Your donor attended medical school and he preferred water polo over football. He's a vegetarian, right?"

She nodded, disbelieving, and added, "He's also ultra-sensitive and he used to work for Greenpeace."

He scrunched his nose.

"He's a doctor," she went on, refusing to believe this man, "and sometimes he works as a clown at the children's hospital because—because he loves kids so much."

She felt the baby kick. He must have felt it too, because he maneuvered his body so he was no longer hovering directly over her. He looked uncomfortable, as if he was in pain. Not that she cared. He deserved to be uncomfortable for spying on her and then dumping too much information on her like he had.

The man was looking at her stomach. The baby kicked again—harder this time.

His eyes widened. "That's amazing."

She smiled. She couldn't help it. Every time she felt her baby kick, it felt like a miracle. "It's as if he's been trying to kick his way out for days now."

"Did you say 'he'? We're having a boy?"

Her heart plummeted at the man's words. "Why are you here? Why would you lie?"

"I'm sorry, I really am. At the time I made a donation I desperately needed the money. I wasn't thinking."

"But CryoCorp verifies all donors' information."

"I have connections."

She couldn't believe what she was hearing. "That's horrible," she said. "You're horrible. You wrote down everything you thought a woman would want in a man—in their own child—all lies—all the way down to the color of your eyes." She frowned. "They couldn't even verify the color of your eyes?"

He shrugged. "I know. I was a little surprised about that myself."

"Is there anything you wrote in the questionnaire that wasn't a lie?"

His forehead crinkled as he tried to think.

"So you're telling me the father of my child is a lying, no-good, compassionless child-loathing, meat-eating, brown-eyed football player?"

"Now wait a minute, what's wrong with brown eyes?"

She laid the palm of her hand on her forehead. She wasn't ever supposed to meet the father of her baby. No man could ever come close to the man she'd imagined was the father of her baby, not even Thomas. Sure, this man was beyond handsome, and she would be lying to herself if she didn't admit he could kiss like nobody else, but a gorgeous and amazing kisser did not a good donor candidate make.

"The father of my baby is a big fat liar," she said as if he wasn't right there. "He's just like all the rest of the men out there—nothing special at all—just an egotistical, selfish, horrible, lying—"

"You've made your point," Derrick cut in, "but like I said, I had misgivings about what I had done. I knew it was wrong, which is why I wrote CryoCorp telling them to take me off of the donor list. I even sent their money back. I do have a conscience."

The ambulance sounded in the distance. She shut her eyes. "Go away. Just leave me alone."

"It's not that easy."

She opened one eye. "What do you mean?"

"You're having my baby, my son. I'm not going anywhere. I can't."

A long low sound of misery erupted as she raised her hands to his chest and pushed at his upper body in an attempt to get him to leave her alone. A pain shot through her belly and she dug her fingernails into his rock hard chest. "Oh, my God!"

"What is it?"

Warm liquid gushed from her lower extremities as her fingernails dug right through his shirt and into his skin. "This can't be happening. Oh, my God! It's too early."

"What's wrong?" Sandy asked, her voice a high shrill.

"My baby," Jill said. "It's coming. My baby's coming!"

In his haste to get away, Derrick Baylor, the man she refused to believe was the father of her baby, fell awkwardly to the floor between her and the front seats, and then scrambled backwards out the door.

~~~

Thirteen hours later, tired of waiting in the hospital reception area, Derrick pushed open the door to Jill's hospital room and peeked inside. Her redheaded friend, Satan, the one who was supposed to keep him updated while he sat in the lobby, had fallen asleep in a chair in the corner of the room while Jill's other friend, the lady in blue, sat in a chair on the other side of Jill's bed.

Despite the paper mask he'd been handed before he entered the room, the smell of antiseptics was strong. He thought Jill might be asleep until the monitor beeped and she opened her eyes. Blindly, she reached out a hand and the lady in blue took hold of it and told her everything would be okay. Jill relaxed, but only until the monitor beeped again. This time her eyes opened wide. She and her friend began to breathe together, exhaling three small puffs of air, inhaling, and then starting over again.

Jill looked as if she'd just finished a day at boot camp without benefit of water: her face pale, her lips dry and cracked. Her hair was damp and pushed back out of her face. Dark shadows circled her eyes. She hardly resembled the woman he'd met earlier in the day.

For a second Derrick wondered if he should go find a doctor or a nurse. How could Satan sleep when Jill was in so much pain? After a few moments passed, the two women stopped the weird breathing thing altogether and laughed instead.

Their actions confirmed his earlier suspicions—they were all nuts.

"What are you doing in here?"

Damn. Satan was awake. "It's been five hours since my last update," he told her. "I thought I'd come in and check things out for myself."

"They never should have let you in here. I'm going to give them a piece of—"

"Sandy," Jill said, her voice hoarse. "It's okay."

Sandy stood and stretched. "Have it your way. I'm going to the cafeteria for some coffee. Scream if you need me."

Derrick ignored her, relieved to see Satan head for the door.

"Wait for me," the other woman said. "I'm starved." She came to where Derrick stood, took his hand in hers, and gave it a good firm shake. "Hi. My name is Chelsey."

He was glad to see that not all of Jill's friends wanted to stick needles in his eyes. "Derrick Baylor," he said. "Nice to meet you."

"You too. I'll be back in five minutes," she said, "but you should know that the last time the doctor was in, Jill's cervix was dilated to five centimeters. She has a way to go and she seems to be having a contraction every ten or fifteen minutes." She pointed to a styrofoam cup. "There are ice chips in there. Feel free to give her as many as she needs. She also likes to have her back rubbed."

"That won't be necessary," Jill said.

"Don't listen to her," Chelsey whispered. "She doesn't know what's good for her. Never has. Never will."

The door shut behind Chelsey before Jill could protest further.

"Sorry about that," Jill said. "You don't need to stay. It could be hours. There's just no telling."

"I want to be here. Tell me if you want me to leave the room though."

"Okay," she said, her gaze falling to her belly and then raising to his face again. "This is strange, don't you think? We've known each other for less than a day and you know more about my cervix than anything else."

He laughed. "I also know that you have scary friends."

She chuckled, blushed, and then looked around the room.

Suddenly he wondered what had possessed him to come into her room in the first place. Calling this an awkward moment would be putting it mildly. He looked toward the door, hoping somebody might enter and save them from themselves. "Parents stopping by later?"

She shook her head. "They're in New York. Busy people."

"Hmmm."

"They're not too happy about the choices I've made," she added.

"I see. And what about Thomas? Will he be visiting any time soon?"

She looked painfully self-conscious, making him wonder why he seemed so determined to make things more uncomfortable every time he opened his mouth. He was usually a man of few words and now he knew why.

"Who told you about Thomas? I'm going to kill Chelsey when she returns—"

"It was you," he said. "You mentioned Thomas. You thought you were kissing Thomas when I set you in the back of my car."

She frowned. "I said his name?"

He nodded.

"I've heard of people talking in their sleep…but kissing in their sleep?" She sighed.

"No worries. I would be lying if I pretended I didn't thoroughly enjoy it—you know—the kiss."

The fluorescent lights reflected off her eyes and made them sparkle.

They watched each other for a moment, sizing one another up before an irritating *beep* brought them back to the moment at hand.

Jill squeezed her eyes shut and dug her fingers into the mattress.

Moving to the side of the bed where Chelsey had been, Derrick reached over the side rail and took her hand in his. "It's okay," he said, although he wasn't feeling okay, and she certainly didn't look okay. It hadn't been much over five minutes since her friends left. *What the hell was going on?*

With her eyes clamped shut and her teeth gritted, the veins in her neck and forehead looked ready to burst.

His heart rate accelerated as he tried to think of something to say to comfort her and take her mind off of the pain. "Maybe we should do that breathing thing," he said.

She didn't answer him, but her fingers squeezed tight about his hand, and damn, she had one powerful grip.

The beeper on the monitor wouldn't stop beeping. That worried him.

Jill brought her knees to her chest, blankets and all.

He leaned closer and rubbed her shoulder. "Is that helping?"

Her eyes shot open, startling him. He wouldn't have been surprised if she suddenly turned her head full circle and spit out pea soup. Instead, she reached out and grabbed a fistful of his shirt along with a little skin and said, "Get your baby out of me!"

He might have laughed if he wasn't bleeding and in pain and if she wasn't pinning him with the scariest look he'd ever seen in his life, which was saying a lot considering his mom had been the queen of scary faces back in her day.

In the blink of an eye, Jill Garrison had transformed from a sweet young lady into a woman possessed by the devil.

"If you don't do something," she said, "I'm going to scream."

"I think we should breathe instead."

"I think you should—" Her face turned scarlet, and she scrunched her nose as if she was chewing on sourballs. And then she did exactly what she said she was going to do. She screamed, an ear-piercing sound that set his teeth on edge and made his brain hurt.

Where the hell was everybody?

Before he could reach for the red emergency button, the door shot open and two nurses surrounded the bed.

"Who are you?" one of the nurses asked him as she checked the monitor and IV hookup.

"The father of the baby," he said.

Jill looked pitiful. Her head was bent back, her neck extended, and she had a white-knuckle hold of his arm, her fingernails clawing into flesh.

The nurses exchanged glances before the one at the end of the bed shrugged, pulled up the sheets and did a quick examination. "Ring for the doctor," she said. "This baby is coming, ready or not."

Derrick would have made a quick exit if Jill didn't have a death grip on his arm. He was pretty sure his chest was already bleeding, and if she kept it up, his arm wouldn't fare much better.

The door swung open again and Sandy and Chelsey rushed in behind the doctor.

"I told you he'd still be here," Sandy told Chelsey.

"Is it a crime for a father to want to see his baby come into the world?" Chelsey asked.

Derrick decided he liked Chelsey.

"Donating sperm to a clinic for money," Sandy added, "does not make him a father."

Satan...not so much.

Chelsey stood close to Derrick's side and leaned over the railing. "You're doing great," she told Jill. "Keep breathing. That's right. You can do this." Chelsey started doing her breathing exercise again and Jill followed along. The doctor and two nurses were taking care of business. Sandy grabbed a video camera and aimed it their way.

He could hear Sandy talking into the camera, muttering words like "ass" and "idiot" every once in a while.

Chelsey was perfectly calm, and she handed Derrick a cool rag and told him to wipe Jill's brow. Glad to have something to do, he used his free hand to try and soothe her. Having no desire to see blood, he decided to focus on Jill's face, which he noticed was heart-shaped. Disregarding the dark circles under her eyes, her skin was creamy and flawless. Although her lips were dry and cracked at the moment, they were also full and had a nice shape to them. She had beautiful eyes when they weren't rolling to the back of her head, and she had high cheekbones and slender brows. There was an understated beauty about her he hadn't noticed earlier.

Jill's cheeks puffed up as she and Chelsey readied for another push and Derrick found himself pushing along with them. The three of them puffed three times, inhaled, three more puffs, inhaled, pushed, and then they all repeated the process for another thirty minutes before the baby finally decided to enter the world.

The baby's cry wasn't anything like the cries of all the other babies he'd heard before. This baby's cry was mild in comparison, bordering on soothing, like music to his ears.

Derrick looked over his shoulder and smiled into the camera before turning back to Jill.

"It's a boy," the doctor said.

"We did it," Jill said, her voice weak.

He thought she was talking to Chelsey until he realized Chelsey had joined the nurses down south.

"*You* did it," he said. He reached for the cup of ice chips and after he'd fed her a few, he gently applied lip balm to her cracked lips. Then he stood back and watched the nurse hand Jill her baby…their baby.

CHAPTER 3

The next day, Derrick ignored the cell phone vibrating in his pocket. He climbed out of his car, grabbed the bouquet of flowers from the backseat, and made his way across the parking lot to the entrance of Sutter Medical. He'd already talked to his mother, his father, Maggie, and four of his siblings. They all wanted to drive to the hospital to see the baby.

Well, everybody except Maggie. Maggie wanted to wring his neck first for not listening to her. Then she wanted to see the baby. Instead, she told him she would see him at the Los Angeles County courtroom at three o'clock tomorrow afternoon if he wanted any chance at all of gaining partial custody of his baby boy.

Now all he had to do was talk to Jill. It was seven o'clock in the evening. He'd planned on visiting Jill much earlier, but after getting little sleep and taking a dozen phone calls, time had gotten away from him. His son had yet to be named since Jill agreed to wait until today to make a decision. He liked the name Joe and Matt, nice healthy strong sounding names, but Jill hadn't seemed thrilled by either of his choices. His sisters, on the other hand, were rooting for names like Colton and Deandre because, according to Mom, they really liked the show American Idol.

He called the hospital this morning and was transferred to Jill's room but nobody picked up. Although he'd only known Jill for a little more than a day, he felt pretty good about her being the mother of his baby. For one thing—she wasn't Sandy; for that alone, he was grateful.

A reporter greeted him about halfway across the parking lot and shoved a microphone in his face. She was tall with dark shiny hair slicked back out of her face. "Hello, Hollywood. Is it true Jill Garrison is having your baby without the benefit of sleeping in your bed?"

The nickname "Hollywood" had been given to him fifteen minutes after he signed his first contract with the Los Angeles Condors, something about his "magnetism."

He remained silent. Reporters were like ants. If they got in his way, he stepped on them. If they kept to the side, he ignored them.

She followed on his heels. "Is it also true that you didn't know Jill Garrison until yesterday when police stopped you for voyeurism?"

Derrick wondered if the reporter had talked to Jill's friend. He kept his eyes focused on the entrance ahead.

She held the microphone higher, closer to his mouth. "Why are you here?"

Derrick merely smiled, mostly because the question was annoyingly amusing.

"Perhaps," the reporter went on, "you're not aware that Jill Garrison left with Ryan Michael Garrison only minutes ago."

He pushed his way through the revolving door, leaving the reporter in the dust.

Ryan Michael Garrison.

No, he hadn't heard, but he wasn't going to take the reporter's word for it. Jill wasn't due to leave the hospital until tomorrow. She told him she'd wait for him to visit today before she filled out any important hospital documents.

Five minutes later, Derrick arrived at Jill's room and found it disturbingly empty. The smell of antiseptics and Pine-sol drifted up his nose. An eighty-year-old candy striper came in after him.

Her salt and pepper hair was tied back with a red ribbon that matched the color of her lips.

He laid the bouquet of flowers on the empty bed. "She's gone," he said.

The nice old lady smiled at him. "She said you would understand since she needed to get started on preparations for your wedding."

"Wedding?"

The woman nudged him with her elbow. "Sorry. I forgot. Her friend said it was a secret." She put her fingers to her mouth and pretended to zip her lips together.

He forced a smile. "Sandy?"

"Yes, Sandy. Nice girl."

"You have no idea." Derrick picked up the flowers and gave them to the candy striper. "These are for you," he said. Then he headed out of the room and toward the elevator. To think Jill Garrison had the gall to call him a liar when all the while she was making plans to run off. Talk about calling the kettle black.

~~~

"I can't believe it has come to this," Jill said. "I feel like a fugitive."

Sandy snorted. "Fugitives go on the run. You're just going home. You've done nothing wrong. That man has no right to collect money for his semen and then ask for it back as if he merely loaned out a sweater or something."

"Mom," Sandy's four-year-old daughter asked from the backseat, "what's a seeman?"

Sandy glanced at Jill and then looked back at the road. "A *sea* man," she explained to Lexi, "is a man who spends his days out at sea collecting shrimp."

"Wike a sea horse?"

"Exactly."

"How's Ryan?" Jill asked Lexi, even though she could see her son perfectly well from her position in the passenger seat. "Does he look like he's still sleeping?"

Lexi looked over at the bundle in the carrier. "Rine moved his weg. I think he wants out."

"We're almost there, honey," Sandy told her daughter. "Just a few more minutes."

"What am I going to do?" Jill asked Sandy as she turned back around. "I can't believe it has come to this."

"You have to stay strong. Derrick Baylor wants his son. I didn't trust him the moment I spotted him at the park sitting in that flashy car of his. Seeing his lawyer on the news confirmed my suspicions. He wants Ryan and he'll do anything, absolutely anything, to take him away from you."

"I don't know," Jill said. "He didn't seem like the type of man who would take a baby from its mother. I should have talked to him before I left the hospital. Grabbing my things and running off a day early seems a little hasty."

"Before you say another word to Derrick Baylor we need to find you a good lawyer. Second, we need to contact CryoCorp and see what the deal is. They're going to want to know if somebody is leaking client information. I, for one, do not want you-know-who—"and they both knew she meant Lexi's biological father"—knocking on my door when I least expect it."

Jill wondered what that had to do with CryoCorp, since Lexi's father was the real deal. Sandy had fallen in love with the man. She'd thought she had found her Prince Charming. But he'd left her soon after Lexi was born. Jill sighed. "You're right. I don't have time to deal with Derrick Baylor anyhow. Chelsey called earlier to tell me that Dave Cornerstone is having major problems with graphics, and I have two contributing authors telling me they haven't received their paycheck. My monthly column is due in three days."

"I know your little guy came sooner than expected," Sandy said, "and having that man pop out of the woodwork like that didn't help matters, but more than anything else right now, you need to stay upbeat. I'm going to help you get through this. Besides, as your editorial assistant, it's my job to keep you happy." She paused and then added, "If things get too crazy, you could always call your mother for help."

"Are you kidding?"

Sandy slowed the car before making a right on West Lake Boulevard. "Maybe now is a good time to bury the hatchet," Sandy advised. "Your parents have more money than The Donald. They can afford to get you the best lawyer."

"I can't do it."

"You mean, you won't."

"I can't and I won't. Since the day I was born, my parents have used money to get me to do things their way. The moment I touch my trust fund, they will have won. Mom and Dad will hop on their private jet and fly over here so fast it'll make your head spin. Then they'll start ordering me around again," she added wistfully. "Before you can count to ten they'll have a man all lined up for me to marry. A clone of every other man they've set me up with: tall; thin, straight nose; impeccably dressed with one of those ultra-short haircuts with too much pomade. I'll never let anybody buy my love again."

"Not even Thomas?"

Something deep inside of Jill twisted. "Not even Thomas."

Sandy pulled the Jeep to a stop in front of the apartment building. "Do you miss him?"

"Not anymore," Jill said. She shifted in her seat so she could look Sandy straight in the eyes. "The man left me at the altar. I thought that was something that only happened in the movies. He didn't even have the courtesy to give me a call. Instead, he left me standing at the church all alone to stare into the face of humiliation."

"He said he had his reasons. Do you know what they were?"

Lexi huffed. "Can I get out, Mommy?"

"In a minute, honey. Take off your seatbelt and gather your things."

Jill felt herself getting all stupid and misty-eyed…and that bothered her. She didn't want to feel bad or sad or anything at all when it came to Thomas. She wanted to forget about him—the man she thought she had loved. The man she had planned to spend the rest of her life with. She wanted to move on with her life. Thomas had made his choice and now she'd made hers. It was over.

~~~

"The court will appoint a mediator within the next thirty days. Until then, case dismissed."

Derrick and his lawyer, Maggie, were excused.

"God I'm good," Maggie said with the same wide smile Derrick remembered all too well.

"You *are* good," he agreed.

She punched him in the arm. "Stop looking at me like that."

"Like what?"

"Like we're teenagers again."

He followed her out of the courtroom and down the hallway. He should have been happy, should have been celebrating the fact that the judge had just granted him a hearing with a court appointed mediator. But in that very moment, there was only Maggie.

Her heels clicked against the floor as he followed her down the hallway. She wore a short-waisted jacket and a snug-fitting skirt that showed off her shapely calves. Her hair was rolled up in a practical sort of bun he wasn't used to seeing on her. He quickened his pace and stepped in front of her before she arrived at the exit.

She stopped and laughed because that's what she did—that was the kind of person she was. She made the world a happier place by lighting it up with her wide smiles and quick-to-laugh nature.

He wanted to kiss her. Aaron was not his biological brother. Hell, after what he did, he wasn't even his friend any longer. They were merely living together. Maggie was still single. Two could play at this game.

"Derrick," she said in her lawyerly voice. "We'll get together next week to discuss our plan of action. I've got to go." When she lifted her chin and their eyes met, he swore she could see right into his soul. Without thinking about what he was doing, he stepped close, raised a hand to the back of her head and removed the pin from her hair. Thick blonde hair fell to her shoulders. "There," he said. "That's the way I remember you."

"Derrick, stop it." She pushed his hands away.

"It's been a long time. I just need to look at you for a moment. I want to thank you for coming all this way. You were always there for me, Maggie. When I needed a friend, somebody to talk to…it was always you."

"You give me too much credit. You had your family and—"

Before she could finish her sentence, he leaned forward and covered her mouth with his, her words disappearing on his lips. Instead of passion-filled bliss, he felt a *thunk* against his shin when she kicked him.

"What the hell is going on?"

Derrick recognized the voice as Aaron's. He pivoted to his right just in time to take a fist to the face.

Derrick staggered backwards before regaining his balance. He raised a hand to the side of his face. "Impressive. I didn't know you had it in you."

Aaron looked wildly at Maggie, ignoring Derrick altogether. "I told you he was still in love with you, but you didn't want to believe me. Tell her," Aaron said, turning back to Derrick. "Tell her you love her. Tell her the truth."

One corner of Derrick's mouth tilted upward. "I don't have to tell her anything."

"Come on," Aaron said, taking Maggie's arm. "Let's go. And you," he said, turning to Derrick. "Get a new lawyer because this is the last you're going to see of us."

As she was led away by his friend, the guy he used to call his brother, Derrick looked at Maggie. Her eyes had a lost, sad look to them.

His hand fisted. He was angry with Aaron, but also angry with himself for not using more self-control. *What the hell was wrong with him?*

That same night Derrick sat in his big empty home and, for the first time since purchasing the eight thousand square foot hulk of a house two years earlier, he wondered what he'd been thinking. He had a big home, nice cars, everything people talked about wanting. He had a career he loved. And yet here he sat, staring out the large paned window, watching the rising tide, and wondering what the hell it was all for? The lights were off but the television was on, giving the room a soft glow and throwing odd-shaped shadows across the walls. He held an ice pack to the left side of his face.

Kissing Maggie had been a stupid move on his part, and yet if he were given the chance, he'd do it again. Aaron was just as much to blame. Aaron knew how he felt about Maggie. Hell, every guy in Arcadia had felt the same way about her. She was pretty and smart, and she was a flirt. Always had been, always would be. They all liked her, which was exactly the reason why they all took a solemn pledge to never take Maggie too seriously. In plain English: she was off limits.

Nothing, especially a female, his brothers had all agreed, would ever come between them. But Aaron obviously didn't understand the meaning of a pledge. After Maggie left for college, they'd all swept their brow with relief. At least he had because he knew then what he knew now: he loved Maggie, and yet he had been willing to give up love over digging a trench between him and his brothers. He thought he'd made the big sacrifice, but now he could see he'd made the worst mistake of his life. He should have gone after Maggie years ago and told her how he felt. He never should have let her out of his sight.

Derrick let out a groan of frustration. He didn't want to think about Maggie, or Aaron for that matter. His head pounded, prompting him to shift his thoughts to Ryan Michael Garrison.

He had a son, a son he had yet to hold.

On the day Ryan was born, a nurse had tried to place his son in his arms, but he'd made up some lame excuse, telling the nurse he had a scratchy throat and didn't want to get the baby sick. The truth was he'd been scared, scared to hold his own son. Now that he thought about it though, he was much more frightened by the idea of *never* getting the chance to hold his son at all.

Outside the window, a wave crashed against the rocks. Derrick rose to his feet and looked around him. Determination filled him as he realized his son gave his life new meaning and purpose. He would fight for Ryan, and he wouldn't stop fighting until he had half custody of his son.

CHAPTER 4

It was noon the next day by the time Jill staggered out of her bedroom and into the family room.

"You're alive," Sandy said.

"Barely."

"Ryan kept you awake, huh?"

"Understatement of the year," Jill said, dropping into the chair across from the couch where Sandy sat. "What have I done?"

"Taking care of a new baby is difficult in the beginning, but things will get better...easier."

Jill shook her head. "You don't understand. I don't think Ryan likes me."

"Of course he likes you," Sandy said with a smile. "Having a new baby just takes getting used to."

Jill blew pieces of straggly hair out of her eyes. "I need coffee."

"I don't think that's a good idea while you're breastfeeding."

"I'm not breastfeeding anymore."

"Since when?"

"Sometime in the middle of the night. And now Ryan is sleeping. He hates me." Jill dropped her face into the palms of her hands.

Sandy came to Jill's side and patted her shoulder. "Oh, honey, he doesn't hate you. Everything will be okay. I'll make you some hot tea and scrambled eggs," Sandy said as she headed for the kitchen.

"I never feel this way," Jill said. "I feel so tired...and depressed. I've felt like crying ever since Ryan was born. What's wrong with me?"

"He's four days old. Give it some time."

Jill could see her reflection in the window. Who was that woman looking back at her? What happened to Jill Garrison, the girl most likely to succeed in high school? What happened to the young vibrant woman who had boys flocking to be her escort at the cotillion in New York City?

Jill stood and curtsied. It was no use. At the ripe old age of twenty-eight she was all washed up.

"Are you okay?" Sandy asked when she peeked out from the kitchen at Jill.

Jill flopped back into her favorite chair. "I'm fine. Just fine."

"Hormonal changes, a little postpartum depression, that's what you have," Sandy assured her. "Nothing's wrong with you. After you eat, you're going to take a shower. You'll feel like a new woman in no time."

Jill's cell phone rang, but before she could answer it, the crying in the other room told her that her time was up. Ignoring the cell phone, she headed for the bedroom.

"It will get better," Sandy called out. "I promise."

Jill didn't believe her. Sandy was just trying to comfort her. If Ryan would just let her sleep for thirty minutes straight, she was certain she could do this.

Just thirty minutes and everything would be fine.

Three hours later, after eating an egg and multi-tasking with a brisk walk around the park while returning phone calls, Jill felt mildly better. At least her hair was clean and she'd managed to brush and floss before Ryan started to cry again. Her baby had a set of lungs that no doubt came from his father's side of the family.

Growing up had been a quiet experience because nobody in Jill's family talked or interacted. On most days you could hear a pin drop. She and her sister were taught to keep their voices and emotions in check at all times. Children were meant to be seen, not heard. If she and her sister were caught being overly rambunctious, or laughing too loud, an uncommon occurrence, they were given ten minutes on the wooden chair.

Jill hovered over the crib for a moment and watched Ryan cry. What had her parents done when she cried as a baby? She had read many books on becoming a new mother. It scared her that she didn't feel the instant bond the nurses at the hospital told her most mothers shared with their newborn babies. She didn't feel a connection, but she wanted to—more than anything. For most of her life, she'd wanted a baby, but now, right this moment, she couldn't remember why.

Her baby didn't even look like her. Maybe she'd brought home the wrong baby. Her heart beat faster. She checked his tiny wristband, comparing the name and numbers to hers. They were a match. "What is it, Ryan? What's wrong?"

She picked him up, kissed his tiny forehead, and breathed in baby powder along with his own baby scent. Then she headed into the family room where Sandy's daughter, Lexi, sat on the floor drawing in a coloring book.

A few feet away, Sandy sat in an overstuffed chair with her legs curled beneath her. She was helping Jill write her monthly column.

Jill hoped someday she and Ryan would look so relaxed, so peaceful.

Sandy placed her laptop to the side and came to her feet. "I'll get his bottle. How's it going?"

"Ryan's doctor said as long as he's been fed and changed, I don't need to worry about his crying too much."

The sound of someone talking outside caught their attention. Sandy went to the window and peeked through the blinds. "Oh, my God! I can't believe it. It's him."

"Who?" Jill asked.

"Hollywood."

"Who?"

"Derrick Baylor. He's talking on his cell," Sandy said. "Oh crap. Here he comes." She squeezed the blinds shut. "Your parents would die if they knew the father of your baby might possibly be a football player."

Sandy's words caused a weird reaction inside her body. Until that very second Jill had no intention of answering the door, but Sandy's words prompted her to change her mind.

Sandy backed away from the window and hid in the kitchen. "Come on. Let's hide and maybe he'll go away."

Lexi rushed into the kitchen, climbed under the table and giggled.

Jill went to the kitchen and handed Sandy the baby. "Take Ryan for me and I'll take care of Derrick."

Sandy held Ryan close to her chest. "Derrick Baylor wants to take your son," Sandy warned in a hushed voice. "You just saw him and his lawyer on the news walking into the courtroom."

Jill looked to the front door. It was true. Jill had been surprised to see Derrick on TV. Before she could blink, he'd run to court. But what Sandy just said about her parents not liking football players had gotten Jill's juices flowing. For the first time in days, everything seemed suddenly clear.

Jill had a plan.

Just this morning, Jill's mom had called to tell her she and Dad would be visiting sooner rather than later. As was the norm, her mom couldn't give Jill an exact day or time of arrival. They were busy people. For Dad, getting away from work for a few days wasn't easy. Sadly, Jill wasn't looking forward to their visit. She loved her parents; she just didn't *like* them very much. Her father was overbearing and controlling, while her mother was merely one of her father's many puppets.

Jill's entire life had been built around her mother and father's wishes. Even Thomas had been their doing. Before Thomas left her standing alone at the altar, though, Jill had begun to think perhaps her parents knew what was best for her after all.

But not any longer.

For twenty-eight years Jill had done whatever her father told her to do. Jill's first act of defiance was moving from New York to California. Her parents would say her second act of defiance was having a baby out of wedlock, but that would be incorrect. Having a baby was a well-thought-out plan on Jill's part. She and Thomas had been dating for many years before he finally proposed. During that time, they discovered Thomas had something called retrograde ejaculation, a disorder that causes some men, like Thomas, to become infertile. There were other related problems, too: problems she didn't want to think about.

For that reason, Jill had spent the last four years visiting sperm banks across the country, finally opting on CryoCorp, the best in the business—or so she thought.

Getting pregnant and giving birth to Ryan had nothing to do with payback, revenge, or even biological clocks. After Thomas abandoned her, she decided to continue with her plans to have a baby. Having Ryan was a well-thought-out choice, a dream come true. She would not apologize to anyone for her decision to become a single mother.

Jill straightened her shoulders and headed for the door just as a knock sounded on the other side.

"Don't answer it," Sandy said.

"I have to." Jill reached for the door handle. Derrick Baylor, she realized, might be just what the doctor ordered. If her parents thought, even for a minute, that she was interested in a football player of all things, they would turn around and head back for home in a New York minute. According to her father, football players were arrogant and overpaid, all ego and no substance, a disgrace to humanity.

Wonderful.

Jill could not have planned this scenario any better had she tried. Derrick Baylor would be the perfect man to get her parents off her back once and for all.

"We don't even know the guy," Sandy said. "He could be dangerous."

"He's not dangerous," Jill said as she opened the door.

"Who's not dangerous?" Derrick asked.

"You," she said matter-of-factly before she waved at her ninety-year-old neighbor, Mrs. Bixby, when the woman peeked out through her apartment door.

Jill gave Derrick a once over. The first day she'd met Derrick Baylor he'd been wearing a nice pair of slacks and a button-down shirt. Today he had on a white T-shirt that showed off well-worked biceps; pre-washed jeans; a pair of sporty-style slip-on shoes; dark sunglasses; and three days' worth of stubble. One hand was tucked in his front pants pocket. His hair was thick, dark, and wavy. Unruly strands hit his handsome forehead from all directions.

If only her parents could see him now.

Her mother would faint.

Derrick was everything her father wasn't: tall, sexy, and from what little she'd heard on the news the other day, Hollywood was a bad boy. A womanizer who had tall, big-busted women lined up outside his door, no doubt.

Looking past him, over the railing, Jill saw his BMW parked at the curb across the street, which explained the flyaway hair. His BMW was a convertible. The same car she'd been in when her water broke. She couldn't help but wonder if he'd had time to take it to a car wash.

Jill stepped outside and shut the door behind her.

Derrick slid his Ray-Bans to the top of his head. His left eye was shaded in pinks and purples.

"What happened to you?"

"Just a little misunderstanding."

"You ruffled somebody's feathers, didn't you?"

"Ruffled feathers?"

Jill rolled her eyes. "I don't have to be Hermann Oberth to see that you have a knack for pushing one's buttons."

"Hermann Oberth?"

"A rocket scientist," she explained. "One of three founding fathers of rocketry and modern astronautics."

Derrick frowned. "You could have just said you didn't have to be a rocket scientist to see that I have a knack for pushing people's buttons."

"So, I was right."

"About what?"

"About you having a knack for pushing people's buttons."

He sighed. "You look different," he said, obviously in an attempt to change the subject.

"I just had a baby."

He cocked his head for a better look. "No, really. Your hair…everything…you don't look like the same woman."

She crossed her arms in front of her chest. "Are you saying I looked fat before?"

"No, of course not, I-I thought you looked great then…you just look different, that's all."

She rolled her eyes because she'd been kidding. "Why are you here?" she asked, giving up on humor since she couldn't even get the man to smile.

"I was hoping we could talk," he said. "I met with a judge and I thought you might want to hear what she had to say."

Jill gave him the twice over as she tried to imagine what her parents would think when she told them she and Derrick Baylor were dating. For some reason, the idea of such a ridiculous notion sent a chill right through her. It had been over a year since she'd been with a man. She'd made love to a total of three different men in her life. Well, that is, if she counted Roy Lester. No, she quickly decided, she didn't want to count Roy. Two men, she amended. She'd made love to two different men in her entire life. Derrick Baylor didn't look like the sort of man who made love. He probably had hot passionate sex every night on the hood of his car. She blushed at the thought.

Sex was dirty.

That's what her mother used to tell Jill and her sister. Thomas had always been a perfect gentleman in bed. Thomas was the cleanest, neatest person she'd ever met, always making sure not to mess her hair or ruin the bed sheets if and when she could manage to get him in the mood.

"Are you all right?" Derrick asked when she failed to respond to whatever he'd said about meeting with a judge.

"I'm fine. I have a lot on my mind and I didn't get much sleep last night."

"Is Ryan okay?"

"He's great. How did you know his name?"

"A reporter told me when I showed up at the hospital as planned."

"Oh." She felt a stab of guilt. "So what did the judge tell you?"

"The judge assigned a court appointed mediator to help us figure out how to deal with our situation."

"Sandy thinks you want to take my baby from me. Is that true?"

"No. Never."

Jill caught a whiff of his aftershave. He had to be wearing Gucci or Chanel. God, he smelled good. She didn't have any shoes on, but either way, Derrick Baylor was tall...very tall. Her neck was beginning to hurt from the strain of looking up.

"Why did you leave the hospital without talking to me?" he asked.

"It's complicated."

"I have time."

The little angel, if you could call it that, sitting on Jill's left shoulder told her to tell him the truth: that she'd been confused and had done what she always did...followed orders. Sandy had told her she needed to get away from Derrick Baylor, and so that's what Jill had done. She'd run.

The devil with the red spiked heels sitting on her right shoulder also told Jill to tell him the truth. But while she was at it, kill him with kindness and make him believe she wanted to be friends. At least until her parents showed up. Then she'd really have to turn on the charm. After her parents flew back to New York, all bets were off. Although Jill knew it wasn't fair to judge a book by its cover, so to speak, she was too tired to care. Her ideal mate could never be an athlete. She preferred intelligent males who kept their hair combed appropriately and wore suits to work.

"All my life," Jill began to explain, "since I was in my teens, I wanted to have a baby."

Derrick raked a hand through thick, unmanageable hair. "Seriously?"

She nodded. "Most girls dream about their wedding day, but not me. I dreamt of having a baby of my own. My sister would ask Santa for a princess dress. I always asked for a baby."

He appeared to be listening intently, which made her wonder about him. Men didn't listen to women rattle on about their wants and desires. Derrick Baylor obviously had a plan of his own. Fine with her. Two could play at this game.

"Fast forward to Thomas," she went on. "We dated for years, but he couldn't—" Jill pulled her gaze from his. "This is too personal. I shouldn't be talking about this with you."

"No, please go on," he said. "Thomas was infertile?"

Jill looked at him skeptically, warily, and then nodded. "We had a long engagement. During that time, I looked for help. I finally found CryoCorp. When things didn't work out between Thomas and me, I knew right away that I would keep my appointment with CryoCorp and raise my baby on my own. No father, no ties, no one telling me how to raise my child. No one judging me. Women all over the world raise their children alone." She crossed her arms over her chest. "I didn't see anything wrong with what I was doing."

"I'm not judging you, Jill."

God, he was good at this, she thought. No yawn; no bored, wandering eyes. "You're not?"

He shook his head.

"It was all supposed to be confidential," she said. "And then you showed up out of the blue. What were the odds?"

"One in a million."

She nodded. "One in a million." She looked into his eyes again, deeper this time, searching. "I never should have left the hospital without talking to you first. But what about you?" she asked. "You never mentioned having a lawyer, or that you were going to court. You weren't exactly upfront with me, were you?" She lifted her chin a notch.

"You're right. I should have told you my plans." He shifted his weight from one foot to the other. "I'm hoping the two of us can work something out."

"Like what?"

He pulled a piece of paper from his back pocket and handed it to her. "Here's the date and time we're scheduled to meet next month for mediation. The soonest date I could get is thirty days from now." He cleared his throat. "I was hoping before that time, you would allow me to spend time with you and Ryan, you know, so we could get to know one another better."

She took the paper and looked it over.

"He's not coming in here," Sandy said from inside the apartment.

Jill sighed. "Do you want to see Ryan?"

He looked surprised. "I would love to."

A loud moan sounded from inside the apartment. "Shouldn't you be practicing your drops? I thought good mechanics were needed on the field?" Sandy asked from the other side of the door.

He smiled—a flash of white teeth and a charming sparkle in his eyes. The man definitely had to have a string of beautiful women falling at his feet on a daily basis.

"Training camp doesn't start for another six weeks," he told Sandy through the door.

"Before we go inside," Jill said, "I do have a question."

"Shoot."

"What happens if we go through with mediation but then fail to come to any mutual conclusion with regard to Ryan?"

"I guess we'd have to take the matter to court."

She liked his honesty, but that didn't mean she liked his answer.

CHAPTER 5

Derrick sat in the middle of Jill's lime-green couch and watched her feed Ryan the last of his bottle. Four-year-old Lexi wriggled around on his left side while Jill sat on his right.

Ryan was a tiny thing, much smaller than his niece, Bailey. "He looks awful small," Derrick said.

"Babies tend to be small," Sandy muttered from the kitchen.

Derrick ignored her. Satan was not happy to have him inside the apartment. Even now he could feel her angry eyes boring a hole through the side of his head.

"Are you sure you don't want to feed him the rest of his bottle?" Jill asked.

"No, thanks. I'm perfectly happy just watching you."

Satan snorted.

"He's afwade of rine," Lexi announced.

"No, I'm not," Derrick answered too quickly.

"Burp him then," Lexi said.

Lexi stood on the couch, her pink sock-covered feet sinking into the cushions as she held onto Derrick's shoulder for support.

"No, no, that's okay. I'll just watch. How do you know so much about babies?" he asked Lexi, hoping to get the little girl's attention focused on something other than him.

"I used to be one," she said.

Sandy laughed.

"Here." Lexi laid a dry cloth diaper on his shoulder and patted it with her hand. "Put Rine's head right here," she told Jill.

The bottle was empty so Jill adjusted herself on the couch so she could do as Lexi said.

"Oh, I don't know," he said nervously as Jill placed Ryan exactly as Lexi had instructed.

The second the baby's head touched his shoulder, Derrick froze—he didn't move one inch.

Lexi giggled and moved his hand so that the palm of his hand was flat against Ryan's back. "Now pat him...softwy," she told Derrick. "You a big guy," she said with a smile. "Don't hurt the wittle baby."

He gently patted Derrick's back. "Like that?"

Lexi's head bobbed. "Yep. Do it 'til he burps."

Within seconds a loud gurgly sound came out of Ryan. Derrick's eyes widened. "It worked!"

Lexi clapped her hands together and squealed.

He smiled at Jill, and then looked at Sandy, which was a big mistake since she was frowning and ruining the moment.

"Mommy, Rine burped!" Lexi shouted in Derrick's ear.

"What did Ryan do?" Sandy asked with a smile, knowing her daughter would shout in his ear again, which she did. Satan was on a roll.

"Rine wikes you," Lexi said as Jill pushed herself from the couch.

Derrick laughed. Despite being the spawn of the devil, Lexi was an adorable kid.

"He don't wike his mommy though," Lexi added.

Jill blushed.

"Of course he likes his mommy," Derrick told Lexi.

"Nope. He don't wike her boobies."

"Okay," Sandy said as she swooped in and ushered Lexi away. "Time for your bath, Lexi."

"Not now. Howiewood said he'd draw pictures with me."

"Maybe some other time," Sandy told her.

"Sweet girl," Derrick said after Lexi and Sandy exited the room.

"She's a hoot," Jill agreed, crossing her arms tightly over her chest.

Derrick didn't know what to do. Ryan was falling asleep on his shoulder. He didn't want to wake him, but his leg was cramping and his arm wasn't faring much better.

It was quiet for a moment while they both stared at Ryan's perfect little head as he rested on his shoulder. "I've never held a baby before today," he told her. "I mean, not in a very long time. It's not so difficult, after all."

"You're a natural."

Derrick tucked his chin into his chest and examined Ryan further. "He's got your mouth," he said.

Jill sat on the armrest of the couch and took a good long look at Ryan too. "Hmm. You think so?"

As he examined her mouth for comparison, she felt ridiculously self-conscious and found herself wishing she hadn't asked the question.

"Definitely," he said.

She looked at Derrick's mouth. "I hadn't noticed that before. You might be right." The thought cheered her immeasurably. "He has your nose, though, that's for sure," she added. "And your big brown eyes."

"The better to see you with, my dear." He wriggled his brows.

She laughed and then stopped when she saw him giving her a strange look. "What?"

"Nothing," he said, looking away.

She thought about coaxing him into telling her what was on his mind, but decided against it. Until things had been sorted out between them with regards to Ryan, it was safest for her to keep her guard up. If she was to convince her parents they were dating she needed to be friendly, but there was no reason to overdo it.

His gaze fell back to Ryan, who was now asleep. "Looks like we wore the little guy out. Should I put him in his crib?"

"I'll take him." She stood, and then leaned low and scooped Ryan up and off of his chest. Her baby smelled like Derrick, musky and masculine. "I'll be right back."

By the time she returned, Derrick was at the door ready to go. She was glad. The man made her nervous. He was handsome and too charming for his own good. This entire afternoon had probably been a sham. He was probably just kissing up to her, befriending her and then when she least suspected, he'd bring in the lawyers and find a way to take Ryan away from her. Men could not be counted on, she reminded herself.

"I was wondering if it would be okay if I stopped by tomorrow."

"No," she said a little too quickly. "I mean, I don't think it would be a good idea." She felt vulnerable and she didn't like the feeling. There was no way she could be his friend and remain strong at the same time. Her plans were quickly dissolving into a pile of mush. She opened the door and after he stepped outside she said, "Maybe it would be better if the next time we see each other it's in the mediation room."

He rubbed his chin, clearly confused. "I know this can't be easy for you, but we're not meeting with the mediator for another month. My parents live less than an hour from here and my family is already on my back to meet Ryan. Let me pick you and Ryan up at, say, ten on Saturday and—"

"No. I'm sorry. I can't." She shut the door, and then leaned against it, her eyes closed tight until she heard him walk away. Everything was happening too fast. She had a magazine to run, a small magazine, but a magazine all the same. *Food For All* was chock full of everything from quick-to-fix recipes to restaurant reviews. The idea for her magazine had come to her five years ago as a hobby when she lived back East, but quickly grew into much more. She'd found a buyer for the New York edition and they agreed that she would start another edition once she moved to California. Finding a readership took time, though. Her savings was dwindling fast. If she didn't find a way to get subscribers, she would be forced to find a job outside of her apartment.

She had an article to finish, emails to read, and a phone to answer. She walked into the kitchen and picked up the receiver. "Hello."

"Jill. It's so good to hear your voice. It's me, Thomas."

~~~

On the way to his car, Derrick found it difficult to wrap his mind around the fact that he had a son. The last few days had been a wild ride of emotions. Before finding Jill, he'd thought a lot about what he would do if he found the woman who had selected him as a donor, and what he would do if she were pregnant.

He certainly never thought he'd feel what he was feeling right now—happy. Spending time with Ryan today had been exhilarating. Even little Lexi had calmed his fears about whether or not he could handle children.

Maybe, he thought, if Maggie could see that he'd changed, that he took his responsibilities seriously, she would see that he was the man for her—not Aaron.

Out of the corner of his eye, he saw a sign: "Apartments for Rent." Turning about, he followed the direction of the arrows, which took him back upstairs. Directly across from Jill's apartment was a FOR RENT sign.

With a smile on his face, he headed for the main office.

~~~

Three days had passed since Maggie and Derrick met in the courtroom. Aaron had insisted she not go, but Maggie went anyhow and now her fiancé was barely talking to her.

Although they had kept their relationship private until recently, she and Aaron had been living together for a few months now. Aaron sat at the kitchen table, his laptop open in front of him—all ten fingers clacking away on the keyboard.

Maggie stood a few feet away, watching him. He was a pharmacist during the day and a law student at night. She loved the way his hair curled around his ears and the way his nose curved just a smidgeon to the left, something nobody else would notice at first or second glance. She hated to disturb Aaron, but he'd been quiet for days and it had to stop. "Aaron," she said.

"Hmm."

"We need to talk about Derrick."

He didn't respond, didn't miss a beat as his fingers continued to hammer away at his keyboard.

"You need to talk to your brother," Maggie tried again, "before he takes that woman to court and embarrasses his family in the process."

"He's not my brother," Aaron said.

Biologically speaking that was the truth, but Aaron had been unofficially adopted by Derrick's family when he was twelve—after Aaron's mother ran off with another man and his father began spending more time in the bar than at home.

"You used to talk about Derrick with pride," she reminded him. "You always bragged about his hard-earned place in the NFL, proudly calling him your brother as you recalled one childhood story or another."

"That was a long time ago—before I found you again. Things are different now."

Ouch. That hurt. Maggie continued to watch him. He had yet to look away from the computer. Ever since he'd punched Derrick in the face, he'd been treating her as if she was the one who did something wrong. "Aaron. Look at me, please."

Finally, he looked up, his eyes cold and unseeing.

"Why are you blaming me for Derrick's actions?"

"The truth?"

"Nothing but."

"I think you *wanted* Derrick to kiss you."

Aaron might as well have punched her in the gut because that's how she felt—sucker punched and sick to her stomach. "Is there more?"

"Yeah. I think you're in love with Derrick. I think you always have been. I think you agreed to marry me to get closer to him."

She didn't know whether to laugh or cry. It was hard to believe he could be so dense. "You don't think I would have approached Derrick if I thought he was the man for me?"

"No. You're a stickler for pride and your pride never would have allowed you to go after him."

Wow. He had it all figured out. She watched him as he set his attention back on his work. She'd grown up with a gaggle of boys, including Derrick and Aaron. They all did everything together. They rode bikes and played football, shot hoops and hiked around town. They joked together, laughed together, played silly pranks on one another. Until she reached puberty, she'd been one of the boys: Connor, Derrick, Aaron, Lucas, Brad, Cliff, Jake, a few neighborhood boys, and Maggie. They were all great friends, at least until her body changed and their voices dropped an octave. For a short time, she'd thought she had feelings for Derrick, but then she'd given him a football for his fourteenth birthday and he'd kissed her. By the time they shared their third and last kiss in the principal's office during their senior year, she'd known her heart wasn't in it.

Derrick was fun and carefree, but he didn't take life seriously. Aaron, on the other hand, had grown up to become a responsible and caring man who wore his emotions like a badge for all to see. She and Aaron had always been great friends. They talked for hours on end and it had only taken one kiss for her to know that he was the one who had her heart, the one she loved.

Yes, she'd heard from Aaron and Derrick's sisters about the ridiculous vow all the boys made back then, a pledge stating that if one of them couldn't have her, then none of them could.

Crazy talk—childhood silliness.

Maggie watched her fiancé and inwardly smiled as she thought about all the lonely nights she'd spent during her college years, dreaming about Aaron someday coming for her. It had taken him a few years longer than she'd thought it would, but he'd come all the same. And she'd been waiting.

"Where are you going?" Aaron asked after she sighed and headed for the other room.

She stopped and looked around the house they'd been sharing for months now. She looked at the roll-top desk Aaron had bought for her before she moved in, to the handmade cushions on the chairs where Aaron sat, the cushions she'd made when they first moved into the house. "I'm going to get my laptop," she said. "I have clients who need me."

"You're not leaving?"

She raised her eyebrows, shocked by his question. "This is my home," she said, tired of his moping. "If anyone's leaving this house, it's going to have to be you. I'm not going anywhere."

"And you have nothing to say on the matter?"

She swallowed the lump in her throat, determined to keep from falling apart, firm in her decision to help Derrick in his time of need. "I'm going to help Derrick to the best of my ability. He's your brother. He's family."

CHAPTER 6

"What did you do to Aaron?"

Derrick grimaced at the front console of his car where the radio frequency miraculously turned magnetic waves into his mother's voice. The wireless phone system in his Chevy Tahoe was supposed to make for a safer ride, but he wondered how safe it was to drive while being lectured by his mother. Keeping his eyes on the road, he said, "I don't know what you're talking about."

"Aaron said he couldn't come to the get-together I'm planning if you were going to be there. He said to ask you about it if I wanted details."

"Not now, Mom. I'm pulling up to my new apartment building as we speak. Jake and the twins are meeting me to help move a few things."

"Why are you moving into an apartment when you have a beautiful home already."

He turned into the parking lot. "It's only temporary. I'm hoping I can make Jill see that Ryan's life will be better with me in it."

"Well, of course, it will be better with you in it. When are we going to be able to meet Jill and our grandson?"

"I'm working on it, Mom. Until mediation next month, I'm going to do what I can to try and see if Jill and I can work something out on our own."

"I don't understand. You were in the hospital room when your son was born, so why can't she see that you're a nice, trustworthy guy? I mean you're not exactly Tom Hanks or Bob Barker, but you've got charisma. Maybe she's wondering why you're still single."

"I would take that as a compliment, Mom, if Bob Barker hadn't been sued by six women from his daytime show."

"Ridiculous. Bob Barker was named the most popular game show host by a national poll."

Derrick chuckled as he pulled into an empty parking slot and slid the gear into Park. "I'll take your word for it. I've gotta go."

"Tell Jake I found the rollerblades he was looking for, and tell the twins dinner will be ready at seven."

"Rollerblades?"

"Jake has a date with Candy this weekend, but you didn't hear that from me."

Derrick lifted his eyes heavenward. "You still cook for the twins? Didn't they turn twenty-five recently?"

"Everybody comes here for dinner on Wednesday. Everyone but you."

Damn. He'd forgotten again. "I'll come next week, I promise."

"I'm going to hold you to that. Don't forget to bring a picture of Ryan."

"I'll do what I can. Talk to you later, Mom." He quickly hit the Off button before she could think of another subject to broach. He climbed out of the car and shut the door.

The layer of marine clouds had disappeared earlier than usual today. The sun warmed the air along with his stiff shoulders. Blue, cloudless skies, not a bit of Los Angeles smog or June gloom in sight. Closing his eyes, he put his face to the sun and inhaled while he stretched his leg - his knee got a little stiff whenever he sat for too long.

A honk sounded as two trucks pulled into the parking lot: an old brown Ford and a newer Toyota model. Three of his brothers had arrived. The twins, Cliff and Brad, owned a construction business and they were in the new truck, while Jake followed behind in the truck he'd borrowed from Dad.

Cliff was the first to find a parking spot and head Derrick's way. At six foot five, Cliff was the tallest of all the brothers. On the basketball court Cliff made a two-handed dunk look easy. He was also the only fair-haired child in the family, which is why they liked to tease him about how much Mom had always liked the fair-haired mailman.

Cliff gestured with his chin toward the apartment building. "So this is your new place, huh?"

"This is it."

"A far cry from your house in Malibu."

"It's only temporary. I've gotta do what I've gotta do."

"And what is it exactly that you have to do?"

Jake and Brad joined them in time to hear his answer.

"I plan to show Jill that I'm a decent guy, you know, make her see that I deserve to be in Ryan's life."

"I never realized you were so eager to be a father," Jake chimed in.

"He didn't have much of a choice in the matter, now did he?" Cliff argued.

"I didn't know how I would feel about it either," Derrick said, "but once I held my son in my arms, I knew that not only did I *need* to be there for him, I *want* to be in his life. I want to see him take his first steps and hear his voice when he says his first words. I want to help him with his homework and throw him a ball at the park. I want to coach him if he decides to play sports and I want to get to know his friends. I want it all."

It was quiet for a long moment.

He could tell by the look in his brothers' eyes that he'd said too much, but he didn't care. Something about being a father had brought out a mushy side to him he hadn't known existed.

"And if Jill sees that you're a nice guy, then what?" Jake asked.

"I have no idea."

Brad shook his head. "What kind of woman would keep a father from his son? So many deadbeat dads out there and then you come along, a guy who wants to be a part of his son's life, and she turns her back on you. I don't get it."

"She's confused," Derrick told them. "From what I've picked up on so far, an incident in her past has left her a little bitter toward men. She didn't plan on having her donor show up at her doorstep, which is why I need to show her that Ryan needs me in his life. I have no intention of taking him away or making her life miserable."

"It's a complicated situation," Cliff agreed.

"What does Jill look like?" Jake asked.

Derrick thought about the first time he saw Jill. All he saw was her belly, at least until she kissed him. He hadn't thought a whole lot about the kiss until now: sexy eyes, full lips, expressive face. "She's cute. Nice, shiny hair; straight white teeth; doesn't wear much makeup."

"Not your type, huh?" Cliff asked.

"I don't have a type," Derrick said.

All three of his brothers laughed at once.

Jake snapped his fingers. "I know what you need to do."

Brad chuckled. "This ought to be good."

"Get her to like you," Jake said. "You know, make her want you, flirt with her, give her compliments, and bring her flowers for no reason at all. Women love that."

Derrick grunted. "I don't want to lead her on."

"Fine. Whatever," Jake said with a shrug. "You can always use my idea as a backup plan."

"Nothing about this situation is going to be smooth sailing," Brad said as Derrick and Cliff headed for the closest truck and began untying the ropes tied across the furniture.

"What if Jill decides to let you into Ryan's life? And then down the road you find out she wants him to go to an all boys' school—"

"Over Derrick's dead body," Cliff interjected.

"What if she gives Ryan a little baby tattoo?" Jake went on, trying to stir up trouble.

"Nobody gives a baby a tattoo," Brad said.

Cliff shook his head. "That's not true. The nephew of a good friend of mine owns his own tattoo shop and he gave his baby a tattoo."

"Jill wouldn't do that," Derrick said, although nobody was listening.

"What if she signs him up for dance lessons?"

Jake looked appalled. "Do they allow boys to take ballet lessons?"

"No nephew of mine is wearing tights," Brad said.

Derrick raised a hand. "You're all getting yourselves worked up for nothing. Ryan isn't even a week old. Besides, if the boy wants to dance, I don't see anything wrong with that."

All three of them got another good laugh at that.

Derrick felt a headache coming on.

"Is she breastfeeding?" someone asked.

Derrick had watched her feed Ryan from a bottle, and he recalled Lexi's comment about Derrick not liking his mommy's boobies. "I don't think so."

"I overheard Grandma telling Mom that she hopes Jill is breastfeeding because otherwise the baby could turn out to be…not too bright."

"Ridiculous," one of them said. "Sounds like an old wives' tale."

"I'm just telling you what I heard."

"Sagging breasts would be the only downfall I can think of when it comes to a woman breastfeeding," Brad stated matter-of-factly.

"A definite downfall," Jake agreed.

"How about Maggie?" someone asked next. "I wonder if she plans to breastfeed?"

"First comes marriage and then comes baby," Derrick growled. "Could we all get to work now?"

"Still a little sensitive when it comes to Maggie, I see."

Derrick finished with the ropes and then headed for the back of his brothers' truck and unlatched the tailgate. "Aaron had no business going after her and that's all I have to say on the matter."

Brad shook his head. "You really do have it bad for Maggie, don't you? I didn't believe it, but now that we're on the subject, what's the deal? If you were in love with her, why didn't you go after her a long time ago?"

"Because I knew I wasn't the only one who had feelings for her. We took a damn vow."

"That was nearly fifteen years ago," they all said at once.

"We were kids," Cliff added for good measure.

Jake shook his head as if Derrick was a lost cause.

Derrick grabbed hold of one side of the couch and slid it halfway off the truck on his own before Jake hurried over and grabbed hold of the center while Brad jumped inside the bed of the truck to get the other end of the couch.

"You've got to let go of your feelings for Maggie," Jake said. "She and Aaron love each other and Aaron deserves to live a good full life with his brothers' support."

"He's not our brother."

Jake glared at Derrick. "That's bullshit. Guess who taught me to swim?"

"Aaron did," Jake said, answering his own question. "Remember the car wreck in West LA, the accident people still talk about: the driver fell asleep and four boys were killed on their way home from Vegas? I never told anyone but I should have been in that car. Aaron caught wind of what I was up to and he wouldn't let me go. He threatened to tell Mom. I was furious, hated him for stopping me. But I wouldn't be here now if it weren't for Aaron. I don't care what anyone says. He's our brother. He's yours too, but for some reason you've got your wires all twisted because if you stopped to think long and hard about the good ol' days you'd see you've got it all wrong. Maggie never loved you or any of us like she loved Aaron. For some reason, though, everyone can see that but you."

"Can we get to work now?" Derrick asked.

"Good idea," one of the twins said.

"By the way," Derrick told Jake, "Mom wanted me to tell you she found the rollerblades you were looking for, the ones you need for your date with Candy this weekend."

Brad made a whooping sound. "Candy Baker? The mean one?"

"The same Candy who ran off with your clothes when you were changing for P.E. when you were still in high school?" Cliff asked.

"It's no big deal," Jake told them. "I happened to run into her the other day."

Cliff scratched his chin. "Rollerblading? Do people even do that anymore?"

They all laughed, except for Jake, of course. And Derrick, because he was too busy trying to figure out why his brothers were so damned blind and forgetful when it came to him and Maggie and what they had shared. Hell, he and his brothers and Maggie had all hung out together twenty-four-seven back then. Derrick couldn't recall one time when Aaron and Maggie had spent more than a few minutes together. The only reason Derrick hadn't gone after Maggie was because of the vow—the vow he now realized nobody had taken seriously except for him.

~~~

It took the four of them about an hour to fill his new two-bedroom apartment with a double bed, dresser, couch, coffee table and forty-inch flat-screen TV. The place had come with a refrigerator and a washer and dryer. Derrick opened the refrigerator and passed out canned iced teas.

"What's this?" Cliff asked. "No beer?"

"Maybe next time," Derrick said as he popped his can open.

"He's trying to set a good example while he's living here," Brad reminded his twin.

"You need some pictures. I have an old poster of Pamela Anderson you can hang above the TV but I want it back when you move out of here."

Derrick ignored them all as he headed to his new bedroom, the one with his bed and dresser, but more importantly, the one with his painkillers stashed in his luggage in the closet. He didn't like taking painkillers. In fact, he avoided them whenever possible. But after lifting couches and tables and walking up and down too many stairs, his right knee felt as if it was on fire. Last week his doctor had offered to shoot his injured knee with steroids to ease the pain, but Derrick figured he'd let the doctor save the needles for someone who needed them more than he did. He'd dealt with worse pain than this during his football career and a little ache once in a while wasn't going to take him out of the game. Football was his life. Football had provided him with a comfortable house, paid off his parents' mortgage, and unbeknownst to Jake, football would see his brother through college. No, he'd never let a few painkillers ruin everything he'd worked so hard for.

"Hurting again?"

Derrick swallowed the pill and took another swig of his iced tea before he turned to his brother Connor leaning against the doorframe watching him.

"I'm fine," Derrick said as he examined his older brother at closer view, surprised to see him, since Connor rarely came around these days. When he did show up he usually had on his scrubs and a white lab coat since he worked ridiculously long hours as a physician. Connor was the handsome one in the family and Derrick and his brothers liked to tease him about his good looks. Today Connor wore a dark-fitted suit and solid blue silk tie.

"Glad you stopped by," Derrick said. "Hot date?"

Connor answered with a crooked half smile. "No date. I was at a conference not too far from here. Mom said you could use some help moving furniture, but it looks like it's all taken care of."

"Thanks anyway. How are things?"

"Fine," Connor said. He nodded toward the luggage in the closet. "If you ever need help getting off those pills, let me know."

"I appreciate the offer," Derrick said, "but I'm fine. The knee is doing much better. In fact, I'll be as good as new before you can say 'preseason.'" Derrick didn't bother explaining that he'd had the same bottle of pills for so long they were nearly expired. He knew his brother had a tendency to think anyone taking anything stronger than an aspirin had a drug problem. Two years ago, Connor had lost his wife to drugs, and he hadn't been the same since. Derrick didn't see any purpose in trying to set him straight. What good would it do? Instead, he ushered his brother out of his bedroom and down the short hallway leading to the main room.

"So, now that you've moved into an apartment the size of your master bedroom in Malibu," Connor said, "what's next?"

"Now I take one day at a time and hope for the best."

"Wook, Mommy! It's Howiewood."

Nobody had bothered shutting the front door. Derrick laughed at the little curly-haired head sticking inside his new apartment. "Hey, Lexi, what's up?"

"Who's that?" Connor asked.

"That's Satan's child," Derrick said under his breath.

Connor angled his head for a better look at the little girl. "She looks sweet enough."

Derrick chuckled. "Don't get me wrong. The kid is great, it's the mother—"

Sandy caught up to her daughter and peered inside the apartment before he could finish his sentence.

"She doesn't look like Satan," Connor said under his breath.

"You can't judge a book by its cover," Derrick said. "Never forget that."

"Sorry," Sandy said as she struggled with bags and packages and at the same time tried to get a hold of Lexi's arm before her daughter could get inside Derrick's apartment.

Too late.

Cliff was in the kitchen putting away plates and utensils while Brad fiddled with hooking up the television. Jake sat on the couch with his iced tea which left Connor to go to the door and free Sandy of her burden.

"I'm fine," she said.

"Not a problem," Connor said, taking her bags anyhow.

Lexi pulled on Derrick's pant leg. "Want to draw? I have new crayons."

Derrick bent down on his good knee so the top of Lexi's head came to his chest instead of his knees. "You're in luck. My brother, Jake, loves to color." Derrick pointed to the couch where Jake sat.

Lexi didn't waste any time taking the crayons and coloring book to him.

Jake paled as the kid crawled onto his lap and got comfortable. Lexi opened her animal coloring book and stabbed a finger at the first picture she came to. "Wets do the wyon first. He says 'roar.'" Lexi roared a couple of times and then smiled, proud of herself.

Sandy stood just inside the doorway and shook her head. "I'm sorry, she's too fast for me these days."

"Jake doesn't mind," Derrick said. "He was the coloring champion in his kindergarten days."

The look Jake gave him told Derrick that his brother would find a way to get him back later.

"Ooooh," Lexi said to Jake. "I wike you."

Jake forced a smile as he took the crayon Lexi stabbed into his hand and started coloring.

Sandy looked around the apartment. "So which one of you lives here?" she asked Derrick.

"Derrick's renting the place for a few months," Brad told her.

"*Really*? Does Jill know?"

"Not yet." Derrick gestured toward Jake, hoping to change the subject. "Sandy, I'd like you to meet a few of my brothers. Jake is the one coloring. Cliff is in the kitchen unloading and Brad is the guy fiddling with the television." All three brothers greeted her with either a wave or a hello. "The well-dressed one with your bags is Connor."

She smiled and made eye contact with everyone but Connor. Derrick couldn't help but wonder if Sandy was being shy. He wouldn't have guessed she had a timid bone in her body.

"Did you say 'a few of your brothers'?" she asked. "Are there more?"

"Three more," Connor said. "Garrett, Lucas, and Aaron— and two sisters: Rachel and Zoey."

"Your mother must be some woman. I have my hands full with one."

"She is," all the brothers said at once.

Sandy seemed like a different person today, Derrick thought. She seemed relaxed, as if her guard was down. Or maybe she'd come to terms with the fact that he was in the picture now and everybody would be best served to make the best of it.

She looked over her shoulder and said, "Oh, look. There's Jill now. Come on, Lexi, time to go."

Derrick swept past his guests and headed out the door where he saw Jill trudging up the stairs to her apartment. Ryan was strapped into a baby carrier.

He greeted her at the top of the landing. "Hi."

She stopped on the last stair. "What are you doing here?"

"I live here now." He pointed to the apartment across the way.

She looked in the direction he pointed and saw Sandy surrounded by men. "What is Sandy doing over there?"

"She and Lexi stopped by to say hello. I was hoping you could do the same." He lifted a finger. "One moment of your time, that's all I ask, just long enough to give my brothers a glimpse of their nephew."

Jill moved past him and set the baby carrier on the welcome mat in front of her apartment so she could sift through her purse for her keys. "You shouldn't have moved here. I can't believe you would stoop that low."

Derrick didn't respond. He didn't want to argue with her because the truth was he'd known she wouldn't be pleased. Instead, he watched Ryan try to stuff his tiny hand into his mouth. It had only been a few days since he saw his son and yet Ryan already looked as if he'd doubled in size. "Hey little guy," he said as he bent down to talk to him. "You're getting big fast, aren't you?"

Ryan's fingers clasped firmly around Derrick's thumb. The little guy smelled like baby powder and formula. "Look at that. He already has a good, strong grip. Someday you're going to play football like your old man, aren't you?"

Jill disappeared inside her apartment and dropped her purse on the coffee table with a purposeful *thunk*.

She came back to where he hovered over Ryan and crossed her arms tight against her chest. "One minute," she said. "That's all you get. And Ryan is not going to be a football player when he grows up."

It took a moment for what she said to register. The football comment had thrown him off, but more importantly, he hadn't expected Jill to agree to his request to introduce Ryan to his brothers.

He stood, figuring he'd better move quickly and take advantage of her agreeable mood. But before he could pick up the carrier, Jill leaned low and scooped Ryan into her arms.

Derrick followed close behind as she headed for his apartment.

Ryan began to fuss.

"Is that Ryan?" somebody asked over the din when Jill stepped inside his apartment.

Brad reached Jill's side first. "Can I hold him?"

"I don't think that's a good idea," Derrick said.

"Of course you can." She placed Ryan in his brother's arms. "Here." She showed Brad how to place his elbow. "You can use the crook of your arm to hold his head up. Yes, like that."

"Look at that!" Brad said. "He stopped crying."

"He don't wike his mommy," Lexi said as she picked a new crayon out of the box next to Jake.

"That's not true," Sandy told her daughter. "What did I tell you about that?"

"You said it's okay cuz wots of babies don't wike their mommies."

"I did not." Sandy looked at Jill and gave her an apologetic shrug.

Jill looked determined to ignore them all as she continued to help Derrick's brother with Ryan.

A knot formed in Derrick's throat. What the hell was wrong with him anyhow? Every time he was around Jill and his son a gushy sappy wave of emotion swept over him.

Cliff and Connor were now huddled around the baby, smiling and making faces at Ryan. "You did good," Connor said to Derrick after taking a quick peek at Ryan.

"He didn't do anything," Jill said.

She was mad at him for renting out the apartment, no doubt about it.

Cliff laughed at her sassiness. "It's pretty amazing how all of that donor stuff works. It won't be long before women don't need men at all."

"You know what they say," Jake said, "you can't live with them and you can't live without them."

Sandy huffed.

"That's what Mom's been telling Dad for years," Brad said before he started making ridiculous goo goo sounds at the baby.

Jill smiled at Brad's antics, a genuine smile that told Derrick she was warming up to his brothers, or at least to one of them.

"I have new crayons, Jill!" Lexi shouted into Jake's ear, making him wince.

"You're a lucky girl," Jill told her. "What are you doing over there?"

"Pwaying with my new boyfriend."

"Okay," Sandy said, shaking her head and trying not to look amused. "I think it's time for us to go."

"Sorry I was late," Jill told Sandy. "You know how bad traffic is at this time of the day."

"No worries. Lexi always manages to find something for us to do."

"I should go," Jill said. "It was nice meeting you all."

"Before you go," Brad said, "Mom would be forever grateful if you brought Ryan to the barbeque at her house this weekend. We'll all be there."

Derrick noticed Jill's eye twitch, a definite sign that she was uncomfortable. He'd seen the same twitch the other day when he showed up at her doorstep unexpectedly.

"I don't think that would be a good idea," Jill said.

"Lexi could ride the ponies," Cliff pointed out.

Lexi dropped her crayon and screamed, "Ponies!" at the top of her lungs.

"And Jake will be there," Derrick told Lexi, causing her to jump up and down in Jake's lap as she clapped her tiny hands in giddy delight, making Jake grimace.

"Your parents have ponies?" Sandy asked.

"They own a pony farm," Connor answered.

"Mom would love for all of you to come for an early dinner on Sunday," Cliff told Sandy, making it clear that she and her daughter Lexi were invited too.

Brad nodded his head. "And we won't take no for an answer."

CHAPTER 7

"Have you ever seen that many good-looking men in one family?"

Jill and Sandy sliced and diced the green peppers and onions for the chili recipe they planned to have on the cover of next month's issue of *Food For All*. Every month they had a theme and this month's focus was soups, stews, and chili. Sandy was an amazing cook and usually didn't bother fiddling with other people's recipes, but the woman in charge of the test kitchen had quit, leaving them in a bind.

Jill reached across the kitchen counter and turned up the baby monitor. They had left Derrick's apartment over an hour ago. Ryan had not stopped crying until five minutes ago. Not a peep while he was being held in Derrick's brothers' arms, but once Jill took her son, all bets were off. He hadn't stopped crying, not until she put him in the crib and let him cry himself to sleep. Lexi was right. Ryan didn't like his mommy.

"Earth to Jill."

"Sorry," Jill said. "What were you saying?"

"All those good-looking brothers in one family and not one of them had a ring on his finger. What do you think that says about men?"

"I don't know, but I suppose you're going to tell me."

"It's proof of what I've been saying all along. Women no longer need men to hunt or bring home the bacon, so what's the point?"

Jill shook her head. "You really need to let go of the weird bitterness you have towards men."

"My father left my mother and me when I was six," Sandy reminded her. "I wouldn't know him if he passed me on the street. What sort of man leaves his own flesh and blood, never to be heard from again?"

"Not all men are like your father or your ex-boyfriend."

"How can you say that after being stranded at the altar? Men are good for one thing and I won't remind you of what that one thing is, but the problem is, men don't have stick-ability."

"It's just a matter of finding the right man," Jill said. "We need to be patient." When Sandy met a man she was interested in, she tended to be controlling and abrasive. Jill figured that Sandy subconsciously sabotaged a relationship right from the beginning, since she didn't believe there was a man in the world who would stick around anyhow. The relationship always fizzled out before it had a chance, confirming Sandy's fears. But Jill didn't want to upset her friend, so she changed the subject. "Did I tell you Thomas called the other day?"

Sandy's eyes widened. "What did he want?"

"He offered to be my lawyer in the event I need help keeping Derrick away from me and Ryan."

"How did he even know Derrick was in the picture?"

"I told Mom and she must have told him. Despite the fact that Thomas left me at the altar, my parents still think he walks on water."

"What did you tell him?"

"I told him I appreciated the offer but I didn't need his help. I also told him that Derrick and I were dating."

"You what?"

Jill smiled "Great idea, don't you think? I wanted to show Thomas that I've moved on. And besides, he'll tell my parents and then hopefully they won't come to visit right away."

"Did he sound upset?"

Jill shrugged and then stirred the ingredients in the pot on the stove. "It was hard to tell."

"Did Thomas mention Ryan, you know, did he ask how Ryan was doing?"

"He congratulated me and said he was sorry for everything that happened between us."

Sandy finished pouring barbeque sauce into a measuring cup and then looked at Jill again. "You're worried about something. What is it?"

"I'm thinking I should seriously think about Thomas's offer in case it turns out that Derrick and I can't work something out when it comes to Ryan. It would be ignorant of me to walk into mediation next month without being prepared."

"True," Sandy said as she tossed onions and peppers into the pot. "I'm curious though. Why do you think Thomas called now after all this time?"

"He called once before, but I didn't pick up."

"Do you still have feelings for him?"

"I've come to realize I need closure and the only way I'm going to get it is if I sit down and talk to him about what happened." What Jill really needed to know was how someone she'd been ready to spend the rest of her life with could humiliate her in such a way. If he'd known he couldn't go through with the marriage, why hadn't he talked to her instead of leaving her standing there like a fool? The question had kept her awake for too many nights. She had trusted Thomas. Never in a million years had she believed he would be capable of doing such a thing. But he had, and he did, and less than a week after leaving her at the church, her parents had invited him inside their home and begged Jill to come out of her room and talk to him. They expected Jill to forgive him without question. That had been the last straw. She'd packed up her things and left for California within the week.

The scent of garlic mixed with onions wafted from the pot as Sandy added white beans to the mix. "I wonder if Connor will be at the barbeque on Sunday?" Sandy asked.

"Derrick's brother?"

Sandy nodded. "Why the surprise?"

"I don't know. I guess I just haven't seen you show interest in a man in a while."

"I'm not interested in Connor. I was just wondering about him because he seemed so quiet…and sad."

If Jill thought there was any chance at all of helping Sandy make a love match, she'd be all over it. But the truth was Sandy was too darn picky, not to mention stubborn and opinionated.

"I didn't notice," Jill lied. "But since we're talking about Derrick and his brothers, I've decided that it's not a good idea for me to attend the barbeque this weekend."

Sandy didn't respond.

"I'm not even sure if it's a good idea for Derrick and me to be friends," Jill added.

"I can't disagree with that," Sandy said as she stirred all the ingredients in the pot together. "You know how I feel about him showing up unexpectedly."

"Exactly. I went through the sperm donor process knowing I would be raising Ryan on my own. But for the record, just because I don't want Derrick Baylor in Ryan's life, that doesn't mean I think he's a bad guy. It's just that I need—no, make that I *want* to raise Ryan on my own. And besides, Derrick is a football player, a celebrity of sorts. He's a good looking man and it won't be long before he'll be married and have a family of his own. I don't want Ryan to ever feel like he's second best. Being friends with Derrick would never work. The man needs to leave us alone."

"Agreed." Sandy put the lid on the chili and turned the temperature to low.

Jill followed Sandy into the family room where Lexi was quietly coloring. She helped her gather Lexi's coloring books and crayons.

"I'm sure Derrick will understand when you tell him you've changed your mind about the barbeque."

"Too bad if he doesn't understand," Jill said, trying to convince herself that not having anything to do with Ryan's father was the right thing to do. "He never should have moved to the apartment next door without discussing it with me first. He's arrogant and pushy. If he thinks he can just—"

A knock sounded at the door.

All riled up, Jill went to the door and jerked it open.

Derrick stood on the other side. His hair was damp. He had on a clean pair of jeans and a blue button-down shirt. He was also holding a crayon. "I thought Lexi might need this."

She took the crayon, thanked him, and tried to shut the door, but he put his hand on the doorframe above her head and used his broad shoulders to prevent her from doing so. "I wanted to thank you for letting my brothers meet Ryan," he told her. "It meant a lot."

"You're welcome."

He peeked his head inside. "Is Ryan asleep?"

She nodded.

He spotted Sandy. "Leaving already?"

"It's getting late," she said. "Jill and I have a lot to do tomorrow."

"Anything I can do to help?"

Sandy smirked at him and then looked at Jill as if to say "tell him to get lost and tell him now."

Ryan began to cry in the other room.

Derrick gestured that way. "Want me to get him?"

"No thanks, I've got it under control."

"Are you still mad at me?"

"Of course I am," Jill said. "A week ago I didn't know you existed, but you've managed to barge into my life without my permission. Everywhere I look, there you are. You've seen me at my most vulnerable and now you've set yourself up so you can watch my every move."

"You think I want to spy on you?"

She raised her chin. "Yes."

"Listen," he said, leaning close enough for her to get a whiff of aftershave. "I'm not spying. I just want a chance to get to know you and Ryan. I swear on my honor, that's all there is to it. I would never try and take Ryan from you. Never."

"You're obviously used to getting what you want."

"I've been sort of pushy, haven't I?"

"That's putting it mildly."

Semi-defeated, he looked at Sandy. "Need any help getting to your car?"

"I think it's safest for me to say 'no, thank you.'"

"I'll be on my way then."

Jill tried to shut the door, but he was still in the way. The man was impossible.

"One more thing…I talked to Mom and everything's set. She's very grateful that you're willing to bring Ryan to the ranch. If it works for you, I'll pick the four of you up at noon on Sunday."

"To ride ponies?" Lexi asked from the family room.

"To ride ponies," he said with a smile.

Jill anchored a strand of hair behind her ear, hating the way she felt all tongue-tied and weak in the knees whenever she was face-to-face with the man. "Why do I get the feeling I don't have a choice in the matter?"

"You have a choice," Sandy reminded her.

A dimple appeared when he smiled. The last thing the man needed was a dimple.

"I won't let anyone hold Ryan unless you give them permission first," he said. "Ponies for Lexi. Great food. Fun people. Short and sweet."

"Ponies!" Lexi shouted.

"Come on," Sandy said to her daughter, "let's go check on Ryan."

Jill sighed as Sandy and Lexi disappeared into the other room.

"You won't regret it," Derrick promised. "Everyone is going to love you."

"Well, I doubt that." *How could they when she didn't even like herself? She was such a pushover.*

"Are you kidding me?" His hand rested high on the doorframe above her head.

She found herself wishing she'd put on heels so she wouldn't be forced to stare at the vee of his button-down shirt where bronzed skin and a feathering of dark hair drew her attention.

"You've got everything going for you," he went on, killing her with kindness. "You're kind, caring, and beautiful. What's not to love?"

The man could charm a worker bee from its queen. She crooked her neck so she could look into his eyes. "Your nickname should be Charmer instead of Hollywood."

"It was already taken."

She smiled at his light-hearted arrogance. "A small family get-together?"

"Under a dozen."

"No fanfare?"

"Over my dead body."

"No balloons or extravagant gifts?"

"No way. Gift giving is overrated."

She crossed her arms. "You're just saying what you think I want to hear, aren't you?"

His brows slanted. "I would never do that."

"Okay," she said, trying not to be amused by the man who was only here because of Ryan. "If it means that much to you, we'll go."

He grinned. "You're a sweetheart." Before she could shut the door he said, "One more thing—something I've been meaning to ask you."

She raised a questioning brow.

"The cute gray-haired candy striper at the hospital told me you had left in a hurry because you needed to plan *our* wedding."

She laughed at the anxious expression on his face. "That was Sandy's doing. She was hoping the candy striper would scare you away so we wouldn't have to."

Derrick frowned. "Your friend has a mean streak a mile wide, doesn't she?"

"She's had a tough life," she said in a low voice so Sandy wouldn't overhear, "but she has a big heart. Besides, you have nothing to worry about," Jill added. "I'll never marry. I have everything I need right here in this apartment."

CHAPTER 8

Six thirty the next morning Derrick walked out of his apartment wearing a T-shirt and shorts, heading for the gym. As he passed by Jill's apartment he heard Ryan crying.

Poor Jill. Every time he saw her she looked more exhausted than the last time. Too bad she was too stubborn to let him help her out while he had the time. In another six weeks he'd be on the training field every day. If he recalled correctly there was a Starbucks around the corner. He walked down the cement stairs, headed for the parking lot and climbed into his car.

Fifteen minutes later he stood in front of Jill's apartment holding a nice warm Grande Mocha. He knocked three times and waited.

The door came open.

Jill stood on the other side, holding a fussy baby in her arms. Pale, expressionless, and wearing a gray sweat outfit with a trail of baby spit-up on the neckline, she looked like a walking zombie. Tangled hair escaped a clip at the back of her head. Her eyes were heavy-lidded and bloodshot. Ryan let out a wail almost as loud as the sirens he'd heard last night.

He held the cup of coffee towards her. "I got you a Mocha."

She looked at his offering with longing. "How did you know?"

"Lucky guess."

Her cell phone rang. The ringtone made a cricket noise. She turned and shuffled away, wearing outrageously fluffy slippers. She held Ryan in one arm and used her free hand to pick up her cell before her phone could play another round of chirping.

Derrick waited at the door. He knew she didn't want his help, but her stubbornness was clearly going to get the best of her. She couldn't exactly conduct business with a crying baby in one arm and the phone in the other. Without asking for permission, he stepped inside, shut the door behind him, and went to the kitchen. He set her coffee on the countertop and then took Ryan out of her grasp. Holding Ryan close to his chest, he rocked him. Ryan stopped crying.

He left Jill in the kitchen and headed for the living room. He didn't bother glancing back to see if she was upset with him for coming inside. Ryan's small body felt warm against his chest. He liked the way Ryan smelled—like baby powder and Jill. Judging from the one-sided conversation he was hearing, Jill's phone call was not making her morning any better. With the phone pressed between her shoulder and her ear, she rifled through a stack of papers. Despite the baggy sweats she wore, he noticed she'd lost a significant amount of weight since Ryan was born. Too much weight, he thought, but with her hair askew and that small up-turned nose of hers she looked downright cute.

"Sandy and I made the chili that's supposed to be featured on next month's cover," she said into the receiver. "It tastes bland—not good at all. I need you to make the chili again, using the exact same recipe as soon as possible." Her voice was lined with panic. "Yes, in the next few hours. Follow the directions to a tee and then bring it to me for a taste test. If it tastes anything like the concoction we made last night we're in trouble." She nodded her head. "Yes. I know I've thrown a lot at you in the past week, but I'm counting on you, Chelsey. Okay. I'll see you in a few hours."

Jill clicked her cell shut and then leaned forward and let her forehead fall flat against the papers on the counter. She stayed that way for a good two minutes.

Derrick noticed her shoulders trembling. He stiffened. Was she crying? Looking around, he wondered what he should do. He had two sisters who rarely cried. He couldn't remember if he'd ever seen his mother cry at all. Crying females made him nervous, made him feel awkward and helpless. Knowing he should comfort her, he inhaled and headed her way just as the fax machine beeped in the other room.

She must have heard it, too, because she was off and running before he could offer any sort of sympathy. *Saved by the beep.*

Ten minutes passed before Jill returned.

Derrick was sitting on the couch. Ryan was asleep in his arms.

Jill extended both arms toward him. "Okay, you can go. I'm ready to take my son now."

A red nose and a slightly deranged look in her big green eyes convinced him not to question her authority. He handed Ryan over and then stood. Before she took two steps, Ryan was crying again. It wasn't a hungry cry either, which he was proud to realize he already recognized. It was a long, high-pitched shriek that reached the core of his brain and made his teeth clench. Without a word spoken, Jill turned about and handed Ryan back to him. Jill's head dropped, her chin hit her chest, and this time she cried in earnest, her shoulders moving in rhythm to her pitiful sobs.

With Ryan in one arm, he wrapped his other arm around Jill's shoulder and pulled her in close, giving her no choice but to rest her head in the crook of his arm while he stroked her upper arm with the pad of his thumb. Before long, she relaxed and he only heard a couple of hiccups and a sniffle here and there.

Ryan wriggled in his other arm, but his son must have sensed now was not the time to fuss because he quickly settled down.

"I don't know what's wrong with me," Jill said as she pulled away.

"I know exactly what's wrong," Derrick told her. "It sounds like you have a case of the ol' baby blues."

She raised a questioning brow, prompting him to gesture toward the book titled *A Mother's Guide to Newborns* sitting on the coffee table. "I looked through it when you were in the other room taking care of business. It says new mothers are often overworked and deprived of sleep. It makes sense—little sleep together with all those hormones and emotions—excitement and joy one moment and then fear and anxiousness the next. It's a wonder you moms survive this stage at all."

She wiped her eyes. "Are you for real?"

He wasn't sure how to answer the question, so he didn't.

"Why aren't you married?" she asked. Then she waved her hands in front of her as if erasing the question altogether. "Don't get me wrong, I already know you're far from perfect."

Although he wasn't sensitive when it came to name calling or character bashing, her statement did make him frown.

"Well, you did lie on your donor application and we've already determined that you can be pushy and overbearing," she said between sniffles. "But you seem like an okay guy overall, so what's the deal?" She hiccupped. "Were you married before? Do you have a fiancée waiting for you back at the Malibu home your brothers mentioned?" She plopped down in the cushiony chair facing the couch and lifted big fluffy pink slippers onto the ottoman. "Out with it. What's really going on here?"

Holding Ryan close, Derrick took his time lowering himself to the edge of the couch, thinking about how he should answer the question. Under any other circumstance, he wouldn't bother, but she was the mother of his son, a son he wanted to help raise. This was his chance to get to know Jill. He couldn't blow it now. "I guess you could say I am married to football," he said, knowing his reasoning might sound lame, but it was the truth. "I'm nearly thirty years old and so far my life has revolved around the game. Football gave me a chance to be close to my dad when he coached Pee Wee football." Derrick took in a breath at the realization because it was the truth. With so many siblings, it wasn't easy to get his father's attention back then. "When some of my friends were getting into trouble in high school, football gave me a thrill like nothing else could. Playing in college and then in the NFL ended up being the icing on the cake. And," he added thoughtfully, "I guess football has kept me busy, too busy to think about much else."

She crossed her ankles. "Lots of famous football players have families."

"True," he said. "To tell you the truth, I wasn't sure how I was going to feel if I found you and you were pregnant. But the moment I saw you standing behind the officer—" He looked down at Ryan. His eyes were open and he was staring at him, seemingly mesmerized. Derrick brushed his finger against the palm of Ryan's tiny hand. "The moment I realized you might be carrying a child that was a part of me...I felt something I've never felt before." He paused as he tried to formulate the words so he could better explain. "Let me put it this way—when I'm playing in a big game and I scramble around guys twice my size and then set and throw the ball across the field with pin-point accuracy, it's like drinking a glass of cold fresh water after a day in the hot desert. It's heaven. It's indescribable." Derrick marveled at Ryan's small fingers wrapped around his finger. "I guess what I'm trying to say is that the moment I laid eyes on Ryan in the hospital I felt that same feeling—only it was different because the euphoric feeling didn't go away after the crowd stopped cheering, so to speak. Holding Ryan and spending a little time with him, knowing he's a part of me, has done something to me. It has made me think differently about life."

He lifted his shoulders in a helpless shrug.

~~~

Jill felt all gushy and wishy-washy inside. Derrick's moving speech had left her with a tight feeling in her chest. She laid her head back against her favorite chair and said, "I think I know what you mean."

He looked relieved. "You do?"

She nodded. "Having Ryan has changed me too." She didn't want to say much more than that, didn't want Derrick to know she didn't feel a connection to Ryan yet, or that most of her thoughts these past few days were filled with doubt and fear. Her parents had always made her feel like second best, like she didn't count. She didn't know what it was like to be a part of a big loving family, but she knew that's what she wanted for her and Ryan. The truth was, before Ryan was born, she'd planned on having at least two more children, which is why she'd bought and stored enough of Derrick Baylor's semen to start a football team of her own. But nobody, including Derrick, needed to know that.

"Let me help you out," he said after a quiet moment passed between them. "Until training begins, I have nothing better to do with my time."

She wanted to tell him no, but nothing came out of her mouth. Every muscle in her body felt weak with exhaustion.

"Since I don't want to be pushy and overbearing I won't insist, but I think a shower and a long nap would do you wonders."

He held her gaze for a long moment, long enough to make her wonder why she had allowed him into her apartment in the first place. The man was gorgeous to look at and he was nice, too. She looked like hell while he looked like he was ready for a photo shoot at *GQ*.

"Just a thought," he added. "It's your call."

She stood and looked toward her bedroom before looking back at him. She knew she should ask him to leave, but a shower and a nap sounded too good to pass up. "You really wouldn't mind?"

He shook his head. "I'm here to help. You can trust me."

~~~

Thomas stood on one side of the mist-filled room and Derrick Baylor stood on the other. Thomas reached out a hand to her while Derrick merely winked. Thomas wore a perfectly fitted suit while Derrick wore slacks, a button-down shirt, and a killer smile.

Jill didn't know which way to turn. Her heart raced as she tried to make a decision, but then Ryan began to cry.

Her eyes shot open and she bolted upward in bed.

She looked about, glad to see that neither man was hovering over her. *Thank God.* She put a hand on her chest above her pounding heart. What the heck was Derrick Baylor doing in her dream? Seeing Thomas made sense since he'd been in most of her dreams since he left her at the church eighteen months ago. But Derrick?

Laughter from the kitchen floated in under the door and to her bed. It sounded like a party out there. She pushed the comforter to the side, slid both legs over the edge of the mattress and wriggled her feet into the slippers on the floor.

She stood at the door and listened for a moment.

The voices all blurred together but Lexi and Sandy's voice were easy to decipher. Ah, and Chelsey. Chelsey must have finished cooking the chili and brought it for a taste test.

She opened the door a smidgeon and peeked toward the kitchen. Sandy's back was to her, but judging by the red pencil skirt and matching jacket she'd come straight from a sales meeting downtown. Her hair was in a neat twist on the back of her head. Sandy had always had a flair for fashion.

Sandy laughed about something and when she walked away, Jill blinked to make sure she wasn't imagining things. As far as she could tell, Chelsey had indeed brought the chili for a taste test and she was spoon feeding the chili to Derrick. He opened his mouth and as he chewed and swallowed he groaned as if he was having a chili orgasm. While Derrick continued to make absurd noises, Chelsey grabbed a napkin and used it to dab at his chin as if they were lovers.

It was all too much. Why hadn't anyone come into her room to wake her up? Why hadn't Sandy kicked Derrick out of her apartment?

Sleepily, Jill trudged into the room. As she glanced around, she plunked a hand on her hip. "Where's Ryan?"

"It's alive," Sandy said as she came to Jill's side and tried to fix her hair.

Jill swatted her hand away.

"Ryan's asleep," Derrick said from the kitchen.

"Then why are you still here?"

"Because he's our savior," Chelsey said with way too much enthusiasm. "He added red and green chili peppers to the chili," she went on, "and it turns out that's exactly what was missing. The woman who sent in the recipe, you know, the one who won all those competitions…well, I just talked to her on the phone and sure enough, she forgot to include a few ingredients when she typed out the recipe for us."

Jill grunted. How could she omit chili peppers from a chili recipe? "Did you tell her how much trouble she's caused us?"

"It's not that big of a deal," Chelsey assured her before she looked back at Derrick and batted her eyelashes."

For the first time since hiring Chelsey six months ago, Jill noticed how perky and cute she was with her blonde curly hair that bounced around her pale shoulders every time she moved. She looked amazing in her sleeveless sundress and strappy sandals. Surprisingly, Jill found herself wanting nothing more than to tell them all to leave. And then she wanted to pick up the phone and call that woman and tell her she didn't deserve to win any ribbons at the next county fair if she couldn't even get one simple chili recipe right.

Breathe, Jill, breathe.

Derrick was right. She had the baby blues, and she had them bad. All of this negative energy was wearing her out. Since when did she care what Chelsey wore or if everybody looked amazing except for her? She wasn't vain like her mother and sister. She didn't have to look perfect every second of the day. For the umpteenth time in the past week, she found herself wanting to cry, which only served to make her want to cry even more because she wasn't a crier by nature. Her hormones were definitely out of control and she didn't like it one bit.

Jill turned away to head back to her room when suddenly Ryan's cry pierced her eardrums. She looked over her shoulder at Derrick. "Your baby is crying. I'm going back to bed."

CHAPTER 9

Thomas stood near the rose garden. Tonight he wore a tuxedo and the moonlight glistened off of his hair and played with the angles of his face, throwing shadows across a nicely shaped jaw and long straight nose.

Across the way, Derrick sat poolside in nothing but a pair of colorful board shorts. His fingers plowed through thick wet hair, sprinkling droplets of water over a bronzed chest and well-worked biceps.

Both men looked Jill's way as she walked toward them, hips swaying.

"She's beautiful," Thomas said.

"Yes," Derrick agreed. "And she's all mine. You blew it, buster."

Jill's eyes popped open. She stared up at the ceiling. What was wrong with her? She hardly knew Derrick and yet she couldn't shut her eyes without dreaming about him. Not once, but twice!

Her heart hammered against her chest as she realized she was absolutely, certifiably losing her mind. There was no other explanation. Derrick wasn't her type. She wasn't attracted to men with deeply tanned bodies and big muscles. Flashing white teeth and sparkling eyes that winked with mischief were not her cup of tea. No sirree. She liked professional men who took life a little more seriously. She preferred a man in a suit who used his brains more than his brawns.

The clock on her nightstand read three o'clock.

She looked back at the ceiling before giving the clock a second look. No way was it three o'clock. It was closer to nine o'clock in the morning the last time she had awakened to the sounds of everybody partying in her kitchen. If it was three o'clock, that would mean she'd slept six hours straight. She'd never taken a six hour nap in her life. Trying not to panic, she flipped off the covers, slid her legs over the side of the bed, slipped her feet inside her big pink slippers, and headed for the door. She listened for a moment.

Nothing. Not a sound.

Ryan. Where was Ryan?

She hadn't spent this many hours away from him since he'd been born. It was no use. Panic hit her like lightning, swooshing through her insides as she shot through the door and ran to the family room. *Where was everyone?*

She ran to the baby's room. Empty.

She ran to the kitchen and saw a note written in cursive.

Took Ryan for a stroll to the park. Hope you don't mind.
—D

Derrick had taken her baby out of her apartment.

How could he?

White-hot flames shot up from the tips of her toes, searing and blistering.

She ran to her bedroom and shook her feet until one slipper flew across the room. The other slipper disappeared under the bed. She shuffled through her closet until she found a pair of tennis shoes and quickly jammed them onto her feet. A glimpse at the mirror above her dresser caused her to make a quick trip to the bathroom where she splashed water on her face, brushed her teeth, and combed her hair back into a ponytail.

The last thing she did before running out the door was grab a sweatshirt from the pile of clean clothes on the wicker chair sitting in the corner of her room.

~~~

Derrick decided they couldn't have picked a nicer day to visit the park. Chelsey was a character with her wide smile and enthusiastic spirit. Sandy, on the other hand, was proving to be a hard nut to crack. No matter how charming he was, she would not cave.

As Sandy and Chelsey passed out coupons to people so they could receive a discount on the *Food For All* magazine along with free samples of the chili, Derrick made small talk with strangers and signed autographs. A woman and her son walked his way. Derrick bent down on one knee so he could talk to the boy. "What's your name?"

The kid blushed and handed him a jagged piece of paper ripped from a magazine. "Eddie."

"How old are you, Eddie?"

"Eight."

"Do you like to play football?"

He shook his head. "Mom says I can't. I'm too thin. She thinks the other guys will break my bones."

"Do you have a football at home?"

He shook his head again.

Derrick signed the piece of paper "Hollywood" and then scrawled his e-mail address beneath his signature. "E-mail me your address and I'll send you a football. It won't hurt you to practice throwing to your friends."

The kid smiled and then looked over his shoulder at his mom to make sure it was okay. She nodded, prompting Eddie to take the slip of paper and run back to her with an energetic hop in his step.

An elderly woman had been waiting patiently for him to sign a coupon Sandy had given her for next month's issue of *Food For All*. He signed it and then hooked his arm around the woman's shoulders as her husband took a picture of the two of them. The couple then reversed positions and took another picture. After they walked away, he glanced at his watch. "It's three o'clock," he told Sandy and Chelsey as they passed out the last of the chili and coupons. "I should head back before Jill wakes up and finds the place empty."

"Jill is going to love what we've done here," Chelsey told him. "Thanks to you we passed out more than 250 twenty-percent-off coupons for next month's issue. We also got the thumbs up from every person who tried the chili."

"I must admit," Sandy said. "This was a great idea. No offense, Derrick, but I had no idea so many people would go out of their way to meet a football player. Jill will be very pleased."

"No offense taken," he said.

Derrick leaned over the stroller to check on Ryan. After having everyone fawn over him for the past two hours, the little guy was worn out. The temperature hovered around the low eighties and high seventies—a perfect day for an outing with his son.

When Sandy and Chelsey had mentioned that they were going to pass out chili along with discount coupons at the mall, he'd suggested they keep it simple and take the chili and coupons to the park. So that's what they did and it hadn't taken long for word of mouth to get out that a pro football player was passing out free chili and taking pictures.

"You have some gall taking my baby without asking me."

Derrick turned to the sound of Jill's angry voice.

Chelsey put a hand on Jill's shoulder. "This was my idea," she said, trying to take any blame off of Derrick. "And you won't be angry once you see what he's done for the magazine. Hundreds of people found out that Hollywood was in town and they came by in droves—all from word of mouth. Once they heard that a celebrity was at the park handing out free chili and autographs, people streamed in and just kept coming. It was fascinating to watch."

Derrick could see it coming, but poor Chelsey had yet to see the power of a woman's hormones after having a baby. Unfortunately Chelsey was about to see the full effects first hand.

Jill pivoted so she was face-to-face with Chelsey, their noses inches apart. "Since this was your idea," she said, "you're fired. No need to return to the apartment. I'll send you your termination papers along with a final paycheck."

School must have gotten out, Derrick noticed, because a group of teenagers were huddled together a few feet away. They were pointing and laughing, talking about women's underwear.

Derrick took a closer look at Jill. Sure enough, there was something pink and lacy sticking out from underneath her sweatshirt. He reached over and grabbed what turned out to be a pair of panties.

The kids laughed some more.

Jill swatted his hand without bothering to see what he was up to. She was too busy ripping Chelsey to shreds.

Derrick stuffed the panties into his front pants pocket.

"Are you kidding me?" Chelsey asked. "Look around you, Jill. We just passed out every coupon we had for next month's issue. We also got high ratings on the taste test we did for the chili that you want to put on next month's cover. Not only that, I took some amazing cover shots that I think you're going to be thrilled with. That's three items off of your to-do-list."

Jill pointed toward the street. "Go."

"But—"

"Nobody takes my baby without asking me. And, in case you haven't noticed, I am the new editorial director."

Derrick kept hoping Sandy would come to Chelsey's rescue, but she was passing out coupons to a family out of earshot and missed the commotion. He was about to step in and try to help Chelsey out himself, but three women, all holding babies, were now surrounding him. Not wanting complete strangers to see Jill's meltdown, he turned to the women and ushered them a few feet away.

"Would you mind if we had a picture taken with you, Mr. Baylor?"

"Not at all." He situated himself in the middle of the women and they all looked toward the camera which was being operated by a man he guessed to be one of the ladies' husband.

"We were watching you with your son earlier. He's adorable."

"I noticed he's not wearing anything on his feet," the curly haired woman said. "Even when it's warm, he should have something covering his feet."

"We also noticed a rash on his leg. I recommend cornstarch to take care of that."

They all started giving him advice at once. He nodded his head as he tried to take it all in: what detergent to use for washing Ryan's clothes, the best brand of diapers, and all the other essential baby items to purchase like carriers and swings.

A finger stabbed into the back of his arm, making him wince. He looked to his right and wasn't surprised to see Jill holding Ryan and giving him a look that could very easily make the devil himself bend to his knees and grovel.

Instead of groveling, he threw an arm around Jill's shoulder and pulled her in close. "This is Jill Garrison," he told the ladies. "Ryan's mom and editorial director of *Food For All*."

"Really?" the lady with curly hair asked as she took inventory of Jill's outfit: a pair of gray sweatpants and faded sweatshirt complete with big-eyed kitten wearing a blue frazzled bow around its neck. "This is your wife?"

The woman next to the curly haired lady blushed at her friend's behavior and said to Jill, "We were just telling your husband what a darling baby boy you two have."

"He's not my husband," Jill growled.

"Sorry. I just assumed."

Jill opened her mouth to say something, but Ryan began to fuss before she could say another word, which Derrick figured was a good thing. No telling what might come out of Jill's mouth. Judging by the deep furrows in her brow, it couldn't have been good.

"He might be colicky," the third woman said, speaking for the first time. "My little guy was colicky for the first three months. It was horrible because I was sleep deprived and for the longest time I didn't think my little Nathan liked me."

In the blink of an eye, Jill's expression went from angry to curious. She looked from Ryan's scrunched-up unhappy face to the woman who just spoke. "Colicky? What is that?"

"My doctor said that Nathan had too much gas, which caused painful cramping."

Jill handed Derrick the baby so she could scoot in closer and hear what the woman had to say. "What did you do?"

Derrick held Ryan in the crook of his arm and smiled at his pitiful scrunched-up face.

"There are lots of things you can try," the woman told Jill, "like keeping your baby's arms close to his body and rocking him gently. Some babies are more comfortable if they are on their stomach and then you can gently rub their back. If all else failed, I used to turn on the radio or even the vacuum cleaner."

"The vacuum cleaner?" Derrick asked.

She nodded. "Some babies are calmed by steady, consistent noises."

"It's true," the curly haired lady said. "My baby loved the wind-up swing. If that didn't work, I sometimes took her on a car ride until she fell asleep."

Derrick watched Jill's features soften. He could only guess she was relieved to know others had been there, done that…and they had survived.

"The most important thing," one of the women added, "is not to take the crying personally. Take deep breaths and try to relax. I know it's not easy, but you don't want to lose yourself in the process. It will get better."

Jill's shoulders relaxed as she released some of that built-up tension the women were talking about.

"And don't be afraid to accept or ask for help from friends and relatives."

Derrick wanted to toss in an "amen" but he remained quiet.

"The doctor will tell you if your baby is colicky," a woman said as she gave Jill a gentle tap on the arm. "When is your next appointment?"

Jill reached for Ryan and Derrick obliged by handing him over to her. "He goes for his first doctor's appointment tomorrow."

"Stay right here," the woman said. "I'm going to ask my husband to scribble down my number so that you can call me if you ever have any questions or problems."

The woman was off and running before Jill could protest.

Fifteen minutes later, Jill waved goodbye to her new-found friends while Derrick helped Sandy pack the dirty pot and unused cups and plastic spoons into the trunk of her car.

"I got a text from Chelsey. I can't believe Jill fired her," Sandy said. "We're short employees as it is."

"I wouldn't be surprised if Chelsey is back on payroll before the end of the day," he said.

"I hope you're right. I also hope you realize that this is all your fault."

"What did I do now?"

"Firing Chelsey had nothing to do with Ryan being brought to the park without her permission and everything to do with Chelsey flirting with you and *you* flirting back."

Derrick shut the trunk and let out a long hearty laugh. "You must not know Jill as well as you think you do. She hates my guts."

Sandy sighed. "I know Jill better than most and I know what I saw today." Sandy peered into his eyes. "If you hurt her in any way, I will do everything in my power to help her keep you away for good."

"I understand. But like I said, you've got it all wrong." He turned toward Jill and watched her lay Ryan in the stroller and rearrange baby blankets until she seemed satisfied. When she finished, she looked his way and their eyes met. The corners of her mouth lifted, her face lighting up as she expressed pleasure and something else he hadn't notice before. *Could Sandy be right?*

CHAPTER 10

Once a week, Derrick and his brothers all met for a game of basketball, playing at his indoor basketball court at his home in Malibu. At the moment, Derrick stood beneath the basket and called for the ball…again. But Brad was a ball hog and instead of passing it like any good teammate would do, his brother dribbled the ball down to the three point line and took another shot.

"Air ball!" his sister Zoey yelled. Both of his sisters, Zoey and Rachel, had offered to take care of his place while he was living at his new apartment. Zoey enjoyed standing at the sidelines, hackling them whenever the opportunity arose.

Playing defense, Derrick ran back to the other end of the court and called "switch!" But he might as well be playing with his sisters because his teammates were not paying him any mind.

Fresh off the bench, his older brother, Lucas, a real life rocket scientist, went in for a layup and scored two points for the other team.

When Derrick finally had the ball and was dribbling down court toward the net, his other sister, Rachel, entered the basketball court and yelled, "Breakfast is ready."

Within seconds the court was deserted. Derrick stopped at the three point line. "Hey! You people can at least wait for the play to be over, can't you?"

Brad grabbed a clean towel from the pile near the door and wiped his face. "Go ahead. Take a shot. I'm watching."

Derrick bent his legs, set his shoulders, and despite the fact that he'd been playing for the past two hours, he took his first *and* last shot of the day.

His form had never been better. The ball swished through the net.

Smiling, he turned toward the door, but Brad had already joined the others. Not a single solitary soul had seen his magnificent shot. If they weren't related, he would have nothing to do with the lot of them.

He made his way to the kitchen where Zoey and Rachel stood behind the stove cooking omelets, while four of his brothers sat at the table eating.

"The usual?" Zoey asked when she spotted him. Zoey and Rachel, although not the youngest of the brood, were still Dad's little girls—the spoiled brats of the family.

"Thanks, but I'll pass," he told her. "I had oatmeal before I came. I think I'll head back to my apartment to get some of my things."

Zoey set the spatula on the granite counter top. "You're not moving back home yet, are you?"

No, he wasn't going anywhere. "Why? Would that be a problem if I was?"

Jake took a swig of his orange juice and then said, "I think Rachel has a hot date tonight with Jim Jensen."

"She better not," Derrick said with a smile.

Everyone became quiet.

A worried frown crossed his sister's face. A wave of heat swept through him as it dawned on him that Jake was serious. Jim Jensen was a rookie quarterback just picked up by the Condors. The kid was just waiting for Derrick to crack a rib or take a bad fall so he could sweep in and take his place as starting quarterback.

"He's never done anything to you," Zoey said.

"That's right," Rachel agreed. "Why do you hate him?"

"The man doesn't have a chip on his shoulder," Derrick said, "he has a boulder, for God's sake."

Rachel plunked a hand to her hip. "And?"

"And he's a player, a snake charmer, a rat. Stay away from him," Derrick said. "You can do better."

"And if I decide *not* to take your advice?" she asked.

Derrick was tired of this. He'd come home today to get away from it all, to give Jill a break—a chance to spend a day with Ryan without feeling as if he was spying on her. Mostly, he'd been afraid of leading her on in case there was any truth to what Sandy had said about Jill having feelings for him. He liked Jill and he wanted to be her friend. Without taking his eyes from his sister, he rubbed his stubbled jaw. "I'm going now. Jensen is not allowed in this house—*my* house."

"You're being childish."

He pointed the same finger at Rachel. "I mean it."

Before she could protest further, Derrick exited the kitchen and made his way across the marble foyer and out the door.

Back at his apartment, it was eleven o'clock by the time he climbed out of the shower. His knee gave, but he managed to get a hold of the bathroom counter and stop himself from going down. Determined to ignore the pain, he stood on one leg in front of the sink and dried himself with a clean towel. Catching a glimpse of shades of color around his eye, he stopped to take a closer look at his reflection. The bruising from the hit he'd taken last week was fading, but there was still enough color to make him look like he hadn't had a good night's sleep in months. His brothers all figured he'd deserved what he got. Aaron had told his siblings to ask Derrick what had happened if they wanted answers, but not one of them had asked him. They just figured he was guilty. Hell, he wasn't going to tell them he'd kissed Maggie. His family already treated him like the black sheep. It was obvious they preferred Aaron over him.

What did he care anyhow? He would do it all over again if he had the chance. Someday, hopefully sooner rather than later, Maggie would come to her senses and see that they were meant to be together. Until then, he had Ryan and Jill to keep him occupied.

Jill, he realized, was pretty much the opposite of Maggie—quiet and sort of shy at times, although she definitely had her moments. Maggie was capable of using words to slice through the air and put people in their places while Jill seemed to think long and hard before speaking, worried about offending. When her hormones weren't spiking, she was sensitive and sweet, which summed her up perfectly: sweet and unassuming—that was Jill.

He finished towel drying his hair. A glint of silver right above his ear caught his attention. When the hell had he grown a gray hair? He wasn't even thirty, for God's sake. He leaned in closer to the mirror, got a good grip on the little bastard, and plucked it out of his skull. *Ouch!*

He was feeling on edge, he realized. His life felt as if it was off-kilter. For starters, Maggie had been avoiding him ever since the kiss in the courtroom. She hadn't returned his last two calls. His mom was angry with him for upsetting Aaron. His sisters and brothers had been favoring Aaron ever since he moved back to town. Jim Jensen's name kept coming up, which was not amusing. His knee wasn't getting any better either. And now Jill might have a crush on him when all he wanted to do was get to know his son and be her friend.

He opened the medicine cabinet and grabbed the cream he used to relieve muscle and joint pain and rubbed some into his knee. He washed his hands and then hopped on one leg to his room and pulled on a clean pair of basketball shorts. His next stop was the kitchen. He filled a plastic bag with ice, hopped to the couch, and then plopped down and placed the ice on his knee. He laid his head back on the sofa and shut his eyes.

Twenty seconds hadn't passed before he heard a knock on the door.

"Come in."

For a moment there he figured whoever had been at his door had gone away, but then the door creaked open and Jill poked her head inside. "Hi there."

He lifted his head. "Hi."

She looked at his knee. "Are you okay?"

"Just a little too much basketball with my brothers this morning."

"Mind if Ryan and I come inside?"

He waved a hand through the air and said, "Be my guest." Then he tried to push himself up from the couch.

"Don't move," she told him. "I can manage."

He didn't like the idea of not helping her with the baby, but then he remembered what Sandy had said about Jill falling for him, and he decided to stay where he was.

She opened the door wide enough to push the stroller inside without disturbing Ryan. "He's asleep," she said with a smile. "A true miracle."

He couldn't stop himself from smiling back at her. She looked happy and that made him happy. "You look great." She looked better than great. This was the first time he had seen her wearing something other than sweats. Her jeans were snug, showing off slim hips and long legs for such a short woman. Her yellow shirt contrasted nicely with her hair, which looked like three shades of brown, depending on the lighting. It was the first time he recalled seeing her hair untangled. It looked soft and shiny, full of body, the kind of hair a man liked to comb his fingers through. He shook his head, attempting to clear his wayward thoughts.

"Thanks," she said. "I feel great." She shut the door and set her purse on the coffee table in front of the couch. "I finally managed to catch up on my sleep yesterday. It's funny, but ever since I talked to those women at the park I've felt different…better. When I called the doctor last week, the nurse told me it was perfectly fine to let Ryan cry sometimes, so when you didn't show up this morning, I let him cry while I took a shower and did my hair. I'm even fitting into my old jeans, which is why I'm here."

"Those jeans look amazing."

When she laughed, her eyes sparkled right along with her straight white teeth.

"I didn't come looking for compliments," she told him, "although I appreciate them all the same. I came to tell you thank you and to apologize for being so rude yesterday. My actions were uncalled for and I'm embarrassed. You'll also be glad to know that I apologized to Chelsey and she's back on the payroll."

"I'm glad. She's a very enthusiastic employee."

She nodded. "I just wanted to let you know that I appreciate all you've done."

"Don't give it another thought. Under the circumstances, I think you've handled everything going on around you, me included, quite well."

"Look at me," she said. "I'm doing it again, blabbing on about myself when you're sitting there in pain. It's that knee again, isn't it?"

"What do you mean again? How could you know about my knee?"

"I noticed you were in pain the first day I met you, the day my water broke and you scrambled to get out of the car."

"We'll definitely have a few good stories to tell Ryan when he's all grown up, won't we?"

Her blush was followed by an awkward bit of silence before she asked, "What can I get for you?"

"If you could grab me a glass of water and that bottle of ibuprofen over there on the counter, I would appreciate it more than you know."

While she busied herself in the kitchen, he watched her through new eyes. She was a ball of sunshine. A little extra sleep had literally transformed her.

"Here you go." She handed him the water and then opened the ibuprofen. "How many do you want?"

"Two would be great."

She handed him the pills, and then waited while he downed them with the water before she took the glass from him and returned it to the kitchen. "Another reason I came," she said from the kitchen, "was to see if you wanted to come with me to Ryan's first appointment with the pediatrician."

Derrick smiled at her and realized how drab his day had been until she walked into his apartment. He wanted to spend time with Ryan. Hell, he realized, he wanted to spend time with Jill, too.

"Your leg hurts pretty bad, huh?"

She was hovering over him now, moving the bag of ice so she could take a good look at his knee. "It is swollen. You should probably stay off of it today."

"No," he found himself saying. "I think going with you and Ryan is just what the doctor ordered." He removed the ice.

"Are you sure?"

"Positive." And it was the truth.

"Here," she said, helping him up. "Lean on me. I'll serve as your crutch so we can get you to the other room so you can get your shirt and a pair of shoes."

"I might hurt you."

"Ridiculous." He was bare-chested but that didn't stop her from taking his arm and placing it over her shoulder. "Now go ahead and walk. Lean on me. It's okay."

He did as she said, surprised by the strength in her small arms as she helped him down the hall to his room. They walked into his bedroom, but as he headed for the bed and she tried to let him loose, he tripped over the backpack he'd taken to the gym earlier, and brought Jill along for the ride. They fell onto the king-sized bed. Instinctively, and in hopes of protecting her from harm, he wrapped his arms around her waist as they fell to the mattress. When they landed, he was on his back and they were face to face, nose to nose.

She laughed, her breath minty as she tried to push off of him.

A creak and then a loud crack brought her right back down on top of him as the old bed frame gave way, bringing them both sliding to the corner of the mattress.

The two of them had become one. "Are you all right?" he asked, his lips pressed against her ear.

"I'm fine," she said. Still laughing, she grabbed one of his pillows and bopped him on the head with it.

"Oh, so you want to play rough, do you?" He rolled to his side and tickled her.

She laughed so hard she could hardly talk. "No tickling," she squeaked. Swatting feebly at his arm, she slunk further into the puddles of blankets and pillows in an attempt to squirm away from him.

Laughing, he tickled her some more, but then pulled his hand away the moment he felt a tightness in his groin. Nothing seemed humorous suddenly as he realized there was no denying the unexpected heat sizzling between them.

Their gazes met and he knew she felt it too. Her eyes were heavy-lidded, her lips plump and full. He already knew he wanted to be her friend, but now he realized he also wanted nothing more than to lean closer and kiss her, feel her lips against his and put an end to the unexpected and tantalizing vibration swirling about inside.

CHAPTER 11

Since entering Derrick's apartment, Jill felt as if everything was happening in slow motion. Getting him ibuprofen, helping him to his room, the frame of the bed breaking, and now this—this wasn't what she had come to his apartment for. But now that she was pressed close against Derrick's hard, naked chest, every part of her felt warm and tingly.

More than anything, she wanted him to kiss her, but he seemed intent on pulling away. Filled with a lustful urge to feel his lips against hers, figuring it was her hormones, but wanting to know for sure, she decided to go for it. She leaned in close and brushed her lips against his. He smelled as good as he looked and the moment her lips met his, and he pressed closer, something snapped. She lost control. It was like awakening after being in a coma.

Letting instinct take over, she wrapped her arms around his neck and brought her body close to his, close enough to feel him thick and hard against her thigh. A whimper escaped her as she brought a splayed hand up and over well-developed back muscles and higher still until her fingers swept a path through his hair. He deepened the kiss. Her leg circled around his. She touched him, devoured him really, one hand sliding across solid abs and lower over the silky fabric of his gym shorts until she felt him hard against her palm.

"What the hell is going on in here?"

The moment Jill heard her father's voice, she knew that her mind had to be playing tricks on her. But then Derrick pulled away and said, "Who are you and what are you doing in my apartment?"

Jill looked over her shoulder and saw her father standing in the doorway. "Dad! What are you doing here?"

Her father walked away. He wasn't angry. He was livid.

Sandy poked her head through the open door next. She looked down her nose at the two of them. "Wow," was all she said before she disappeared too.

Derrick pushed himself to his feet. Once he was on sturdy ground, he helped Jill up, and she found herself peering into gorgeous eyes.

"I'm sorry about all of this," he said. "I don't know what came over me."

I'm sorry? She'd already been fantasizing that the kiss might be the beginning of something wonderful, while he, on the other hand, felt the need to apologize. She dropped her gaze from his. "I better go check on Ryan."

He didn't protest. Instead, he said, "I'll get dressed and be right out."

She slipped out of the room and made her way down the hallway. Everybody was gone, including the stroller with Ryan in it. A glance out the window told her Sandy had taken everyone back to her place.

Pacing the floor, she suddenly regretted wearing tight jeans and shoes with heels instead of sweatpants and her comfortable sneakers. Earlier, when she had squeezed her bottom into ridiculously tight jeans, she had been so excited to fit into her pre-pregnancy clothes, she hadn't thought twice about what Derrick's reaction might be.

But what was she doing? Why had she come to his apartment in the first place? Only a few days ago, she'd wanted Derrick Baylor as far away from her as humanly possible. And now suddenly she wanted him to take her in his arms and ravish her.

She palmed her forehead in disgust.

The expression on his face after he'd lifted her from the floor spelled *R-E-G-R-E-T* in capital letters.

She looked around his apartment. *Now what?* She needed to get out of here, and fast. She grabbed her purse from the coffee table, left his apartment, and shut the door quietly behind her. Her eyes stung at the realization she'd made a fool of herself.

"Mom," she said as she came through the door to her apartment. Forcing a smile, she took her mother into her arms and gently squeezed her bony, rigid body. Her sweet smelling perfume was overwhelming and it took everything in her power not to cough and wheeze.

Sandy was sitting in Jill's favorite chair, holding Ryan while Lexi sat on the floor close to Sandy's feet. With a crayon in each hand, Lexi busily colored in her books.

Jill set her gaze on her father. He looked out of place on her lime-green couch. And yet, oddly enough, he looked the same as always: the same perfectly fitted dark suit, the same starched button-down shirt, the same disappointed frown. He would be turning sixty this year. His hair was thick with very little grey. There wasn't a hair out of place. If he didn't always look so angry, she might consider him to be a handsome man.

"What was that over there?" he asked, his voice as stiff as her mother's posture.

Jill sighed. "I thought you knew."

"Knew what?"

"I told Mom I was dating Derrick Baylor, quarterback for the Condors."

"She mentioned it," her father said. "He is an athlete. I guess I should have expected to find you in a compromising position on the floor of his bedroom. From the looks of it, you two are getting along just fine."

Jill felt a burst of heat creep into her face. "We're doing well," Jill lied, "but what you saw over there isn't what you think.

Derrick has a bad knee. I was helping him to his bedroom when he tripped and we both fell and then the frame broke—"

"Stop with the stories," he interrupted. "Your mother has been trying to convince me that you've grown up. I've been in California for less than an hour and I can already see that nothing has changed. I'm very disappointed."

Jill lifted her chin. "I'm sorry you feel that way," she said, but the truth was, she'd heard it all before. She'd always been one big disappointment to her father. Never mind that she'd never once been caught in a compromising position before. It's just the way it was. Jill was only thankful that her younger sister, Laura, hadn't joined them. Jill loved her sister, but the pressure her parents put on Jill to be like Laura was too much. She loved her family, but all three of them had a way of making her feel small and unworthy. It had taken her father five minutes to cause all of her insecurities to come rushing forth.

"I canceled more than one important meeting to make this trip," her father cut into her thoughts. "We wanted to support you and your new baby—"

"Your grandson's name is Ryan," she cut in.

"I can see now," her father went on, "that believing you might have grown into a responsible young lady was only wishful thinking on our parts."

"I need to go," Jill said right before she heard a knock on the door. "Come in," she said.

"Howiewood," Lexi shouted when Derrick entered the apartment.

Derrick smiled at Lexi. His limp was no longer noticeable as he entered. He looked about the room and extended his arm toward her father, ready to shake his hand. Her father would have nothing to do with him. Simply put, her father was a snob.

Straightening, Derrick's arm fell back to his side before he headed for her mother instead. Jill's mom was as friendly as a two by four, but at least she managed to place a limp hand in Derrick's palm. Once her mother had her hand back, she pulled a tiny bottle of hand sanitizer from her purse and wiped the germs clean.

Jill had already had enough. Besides, she was going to be late for Ryan's doctor appointment if she didn't leave soon. "If I had known you two were coming," Jill said, "I would have had time to prepare, but as things stand, Derrick and I are on our way to Ryan's doctor appointment. We need to go."

"You're not going to say hello to your sister?"

Jill's eyes widened as she looked at Sandy.

Sandy nodded. "She's in the other room, washing up."

"She's distraught after seeing you copulate on the floor with that man," her father said.

"He has a name," Jill said.

"Howiewood," her father said as he smiled at Lexi. "Isn't that right?"

Lexi nodded, happy to oblige.

"Copulate?" Derrick repeated. He looked at Jill. "Is he serious?"

Jill answered the question with a tight nod and even tighter smile.

"How could you?" Jill's mother asked.

"We were not having sex," Jill said, exasperated.

"You told me you were dating a football player," her mother said, "but I had no idea you had taken it to the next level. It's no wonder Laura is bawling her eyes out in the other room."

"I wasn't crying," Laura said as she joined them. She looked at Derrick and her mouth dropped open. "Is this the guy you were banging over there?"

Jill couldn't believe her ears…or her eyes. If Mom hadn't just told her that Laura was here, she would never have guessed that the twenty-six year old woman standing before her was her younger sister, Laura. She hadn't seen Laura in nearly a year, but that didn't explain the transformation. Her sister used to wear pencil skirts and cashmere sweaters with tiny pearl buttons. Today she was dressed in all black, the fabric hugging her body like a second skin. The girl standing in front of her looked more like Lady Gaga than Laura. "Are those leather pants you have on?"

Laura smiled brightly. "Aren't they great?"

Jill didn't know what to say. She was confused and she needed to go. "I hate to run, but Derrick and I need to take Ryan to the doctor's. Why don't you come with us, so we can catch up?"

"I would love to join you."

Jill looked at Derrick. The poor man looked as if he was afraid to make another move. "Could you grab the stroller and the baby's bag?"

He did as she asked while Jill took Ryan from Sandy.

"I'll lock the doors for you and then call you later," Sandy said.

Jill thanked her before gesturing toward her sister and heading for the door. "Where are you staying?" Jill asked her mother.

"At the Amarano."

"We have reservations at the Sky House for 7 pm," her father said. "We will see you there."

It was *not* a request, Jill realized. It was an order.

~~~

"It's nice to finally meet you," Derrick told Laura as they headed for the parking lot. "Jill has told me all about you."

"Liar," Laura said.

He laughed.

Jill unlocked the door to her Volkswagen Jetta. Derrick took Ryan from her and while he strapped Ryan into the car seat in the back, Jill pulled her sister to the side. "What's with the new look?"

"I'm just having fun," Laura said. "For the first time since I was born, I'm doing what I want to do."

"And what is that exactly?"

"I'm singing in a rock band."

"You can sing?"

Laura laughed as she nodded. "After dinner tonight, I'll be heading home. Mom and Dad don't know it, but I'll be long gone before they return home."

"Where are you going?"

"The band and I are traveling around the world."

Jill didn't know what to think. "You're serious, aren't you?"

"I've never been more serious in my life." Laura clasped Jill's hand in hers. "I've also never been happier. I came to California because I wanted to see you before I left."

Jill shook her head. "I don't know what to think."

"I'm sure you'll hear horrible things about me from Mom and Dad once they know what I'm up to, but I wanted you to hear it all from me first."

"I wish we had more time to talk."

"I do, too, but don't worry. I'll call you from the road and email you updates."

Jill took her sister in her arms and hugged her tight.

"We should have stood up to Dad years ago," Laura said, her voice growing serious. "We always gave up too easily. Some things," Laura said, glancing at Derrick, "are worth fighting for."

"I'm glad you're happy. You promise to stay in contact?"

"I promise." They hugged for a long moment before Laura turned back to the car and climbed into the backseat next to Ryan's carrier.

Derrick was folding the stroller at the back of the car and Jill joined him. He placed a hand on her arm before she could get away. "You ran out of my apartment because of the kiss, didn't you?"

"I don't know what you mean."

"That kiss threw both of us off guard," he told her, "but I want you to know that it won't happen again. If we're going to be friends, then we need to keep things cordial between us. It was a mistake and I take full responsibility."

Great. Just great. "I think that would be best," she lied. "Let's keep things *cordial*." She put out a hand for him to shake. "Deal?"

He shook her hand as if they were good pals. "Deal."

Jill tried not to show any emotion as she climbed in behind the wheel and turned on the car. She watched quietly as Derrick squeezed his six-foot-two inch, two hundred and twenty pound body into the passenger seat of her Jetta.

He looked ridiculously squished. "You don't have to come. I have Laura to keep me company."

"A team of wild horses couldn't stop me from coming to Ryan's doctor appointment," he said, and he must have meant it, because his knees, the good and the bad, were pressed against the glove box and his head was only a quarter of an inch away from hitting the ceiling.

The engine purred as Jill merged onto the main road.

"What's going on between you two?" Laura asked. "You're not really dating, are you?"

Jill didn't say a word.

"You two can't fool me," Laura added.

"You're right," Derrick said, "we're not dating." He looked at Jill. "What was all that talk in your apartment about the two of us dating, anyhow?"

Jill swished a hand through the air as if it was no big deal. "I told Mom we were dating in hopes that my parents wouldn't come to visit."

Derrick frowned. "Why would our dating cause your parents to stay at home?"

"Ridiculous, I know," Jill said, "but the truth is my dad doesn't like football players."

"He thinks athletes are worthless creatures," Laura added with a laugh.

Not too surprisingly, Derrick didn't laugh with her. The moment Jill was alone with her sister, she planned to ask Laura what she had done with her real sister—the bashful, quiet sister who never wore mascara, let alone false eyelashes. *What the heck was going on here?*

"Let me get this straight," Derrick said. "You told your parents that we were dating in hopes that they would stay away."

"Yes," Jill answered.

"But you plan to straighten them out the next time you see them?"

"No," Jill said.

Laura laughed again.

"Why not?"

"Because for the first time in my life I don't care what they think about me." Jill used the rearview mirror to glance at her sister. "How long are Mom and Dad planning on staying?"

"Two or three nights," Laura said. "I think Dad has business in San Francisco." She reached forward and put a hand on Derrick's shoulder. "Don't worry, Hollywood, a few outings, a dinner or two, and it will all be over before you know it."

"I'm not worried," he said, "because there's no way I'm getting involved in your family problems. No outings or dinners for me."

Jill tightened her grip on the steering wheel. "If you don't come to dinner with me and my family tonight, then Ryan and I will not be attending your family barbeque this weekend. What's good for the goose is good for the gander."

He frowned. "The idea that you were dating me obviously wasn't scary enough to keep them away. So what's the point in keeping up the charade?"

"I think they're calling Jill's bluff," Laura said. "They didn't believe Jill would stoop that low, so they came to California to see it for themselves."

As Jill nodded in agreement, a glance his way revealed an unyielding jaw. Derrick was not happy with the fact that as far as her parents were concerned, he was pond scum. Well, that was just too bad. Jill figured if she had to suffer through a dinner or two, then Derrick might as well suffer, too. "You did say you wanted to be a part of Ryan's life," Jill said. "Be careful what you wish for."

"Okay," he said under his breath. "I'll do it."

Laura clapped her hands together, making Jill feel as if she had Lexi in the backseat of her car instead of a grown woman.

Keeping her eyes on the road, it didn't take long for Jill's thoughts to meander to the kiss. She could still taste him on her lips. Hoping to take her mind off of the heat sizzling within, she turned on the radio and rolled her eyes when "This Kiss" by Faith Hill belted out from the speakers:

I *don't want another heartbreak*

I don't need another turn to cry, no
I don't want to learn the hard way

She shut the radio off.

"I never would have figured you for a country girl," Derrick said.

"That's because you don't know anything about me," Jill said, annoyed by the entire state of affairs. "I'm a little bit country and I'm also rock 'n' roll all in one. I'm a wild woman, Derrick Baylor. A wild, wild woman."

"Is that right?"

"She's kidding," Laura said, ruining Jill's fun. "Jill has never done anything remotely wild. Never jumped out of a plane or skied down a Black Diamond trail. She never smoked a cigarette, let alone a joint. I can't even recall ever seeing my sister on the dance floor."

"Who are you?" Jill asked her sister, wondering if she had fallen into some sort of black hole.

"How about skinny-dipping?" Derrick asked. "Everyone has skinny-dipped at least once in their life?"

"Nope, not Jill," Laura said. "She's safe and predictable. No surprises there."

"I have a voice," Jill reminded her sister as she came to a stop at the light.

"Okay," Laura said with a shrug. "Let's hear it. Have you gone skinny-dipping?"

"That's none of your business."

Derrick looked over his shoulder at Laura. "Your sister just had a baby. Her hormones are still a little wacky."

Jill rolled her eyes.

"Don't get me wrong," Laura said. "Jill has a lot of good qualities. Despite what my parents believe, she's dependable and responsible. She's compassionate, too. She's just lacking a little when it comes to adventure."

The light turned green and Jill stepped on the gas. "When Ryan is older," Jill said, "the two of us are going to do many adventurous things together."

"Sounds like Ryan is in for a good time once he gets out of those diapers," Derrick said with a smile.

Laura chuckled.

Jill looked over at him and scowled. The sun was coming through the window and hitting his handsome face just so: sparkling eyes and dimples—a deadly combination. If Ryan looked anything like his father when he grew up, she wasn't going to have time to ski down the Silverfox in Utah, learn how to rock climb, or bungee jump off of a tall bridge, because she was going to be too busy fighting off all the girls vying for her son's attention.

The ride to the pediatrician's office felt like hours instead of the twelve minutes it actually took to get there. The streets were crowded for a weekday, Jill thought, as she pulled into a parking space reserved for patients of the medical building. Derrick had a tough time getting out of the passenger seat, but she decided not to worry about him. He deserved to be uncomfortable for setting off fireworks inside of her and then dousing them with cold words and a handshake.

~~~

Although he did his best not to show it, Derrick felt like a heel. Sandy had warned him of Jill's growing affections and yet he hadn't tried to stop her earlier from pressing up close and kissing him. He already knew she could kiss like an angel, but he hadn't known until today that she was a dozen sticks of dynamite waiting to be ignited. If it had been anyone but Jill Garrison, the mother of his child, throwing herself at him, he might have taken what she offered, and then some.

Hell, he never proclaimed to be a saint.

But Jill was nothing like the women he had spent time with over the years. Jill was way too sweet and innocent for the likes of him.

And besides, his heart belonged to Maggie.

Jill deserved to be with someone who could give her one hundred percent, someone who would always be there for her. If not for Maggie, he might think twice about applying for the job. But Maggie was always there, floating in his thoughts—even when he didn't want her to be. Deep down, he knew his brothers were right. He needed to forget about Maggie—cut all emotional ties and let her go. But he'd already tried that and it hadn't worked. Loving Maggie was like being addicted to drugs. He needed a twelve-step program if he ever wanted to break free.

There was an art festival taking place downtown and it took a few minutes to weave through the crowds and into the building. Before long, Derrick and Jill were in the examination room waiting for the pediatrician, while Laura waited in the lobby.

Derrick was glad he could finally feel the blood pumping through his legs again. Being in Jill's car could be compared to being squeezed into a sardine can.

Jill paced the tiny room, back and forth, while Ryan cried his heart out.

"If you hold him closer to your chest, a little further to your right, I think he'll—"

"I know how to hold my baby. Thank you very much."

Stretching, Derrick hid a smile behind a feigned yawn.

"I'm glad to see you're amused," Jill admonished, "although I really can't imagine how you could find Ryan's discomfort comical."

"That's not why I'm smiling." What amused him was the way her eye twitched and her lip curled just the slightest bit whenever she was annoyed. He also couldn't stop thinking about Jill's reaction to what her sister had said about Jill not being adventurous. Jill clearly wanted to change all of that. He had some good ideas to help her break out of her shell. "I was just thinking about your family showing up out of the blue. Your sister is quite a character."

"That woman waiting out there in the lobby is not my sister. My sister is graceful, delicate, and quiet to a fault. She sips Ming Cha tea and nibbles on watercress sandwiches. She never curses and she certainly doesn't own a pair of leather pants."

"She eats watercress sandwiches?"

The doctor walked in before Jill could respond. The pediatrician was a man—a young man Derrick guessed to be in his early thirties—a man who looked ridiculously pleased to see Jill.

"Jill! It's great to see you again."

Jill's eyes lit up. "Nate Lerner," Jill said. "I'm so glad you made it back in time to be here for Ryan's first appointment."

Before Derrick could introduce himself, Jill handed Ryan to him and then turned back to the doctor and practically leapt into his arms, hugging the man as if he were a long-lost brother finally returned from war. After she finally broke free, Dr. Lerner took a step back so he could take a good long look at Jill. "You look amazing. Absolutely stunning."

Derrick held Ryan close to his chest and rocked him until he quieted.

The whole scene with the doctor and Jill seemed a little off, maybe because Jill hadn't said a peep about Dr. Lerner and now suddenly the two of them were practically getting it on right here in front of him, as if he wasn't even in the room. Derrick knew firsthand how out of whack Jill's hormones were and he really didn't want to stand here and watch her get all hot and bothered.

Jill put a hand to her chest. "You look exactly like your father." She shook her head in disbelief. "It's uncanny."

Derrick cleared his throat, but nobody paid him any mind.

"We'll have to get together soon and catch up."

"I would love to," Jill said with the brightest smile Derrick had ever seen as she clasped the good doctor's hands between hers.

"So who do we have here?" the doctor asked, after thoroughly checking out Ryan's mother.

"Nate, I'd like you to meet my friend, Derrick, and my son, Ryan." Without making eye contact, she took Ryan from Derrick and cradled him in her arms in such a way that Nate could get a better look at her cleavage.

The doctor gestured toward the examination table and Jill obediently followed him that way.

"He's a handsome boy," Dr. Lerner said. "Let's take his measurements."

"Should I undress him?"

"Please."

She took her time slipping Ryan's tiny arms and legs from his blue cotton sleeper.

Derrick stayed where he was, watching from afar while the doctor measured the circumference of Ryan's head before checking his soft spot.

"His fontanel is just as it should be," the doctor said. "It's safe to touch and should disappear in twelve to eighteen months." Next, he measured Ryan's length from toe to head, checked his charts, and then asked Jill to remove his diaper so he could weigh him. Dr. Lerner proceeded with additional tests while Jill fawned over the doctor and Ryan in equal doses. With adoring eyes, she watched Dr. Lerner as he used an instrument to look inside Ryan's ears.

It was enough to make Derrick want to gag. Instead, he took a seat in the corner of the room. His muscles felt tense and it dawned on him that he was behaving like a jealous fool. The emotions he was feeling were absurd and completely out of character. He had no reason to be jealous because he didn't feel *that* way about Jill. As she had just told the doctor, they were friends. Yes, Derrick liked her, and yes, she looked amazing today, but she looked amazing every day, whether she wore a sweat outfit covered with spit-up or baggy pants and fuzzy pink slippers.

After analyzing the situation, Derrick convinced himself that what he was feeling was perfectly acceptable and normal. He wanted to protect Jill. She was the mother of his son. Any man she showed interest in could be a potential father to his son. It made perfect sense that he might feel anxious under the circumstances.

It wasn't long before the doctor was finished and Jill was pushing Derrick out the door.

"I'll catch up," Jill told him, leaving Derrick and Ryan to fend for themselves as he guided the stroller out of the examination room and toward the lobby.

Laura came to her feet the moment he appeared. "Where's Jill?" she asked.

"She and the doctor had some catching up to do. Why don't we head on outside and get some fresh air while we wait?"

By the time Jill caught up to them, Derrick and Laura were outside and in the middle of the art festival. Brightly colored chalk drawings covered the walkways and vendors behind their exhibition booths were lined up on both sides of the street.

"Sorry I took so long," Jill said as she anchored strands of hair behind her ears. "What did you think?"

"Of what?" Derrick asked.

"Of Nate?"

"I think he's dreamy," he offered.

Jill laughed. "I mean as a pediatrician. Don't you think he's thorough and professional? A doctor we can trust to take care of Ryan?"

"I can't say I have met a lot of pediatricians in my day. I have nothing to compare him to, sorry."

"Sounds like I missed all the fun," Laura said.

"You two got along well," Derrick said. "I suppose you and Nate have a date?" he questioned, although he was only teasing.

Jill's eyes flashed like neon lights in Vegas. "As a matter of fact, yes, we do. We're going to a movie Friday night."

Derek felt a little nauseated and he wasn't sure why. Jill was on one side and Laura was on the other while he guided the stroller through the main part of town. He didn't have a destination in mind. Jill's car was back the other way. He just kept walking, trying to keep his cool since he knew he had no business getting bent out of shape.

"Do you think you could babysit that night?" Jill asked.

"He's my son. Of course I can watch my son. What time?"

"How about four o'clock?"

For some ridiculous reason he felt better knowing it would be earlier rather than later.

"That will give me time to take a shower and get ready. Nate is taking me to Crush, a new restaurant on Jasmine Street. I've wanted to go there ever since they opened six months ago."

They stopped and waited for Laura, who they lost a few vendors ago. She was looking at handmade purses and bargaining with the salesperson.

"I thought you were going to an early movie?"

"I didn't say that. I said we were going to a movie, which we are—after dinner."

"How late do you plan on staying out?"

"Why? Do I have a curfew?"

"Of course not, it's just that I thought you said that you and Sandy had a lot of work to do on the magazine."

"Thanks to you, we're all caught up. Sandy helped me write my column and Chelsey brought the pictures by late last night. You know—the pictures she took at the park the other day. We have lots of great photos to pick from. According to Sandy, the chili received rave reviews and so that's a go, too." Jill smiled. "I'm beginning to feel like my old self again." She swung herself in a circle, arms in the air, face to the sun. "What a beautiful day."

Yeah—a beautiful day.

"Wow, look at that." Jill headed across the street to one of the exhibition booths.

Derrick watched as she oohed and aahed over the ugliest bronzed figurines he'd ever seen. She brought one of the figurines over to him and held it up so she could show him the details. "That's what I call artwork."

His mother's words rang in the back of his head: *if you have nothing nice to say, it's best to say nothing at all.*

"What's wrong?"

"Nothing. Why?"

"I don't know," Jill said. "Ever since we met with Dr. Lerner you've been acting like a big gloomy rain cloud on a sunny day."

"Maybe it's because I'm wondering why you were kissing me one minute and then all but drooling over the good doctor in the next."

"I wasn't drooling. Besides, you made it perfectly clear that the kiss we shared was a great, big foolish mistake. So, why would you care about my interaction with Dr. Lerner?"

"I don't know," he said. "Forget I said anything."

"Are you jealous?"

Nervous laughter escaped him. "Of course not. I just don't think Dr. Lerner is right for you."

That made her smile.

"What?"

"Dr. Lerner used to be on one of those Abercrombie and Fitch shopping bags."

"On a what?"

Her eyes twinkled as she said, "All the hot guys are displayed on the A&F shopping bags."

"What does that have to do with him not being right for you?"

She shrugged. "Just thought I'd mention it."

"So you think he's hot?"

She snorted. "Duh."

"Is that why you like him? Because he's hot?"

"It never hurts to be hot, but no, that's not the only reason I like him."

He felt as if he was pulling teeth. "So what else do you like about him?"

Derrick followed her back to where the woman waited patiently for Jill to return her piece of artwork.

"Beautiful work," she told the artist.

The artist was an older woman with long gray curls that hung over her shoulders. "I use clay and bronze and I spend hours on each piece, trying to capture the innocence and grace of the female form."

"Your passion shows in your work," Jill said. "How much is this one?"

Derrick waited patiently for Jill to look around.

"The one you have your eye on is five thousand dollars. This one over here is thirty-five-hundred."

Derrick nearly fell over backwards.

"I'll have to think about it," Jill said, "but if you have a card I would love to keep track of where you'll be showing more of your work."

The woman pulled a business card out of the front pocket of her apron and passed it on to Jill.

Derrick peeked into the stroller at Ryan and then started off again. "Why don't we grab something to eat at the café across the street while Ryan is sleeping," he said.

"That's a terrific idea. I'm starved. Look at this," Jill said, holding up the business card. "The woman is from New York City. She's come a long way to sell her figurines."

They stopped at the street corner and Jill pushed the button on the pole. As they waited for the Walk sign to turn green, she sent a text to her sister letting her know they would be in the café.

"Are you going to answer my question?" he asked.

The light turned green and she started off across the crosswalk. "No."

"Why not?"

"Because whether you're my friend or not, who I choose to go out with is none of your business." She held the door to the café open and waited for him to push the stroller through.

The waitress took them to the booth in the far corner, handed each of them a menu, and told them she'd be back in a few minutes.

Jill readjusted the blanket, making sure Ryan wasn't too hot. "Dr. Lerner said Ryan was short for his age."

Derrick grunted. "He's hardly two weeks old. I think it's a little soon to be—" He stopped in mid-sentence when he spotted Aaron putting a tip on the table across the way. "Just one minute." He stood and headed that way. "Aaron," he called.

Aaron turned toward him. His shoulders sank and his expression told Derrick he had already seen him and was trying to escape unnoticed. Derrick looked around. "Where's Maggie?"

Aaron shook his head at him.

"I'm only asking because I was hoping you and Maggie could meet my friend, Jill, and our son, Ryan."

"Maggie's already halfway to the car and I really don't have time."

"Just give me one minute."

Aaron raised his hands in surrender and followed him back to where Jill sat studying the menu.

"Jill, I'd like you to meet my brother, Aaron."

Jill smiled as she came to her feet and shook his hand. "Nice to meet you," she said. "I believe I've met all of the brothers now, haven't I?"

"You still haven't met Lucas or Garrett," Derrick told her.

"I'm the misfit of the family," Aaron told her. "We're not brothers in the true sense of the word."

"You're not?"

"He's adopted," Derrick added.

Aaron peeked inside the stroller at Ryan. "So this is the little guy we keep hearing about, is it?"

"We just finished with his first check-up," Jill said.

Aaron raised a brow. "Who's your pediatrician?"

"Dr. Lerner." She pointed out the window and toward the building they had just left. "Right over there."

"I went to college with Nate," Aaron said. "What are the odds?"

"I've known him for years," Jill said excitedly. "He's very competent and knowledgeable."

"Yeah, he's a good guy. He and I went golfing before he left for Europe. He has a great swing."

"Is there anything that man can't do?" Derrick asked.

Aaron angled his head as if he was thinking about asking Derrick what he meant, but then thought better of it. Instead, he looked at Jill. "It was nice meeting you. I better get going. My fiancée is waiting in the car. She's probably wondering what's happened to me."

Derrick offered a hand, but after Aaron pretended not to notice, he shoved his hand into his front pants pocket and let it go. Derrick was beginning to feel like a leper. "Tell Maggie I said hello."

"I don't think so," Aaron said with a frown. "But I am glad to see that the discoloration around your eye has almost disappeared. Maggie has been worrying about you ever since we saw you last. Speaking of which, I guess you won't need her services since the two of you," he said, wiggling a finger between him and Jill, "seem to have worked things out."

"Is your fiancée Derrick's attorney?" Jill asked.

"To tell you the truth," Aaron said, "I'm not sure what their working relationship was…or is." He let out a short caustic laugh and took a step away as he pointed a finger at Derrick. "Watch this guy though," he told Jill. "He's quick on his feet—on the field and off the field." He continued to wag the same finger. "You never know what he's going to do next."

With that final cryptic message, Aaron walked away.

Once Aaron was out of sight, she took her seat and said, "Wow, somebody is angry with you. Is he the one who punched you in the eye?"

Derrick nodded. "He's had a chip on his shoulder for as long as I can remember."

Derrick glanced out the window and wondered how Maggie was getting along. He took a seat across from Jill and opened his menu, but it might as well have been written in Chinese because he couldn't concentrate.

CHAPTER 12

Jill's father had managed to get reservations at the Sky House downtown. They dined on prime rib eye with pommes frites, asparagus, and béarnaise sauce. There was a dance floor in the bar, and unlike their small group, the people on the other side of the room seemed to be having a good time.

Sandy had offered to take care of Ryan and Jill realized she missed her son already. This was the longest she'd been away from Ryan since he was born, not including the time he was kidnapped and taken to the park.

Jill's parents had not been happy to learn that Derrick would be joining them for dinner, but now that they had all suffered through an awkwardly quiet meal, her parents seemed intent on making up for lost time before dessert was served.

"Your mother mentioned that Thomas has been trying desperately to get in touch with you."

"I talked to him last week," Jill offered.

"I heard that you were abrupt and cut the conversation short."

Jill stiffened. "There really isn't much for the two of us to say to one another."

"He wants you back."

"Maybe she doesn't want him back," Laura said before she raised her glass to her lips and finished off the rest of her wine in one long gulp.

"Thomas was recently appointed partner at the firm. He regrets what he did and he wants nothing more than to make it up to you."

"I didn't come here tonight to talk about Thomas," Jill said, trying to keep her composure.

"Your apartment is small and the location is questionable at best. Come back to New York with us. We'll set you up in a comfortable apartment where you'll have help so that you can have fun with your project."

"My project?"

"Yes, your little publication."

Jill did her best to remain tight-lipped as her father droned on.

"Once we get you and Ryan set up properly, you might be frowned upon in the beginning, especially considering your choice to be a single mother, but once the other young couples learn that you come from good stock and see that you're respectable and—"

Laura's laughter cut into her father's ridiculous oration, stopping him short.

"And what, might I ask, do you find humorous?" her father asked her sister.

"Good stock?" Laura repeated. "Are you kidding me? Why do you think Jill moved so far away in the first place? To get as far away from the three of us as possible," she said, answering her own question. "You've been micro-managing both of our lives for too long." Laura directed her gaze at Jill. "Did you know that Mom and Dad wanted Thomas in the family so badly that they tried to push him off on me?"

Derrick noticed Jill's face turn bright red, and his heart went out to her.

"And worse than that," Laura went on, "I fell for it…hook, line, and sinker. They went so far as to convince me that he left you at the altar because he was interested in me."

"That's enough," Jill's father said. "You've had too much to drink and you don't know what you are saying."

"Well, you, Father, have not had enough to drink because you still have that same stick up your ass. The good news is," Laura told Jill, ignoring her father's horrified expression, "is that Thomas ignored my advances and even revealed that he had made a horrible mistake when he left you." Laura looked around for the waiter. "Where is everyone? I'm going to the bar to get a drink." She left the table and headed for the bar where people of all ages danced beneath dim lights.

"Your poor sister," her mom said the moment Laura was out of earshot.

"What do you mean?" Jill asked.

"It's obvious, isn't it?" her father asked. "Thanks to you, she's a complete mess."

"Soon after you left," her mother added, "she became argumentative and defiant."

"And this is somehow my fault?"

"Of course it is," her father said under his breath.

Derrick put a hand on Jill's shoulder. She wore a black sleeveless dress, and he brushed his thumb over her soft skin. He wasn't sure if the stunned look she wore had to do with her sister's bluntness or the idea that her parents might have tried to hook up her ex with her sister. He wanted nothing more than to tell these so-called aristocrats to stuff it and then lean down and nibble on her neck, but for Jill's sake he kept his opinions and his urge to nibble to himself.

Mrs. Garrison's stone-cold gaze burned a hole into the hand he had on her daughter. "Tell me again," she said, "how did the two of you meet?"

"When Derrick was in college," Jill offered matter-of-factly, "he made a donation to the sperm bank. Eighteen months later, he changed his mind and sent them their money back along with a letter letting them know where he stood on the matter."

"And where exactly *did* he stand?" her father asked.

Derrick held out a hand, letting them all know he could speak for himself. "Although I needed money at the time," he said, "I realized I didn't like the idea of having my biological children out in the world, knowing I wouldn't be a part of their lives."

"How did you find Jill?" Mrs. Garrison asked. "Those places are supposed to be discreet about these things."

"I hired a private investigator."

"Do you two plan to marry?" her father asked next.

"Not at this time."

"Why not?" he asked, obviously trying to make Derrick look like the bad guy.

"Because we've known one another for less than two weeks."

"She's raising your baby. That's not good enough for you?"

Jill tried to get a word in, but Derrick was too quick. "It's not good enough for your daughter. She'll decide when and who she wants to marry when the time comes."

"Maybe she chooses you," Mr. Garrison said. "Have you asked her to marry you?"

Derrick looked at Jill and said, "Jill, will you marry me?"

"No, but thanks for asking."

Derrick looked back at her father and shrugged his shoulders.

"You're trying to be cute with me?"

"No, sir, I'm not. I was only trying to prove a point."

"Which is?"

"Your daughter is old enough to make her own decisions. She knows what she does and doesn't want."

"And apparently she doesn't want you."

"Dad," Jill said. "That's enough. If we can't all sit here and enjoy a nice dinner, then maybe Derrick and I should leave."

"Thomas still loves you," her mother said, desperation lining her voice. "He regrets what he did."

"Did you really try to set him up with Laura?" Jill's eyes could not conceal the hurt she felt by their betrayal.

"Whether we did or not is neither here nor there," her father said. "The fact is he only wants you."

Jill stood and looked at Derrick. "Let's dance."

Without hesitating, Derrick came to his feet and led her to the dance floor. Billy Joel's soft ballad "Just The Way You Are" played from the speakers, which was a good thing because his knee was acting up again. The moment they hit the dance floor, Derrick took Jill into his arms and held her close as they swayed to the music. No words were said between them. No words were necessary.

~~~

Seventy-two hours after their dinner from hell, Jill held Ryan in her arms and knocked on the door to Derrick's apartment. It was Friday, 4pm, and she was excited at the prospect of a night out without Mom and Dad questioning her every move. Once her parents realized Jill was not going to return to New York, they dropped Laura off at the airport, having no idea they wouldn't be seeing their youngest daughter for a while. Then her parents headed for San Francisco, telling Jill they would be returning next weekend to say goodbye before they returned home. Jill didn't know what to think about her sister running off with a band, but Laura seemed genuinely happy and that's all that mattered.

The door came open and, as always, Derrick looked ridiculously crazy, take-your-breath-away handsome. Never mind that he wore a simple pair of gray sweatpants and a clean white T-shirt. Thick dark hair curled around his ears and when his gaze fell on hers, his brown eyes appeared darker than she remembered. The expression on his face was hard to read, and he had a dangerous edge to him that never failed to make her insides quiver.

He took the baby bag out of her hand and gestured for her to come inside.

"I thought I'd bring Ryan to you first and then go back for the portable crib," she said as she stepped inside.

"No need." He leaned forward and for a fleeting moment she thought he was going to kiss her. Instead, he planted his lips on Ryan's forehead.

Inwardly, Jill scolded herself for thinking that Derrick was going to kiss her. Even more ridiculous was the fact that she was going to let him. He'd been more than gracious at dinner with her uptight parents, handling their rudeness with aplomb, letting their offensive questions and rude comments roll off of his back like water. Derrick had been kind and courteous. And the best part of the night had been when he followed her to the dance floor without question and held her in his arms, calming her nerves and making her feel safe.

And that was the moment she knew she was in big trouble.

She'd never believed women who insisted they fell in love within days of meeting a man. But now Jill knew that it could happen because it was happening to her. She was falling fast and hard for Derrick Baylor.

And she needed to put a stop to it.

Derrick shut the door behind her. "Come with me," he said. "I have something I want to show you."

She followed him down the hallway. On the way, she peeked inside his bedroom and noticed he'd fixed his bed frame since she'd been here last. The memory caused her cheeks to burn while her insides fluttered.

When she entered the last room where Derrick waited, her eyes widened in surprise. The guest room had been made into a baby's room. Two bands of blue lined the wall. There was a blue rug with a choo choo train and white shelves filled with stuffed animals. "It's beautiful. When did you do this?"

"Today."

"Is this why Maggie was here earlier? To help you decorate?"

He looked surprised and maybe even uncomfortable.

"I saw her leaving your apartment," she explained.

"How did you know it was Maggie?"

"I saw you with her in the courtroom when you were on the news."

"Ahh," he said. "I designed the room myself, although Maggie did suggest I hang the animal mobile higher so Ryan wouldn't be able to reach it."

"You and Maggie have been friends for a while?"

"Practically forever," he said. "Growing up, she was like one of the boys."

The Maggie she had seen looked much too serious to play with boys.

"That was years ago. She's changed since then." He left it at that and went to the crib. "They call this the four-in-one sleep set. It reassembles to grow with your baby. The mattress has a thick foam layer inside and it's hypoallergenic. What do you think?"

"It's stunning. I love the cherry wood." Jill looked from the matching changing table to the tall dresser and the plush bedding, a mixture of soft suede and cotton. Everything from the window valance to the diaper stacker matched perfectly.

Derrick opened up a dresser drawer. "Everything Ryan could possibly need is right in here."

Holding Ryan close, she reached out her free hand to touch a sweater. "This is cashmere."

He nodded. "I liked it because it was soft."

There were at least three cashmere outfits and then soft cotton one-pieces in every color imaginable. There were also cashmere hats and socks, long-sleeved shirts and short-sleeved shirts, corduroy pants and matching tops. "Ryan is going to be the best dressed baby this side of Los Angeles."

"You think so?"

She laughed. "I think you got carried away. He's an infant now, but later on, too much of this sort of thing could spoil a kid rotten." She looked inside the closet where he'd stacked every baby accessory imaginable. "You must have spent thousands."

"He's worth every penny."

"Of course he is, but that's not the point." Derrick was a good man and a naturally good father, too. Earlier today, when she'd heard voices and then glanced out the window, she'd seen Derrick holding Maggie close as they said goodbye. Instantly, she'd felt a wave of resentment and envy. Who Derrick spent his time with should be no concern of hers. She needed to rein in any feelings she felt toward him since he'd made it clear he wanted the two of them to be nothing more than friends.

She placed Ryan on the center of the mattress inside the crib and smiled when he kicked his legs as if he was riding his first tricycle. "Looks like you won't need the portable crib, so I guess I'll be on my way."

Derrick turned on the musical mobile. "Look at that, would you? He likes it."

She swallowed the knot in her throat. "If there's anything else you need, you should find it in the diaper bag. My cell phone number is in there, too, in case you have any problems."

He walked her to the door.

"I'll be across the way getting ready if you need me before then."

"Are you sure you want to do this?"

"Do what?"

"Go out with this Nate guy."

She smiled. "Of course I do. He's been on a shopping bag, remember?"

"That's a dumb reason to go out with a guy."

"I'm only teasing. He's a wonderful man. Besides," she said over her shoulder as she headed back to her apartment. "Nate Lerner could be the *one*."

~~~

A little powder on her nose, some lipstick, and she was ready to go. Turning toward the full-length mirror, Jill gave herself one last look. She wore a pair of white stretch pull-on jeans and a Marc Jacobs V-neck black tank. She'd bought the outfit a few weeks before she found out the insemination process had been successful and she was pregnant. She turned to her right and then to her left. Between stress and hormonal changes, she weighed three pounds less than she did before her pregnancy. Even though she wasn't breastfeeding, she was still almost a cup-size bigger. "Not bad."

Nate wasn't due to pick her up until six thirty, which gave her another ten minutes. She had dropped Ryan off early since she'd wanted enough time to take a nap and a long hot shower. Her skin was glowing, and she felt rejuvenated. Satisfied with her hair, she went into the bathroom and unplugged the flat iron. Another swipe of Burt's Bees Super Shiny lip gloss and she was ready to go.

A knock at the door told her he was early. It was date time. She was nervous and yet excited to spend some time with Nate so that she could begin to get Derrick Baylor out of her head for good. She didn't waste any time getting to the door.

Only it wasn't Nate.

"Great. I'm glad you haven't left yet," Derrick said. "I had to show you this."

He held Ryan upward and outward.

Her poor baby was covered from head to toe in some sort of weird looking fur.

"What is he supposed to be?"

Derrick made a tsking sound. "A porcupine, what else? Look at how the fur actually sticks up in spikes." To demonstrate, he fluffed up the fur around Ryan's head.

"I don't know if that will fit him by the time Halloween rolls around."

"You don't think so?"

She slipped the spikey hood off of Ryan's head so she could read the tag. "This costume is for infants. He'll be wearing big boy clothes in five months."

"Well, either way it's awfully cute, don't you think?"

"It's adorable," she agreed, "but I really need to go now. I need to finish getting ready before Nate gets here."

"That outfit you have on is a little on the revealing side, don't you think?"

"Not at all."

"All I can see is cleavage." His gaze traveled lower. "I also see that you borrowed your sister's leather pants."

"These are jeans, not leather. They're white, not black. Nice try."

"The truth is," he went on, "Ryan and I were just talking and we both think it's too early for you to be out gallivanting around town. You just had a baby, for God's sake."

"You're not my father or my brother or my boyfriend. In fact, I'm having a difficult time having you as a friend. So knock it off. I refuse to let you ruin my first night out."

"You enjoyed a nice dinner two nights ago."

She laughed. "It was three nights ago and if that's your idea of a good time, then you need to have your head examined."

"The guy is late, isn't he?" Derrick asked. "Maybe he stood you up. I knew there was something fishy about that guy."

Looking over Derrick's shoulder, Jill waved. "Hi Nate."

Nate looked absolutely dashing in dark slacks and a striped button-down shirt that fit him like a glove.

Trying not to laugh at the annoyed expression scrawled across Derrick's face, she moved around him so she could greet Nate properly.

"Look at that," Nate said after she gave him a hug. "A porcupine." He touched the tip of Ryan's nose. "A little early for Halloween, isn't it?"

"So we've been told," Derrick said. "Don't keep her out too late. She's got a magazine to run and a baby to take care of."

"Don't listen to him," Jill said as she grabbed Nate's hand and pulled him inside her apartment. Recognition hit Nate, and he snapped his fingers. "He plays for the Condors, doesn't he?"

"That's right," Jill said. "He's a football player."

"Ahh," Nate said. "I thought I recognized him the other day."

When Jill turned about and saw Derrick still standing there, she shooed him away and then gently shut the door in his face.

~~~

Derrick heard another noise and peeked through the curtains. He looked toward Jill's apartment but nobody was there. The plastic clock hanging on the kitchen wall mocked him with its tick tock, tick tock. It was only nine o'clock. Jill wouldn't be back for hours.

He took a seat on the couch, picked up the remote, and did a little channel surfing. Ryan had fallen asleep over an hour ago.

He was bored out of his skull. But then he heard keys jangling outside and this time he knew he wasn't hearing things. Jumping to his feet, he went to the door and opened it.

Jill had returned, and she was unlocking her door.

"Back so soon?" he asked.

"Are you keeping tabs on me?"

"No, of course not. I was just sitting here watching a little television and I heard a noise. So where's pretty boy?"

"He was called to the hospital for an emergency."

"How rude," Derrick teased.

"He's a doctor," she reminded him. She looked at Derrick for a moment longer. "Is everything all right? Is Ryan okay?"

"He's fine."

"Wonderful," she said before turning about and disappearing inside her apartment.

Derrick stood at the door for a moment, figuring she would reappear since she hadn't bothered to say goodnight. When she failed to return right away, he quietly shut the door to his apartment and went to Jill's door. Without knocking, he opened the door to her apartment and stuck his head inside. Her purse was on the floor and her wallet and keys made a haphazard trail around the corner. "Jill?"

The beat of his heart doubled in rhythm. Afraid somebody had been waiting for her inside and dragged her to one of the bedrooms, he headed that way. The door to her room was open and there she was wearing nothing but a pair of lacy thong underwear and matching bra.

Damn. Shapely legs and curvy hips were going to make it difficult for him to look her in the eye next time they had a conversation.

"Oh, my God! What are you doing in here?" She reached for her clothes and held a shirt in front of her.

With his hands held out like a traffic cop, he backed away from the door. "Sorry. I just came over to see if you wanted to watch a movie with me. I saw the contents of your purse scattered across the floor and I thought you had been accosted."

She shooed him away. "Why don't you go back to your apartment and I'll be right over to get Ryan."

"What about the movie?"

"I don't think so."

He stayed in the hallway as he continued the conversation. "Ryan is asleep. He won't be awake for hours. I'll make popcorn and I have a bottle of chardonnay that I want to share with someone."

"Just go, okay? I'll be right there."

"Great. I'll see you in a few minutes."

Seventeen minutes later, not that he was keeping track, Jill knocked on his open door.

He stood and gestured for her to come inside. "Welcome."

She entered his apartment, but she wasn't smiling. She swept past him, heading straight for the baby's room. A few minutes later, she returned empty handed. "He's so cute when he's sleeping."

He imagined Jill was probably cute while she slept, too. The pink sweat pants and loose, long-sleeved T-shirt didn't do her curves justice now that he'd seen her in a thong and a push-up bra. All he had to do was shut his eyes to call forth the vision.

"What are you doing?"

He opened his eyes. "Nothing."

"Your eyes were closed."

"No they weren't." He pointed at the leather binder filled with DVDs, the binder he'd brought from his Malibu home. "Why don't you pick a movie while I open up the bottle of wine and fix us some popcorn?"

She took off her sneakers and left them side by side at the door. Then she picked up the binder and brought it with her to the couch. She tucked her feet under her bottom and flipped through his DVD selection. "*Sin City, The Terminator, Pulp Fiction, Bourne Identity, Blade*…oh, this one is perfect." She pulled out a DVD.

He handed her a glass of wine and set a bowl of microwave popcorn on the coffee table. Then he took the DVD she had selected to see what she had chosen. "*The Notebook*? How did that get in there?"

"It's one of my favorite movies of all time. I'm so glad you suggested I come over." She lifted her glass as if to say cheers and then took a sip of her wine.

Damn. She knew she had him right where she wanted him.

He slipped the DVD into the machine and hit the Play button, figuring one of his sisters must have stuck that particular movie into his collection. With wine glass in hand, he took a seat on the couch next to her. Jill's gaze was directed at the coming attractions while his gaze fixated on her. Truthfully, he didn't care what they watched. He liked how this night was playing out. Enjoying a quiet night with Jill, knowing his son was right down the hall, felt like coming home after a long journey on the road.

Strange, he thought, that he couldn't remember the last time he'd felt so content.

CHAPTER 13

The next morning, when Jill opened the door to her apartment, Derrick took a step back so he could get a good look at her. "You look great."

"Thank you."

She was wearing a pair of white slacks, not as snug as the ones she wore on her date, and a cute little forest green sleeveless number that made her green eyes look even greener. Her hair was curly today. There was always something refreshing about seeing Jill, he realized. Yes, she had flawless skin and a cute turned-up nose, but it was more than that. There was something about the way her eyes lit up every time she looked at him that made it difficult for him to look away.

He looked down at his blue short-sleeved button-down shirt, the one his sisters had given him last Christmas. It wasn't horrible, but he could have done better. If he'd known Jill was going to go all out, he might have taken a little more time getting dressed this morning.

"Howiewood!" Lexi said, hopping around Jill so that she could latch onto Derrick's leg.

Jill winced. "Is that your bad leg she's holding onto?"

"No worries," he said as he patted the bouncy curls on Lexi's head. "I took a couple of ibuprofen, and besides, the little squirt is a lightweight."

Jill smiled again and this time a cute little dent appeared below her left eye, something he hadn't noticed before.

Sandy came to the door next. She was holding Ryan in one arm and a large bag stuffed with baby bottles and diapers in the other. "Here's your son," Sandy said as she handed Ryan over to Jill. "Lexi," she said, "go get your coloring books so Hollywood can keep his promise and color with you today."

Lexi let go of his leg and ran back into the apartment.

"Are you sure your parents don't mind Lexi and I coming along?" Sandy asked.

"Positive," Derrick said. "Mom's a big believer in 'the more the merrier.'"

"Do you have extra diapers at your apartment?" Jill asked. "I was going to call you, but I didn't have your number."

He pointed inside Jill's apartment. "I'll go inside and write my number down for you."

"You don't have to do it now," she said. "I can get it from you later."

"I'll do it now before I forget."

"We have to wait for Lexi anyhow," Sandy added.

He went to the kitchen where he knew he'd seen a pad of paper the last time he was here. While Jill and Sandy fussed over Ryan, he opened a couple of kitchen drawers until he found the paper. He also found a picture of Jill. She looked like a million bucks dressed in a long formal gown. Her hair was pulled up and lots of jewels glittered from her ears and neck. The guy next to her looked like a weasel, tall and reed thin with slicked back hair and big ears.

Lexi appeared out of nowhere and said, "That's Tommy. He's bad cuz he makes Jill cry a wot."

"A *LLot*," Derrick repeated with emphasis on the L sound as he bent down so he was eye level with the kid. "See how my tongue hits the back of my front teeth when I say a word that starts with 'L.' A *Lot*," he said again so she could see. "A *Lot*. See? It's easy."

Lexi opened her mouth wide and put her tongue on the back of her teeth like he had done and said, "A Wot. A Wot. A Wot." Then she smiled.

"Yeah, keep working on it kid." Lexi was stealth, sneaking up on him like that. She was also very perceptive for a four-year old. He wiggled the picture and said, "Jill must like him a Lot if she keeps his picture around."

Lexi shook her head.

If anyone knew what was going on around here, he was confident it was Lexi, and her head shaking told him Jill was through with ol' Tommy Boy. For reasons he couldn't explain, he was glad.

"She doesn't wike him," Lexi explained, "she WUVS him."

Derrick dropped the picture back into the drawer, and then rifled around for a pen. "That's too bad," he said, and he meant it. "Jill deserves someone a Lot better than that weasel."

"Do you make Jill cry?" Lexi asked.

"Never."

Lexi's eyes grew round. "Maybe you can WUV Jill and then she can fowget Tommy."

He looked seriously at Lexi for a moment before he burst out laughing. Rubbing the top of her head, he said, "You're a funny girl, a very funny girl."

Forty-five minutes later, Derrick didn't think Lexi was very funny anymore. If he had to listen to another round of "Old MacDonald" on his CD player, he was going to have to pull off at the next exit and call her and her mother a cab. He had hoped to have a conversation with Jill and Sandy on the ride to his parent's pony farm—get to know Jill's friend a little better before they all spent the day with his family. He could only hope his brothers and sisters would be on their best behavior, although the odds were against it. The law of attraction must be at work, he figured, because just as he thought of his family, the music shut off and the console rang.

He hit the On button and like magic his mother's voice replaced *the moo moo here and the moo moo there, here a moo, there a moo, everywhere a moo moo.* He'd never been so relieved to hear his mother's voice—that is, until she finished her first sentence.

"Hi, son. I wanted you to know I went to the store for the really good kind of anti-bacterial soap. I made everybody scrub up. Your sisters even gave us all manicures to make sure we're all good to go. No horse manure smells inside or out. Do you think Jill will let us hold the baby if you tell her we all scrubbed clean?"

He glanced at Jill and noticed her blossoming cheeks. "No need for me to tell her, Mom. We're on speaker phone."

"Oh, hello, Jill."

"Hello, Mrs. Baylor."

"Please, call me Helen. I hope I didn't say anything that might offend you in any way. I just wanted—"

"Mom," Derrick interrupted. "We'll be there in five." He shut the Off button just in time to hear the pig oinking here and there and everywhere. He was about to sing along when Jill reached over and shut off the music. He glanced in the rearview mirror in time to see Sandy cross her arms and raise both brows for good measure.

Jill huffed. "You told your mother they couldn't hold Ryan because they didn't have clean enough hands?"

"I didn't put it exactly like that. Don't forget, they live and work on a pony farm."

"Ponies!" Lexi shouted loud enough to make Derrick's ear drums hurt.

Jill released a long sigh.

"I told Mom and Dad that you didn't want them to make a big deal about your visit—you know—no signs, no balloons, no fanfare," Derrick said. "I also told them you didn't feel comfortable passing Ryan around—you know—like a football."

She groaned.

Sandy continued to glare at him via the rearview mirror, eyes narrowed, lips tight.

Lexi laughed and said, "Howiewood called Tommy Boy a whistle," Lexi said with glee in her voice, making Derrick realize the apple truly didn't fall far from the tree.

Jill frowned. "Tommy Boy?"

"Thomas," he said.

"A whistle?" Sandy asked.

"A weasel, not a whistle," Derrick corrected.

Jill snorted. "Oh, that's much better."

Sandy laughed.

The sound startled Derrick because even though he knew Sandy was slowly softening toward him, despite the occasional dagger eyes and before his mom ruined everything, he still hadn't thought Sandy was capable of laughing.

Sandy looked into the rearview mirror and wrinkled her nose. "What are you looking at?"

"Just checking to see if you're laughing at my expense."

She laughed some more. "Definitely."

"It's not funny," Jill told Sandy. "Tommy Boy—I mean, Tommy—I mean Thomas— is not a weasel."

"But he makes you cry," Lexi said, her voice much too serious for a four-year old.

"Not any longer," Jill said.

"Howiewood said he would never make you cry. I think he wikes you."

Although he kept his eyes on the road, he figured Jill was looking his way—probably trying to figure out what his problem was. Sandy had already made it clear that he was a dead man if he ever hurt Jill. At least they were no longer focused on what Mom had said about his entire family sterilizing their hands before they got there. No matter how he looked at it, there was no getting around the fact that this was going to be a long day.

It wasn't long before Derrick parked the car on the curb outside his parent's ranch house. The first sign he might be in bigger trouble than he already was came in the form of an assortment of foil, Mylar, and latex balloons—in every shape, size, and color. The second sign was an actual sign—a ten-by-three foot expanse of white paper hanging over his parents' front door with big red letters that spelled out, "Welcome, Jill and Ryan!"

He figured Jill hadn't noticed since she had already climbed out of the car and was busy fiddling with the buckles and belts on the child seat. When she was finished, she kissed Ryan on the tip of his nose and then handed Ryan to him.

As he held Ryan in his arms, he gazed upon his son for a long moment, almost as if he was looking at him for the first time. It hit him like a bolt of lightning. His son was here to meet his parents for the first time. Why that particular thought would make him feel as if a multitude of moth wings were flittering around inside his gut, making him feel all woozy and emotional, he didn't want to know. He'd never been big on emotions. He didn't do woozy and emotional, and he certainly didn't see any reason to start now. Swallowing the knot lodged in his throat, he blinked a couple of times to get control of himself.

Jill collected Ryan's things and then looked at him. "Are you okay? You look pale."

"We never should have brought him here."

She smiled. "You're the one who was worried about clean hands. Don't worry," she said, "your secret is safe with me. And stop worrying about Ryan. He'll be fine."

Derrick grabbed her arm, stopping Jill from heading for the house. Sandy was already chasing Lexi across the yard. "I've wanted to tell you all morning how much I enjoyed last night." He shifted his weight from one foot to the other. "I've seen better movies, but never with better company."

That cute little dent of hers appeared again...until she frowned. "What is wrong with you? You look as if you're about to take the death march."

"You haven't met the entire family all at once."

"I thought you were excited about this—about your family meeting Ryan?"

"You're right. I am excited. I'm fine. They'll be fine. You'll be fine. Everything will be fine." He let go of her arm and then looked at Ryan, who seemed to be growing at the speed of light.

"Come on, Howiewood!" Lexi shouted.

"We're coming," Jill answered.

Ryan was sucking on his fingers again.

"I think the little guy is hungry," Derrick said as they headed for the house, hoping to distract Jill in case she hadn't noticed the assorted balloons affixed to the mailbox or the big Mylar ones swinging from the branches of the elm tree in the front yard.

"We can feed him when we get inside." She looked over her shoulder at him. "No signs, no balloons, no fanfare?"

"You noticed, huh?"

She rolled her eyes. "I'm surprised the local news trucks aren't here for the big event."

"I think aliens abducted my family. Not once in my life have I seen a sign, let alone balloons, in a quarter of a mile radius of my house before today."

"I wike balloons!" Lexi said, running toward the tree. Sandy continued to chase after her.

The door to his parents' house came open and his mom and dad stepped outside, followed by his brother Lucas, and then Jake, and his sisters Rachel and Zoey.

Once again Derrick found himself hoping that it wasn't a mistake bringing Jill to meet his family. After today, Jill might waltz into the mediation room next month with enough ammunition against him to convince the mediator to never allow him to see his son again.

His father had stopped to talk to Lexi and Sandy while his mother headed straight for her grandson. She and Jill hugged, squeezing the life out of one another since they were both natural-born huggers. They released each other long enough for his mother to turn toward Derrick and focus her full attention on Ryan. With a hand over her heart, Mom let out a noise that sounded like she'd died and gone to heaven right then and there. "He's the most perfect baby on this earth," she crooned.

"That's what you said about Garrett's baby," Derrick reminded her.

"True, but now we have one perfect little girl and one perfect little boy."

Mom looked squarely into Jill's eyes. "I can't thank you enough for allowing us to meet Ryan today. I thought my heart would burst if another day went by without getting to see him."

Before Jill could respond, she was bombarded by the rest of his family, everyone asking questions and talking at once. His sisters oohed and ahhed at the baby as they all moved up the walkway and through the double doors leading into the house.

Derrick hardly had time to finish introducing Jill before Mom ushered everyone out the sliding glass door and into the backyard for a feast of finger foods, including cream cheese and garlic crostini and overcooked hamburgers and hotdogs. His mom had taken his son from him before he could stop her. She was holding Ryan close to her chest as she walked side by side with Jill, heading for the picnic benches.

While Derrick watched the subtle sway of Jill's hips as she moved across the yard, one of his brothers shoved a plate into his hands and pointed to the food, telling him to eat. Derrick had no idea where Sandy and Lexi had disappeared to, because from the looks of things, more and more people were pouring into the backyard with every passing minute.

First to enter through the side gate were Mr. and Mrs. Cooley from across the street. And he was pretty sure the man with the moustache and squinty eyes who came in behind them was Dr. Frost, his dentist from way back. Two elderly ladies entered the backyard from the kitchen sliding door. One woman he didn't recognize and one he did: Grandma Dora was here—and that meant trouble.

Judging by the never-ending line of people streaming into the backyard, Mom had invited most of Arcadia. Figuring he better eat before making the social rounds, he placed a crostini, which was basically cream cheese and onion on bread, and a ham roll next to his overdone hamburger. His parents weren't the best cooks in town, but they always had two or more long tables covered with enough food to feed the neighborhood.

After chatting with Mr. and Mrs. Cooley for a while, Derrick sifted through the crowd. As far as he could tell, Jill had found something to nibble on while his mother and sisters hovered around her and the baby. He spotted Sandy across the yard and noticed that she had made a friend of his brother, Jake, which worried him a little because as much as he liked Lexi, he couldn't imagine coming to his parents' get-togethers only to be scowled at for the rest of his life. Besides, Jake was too young for Sandy.

Mom must have already eaten because she looked more than content sitting next to Jill and feeding Ryan a bottle while introducing Jill to everyone who stopped to take a peek at her new grandson.

A big hand settled on his shoulder and he turned to see who was there. "Hey, Dad. What's up?"

Dad shook his head as if he couldn't find the words to express whatever it was he wanted to say. Finally he coughed and said, "My little boy is growing up."

"Dad, are you serious? I'll be thirty soon. You're not going soft on me, are you?" His dad had retired from his position as bank manager two years ago. It suddenly occurred to Derrick that he hadn't taken his dad golfing in a while. Obviously, it was time he did.

Dad blinked a couple of times, reminding Derrick of his own breakdown earlier when he'd realized he was here to introduce his son to his family.

"Holy shit," Derrick said. "You're crying, aren't you?"

Dad stiffened. "You have a son now. No more cursing."

"Okay, you're right. No cursing." Derrick pointed a finger at him. "But no crying either."

"Don't be an ass. I wasn't crying."

Derrick inhaled and decided to let it go—the crying and the cursing. "Quite a spread Mom prepared for us today," he said.

"Yeah. Just don't eat the ham rolls," Dad said. "They taste like fish."

Ah, much better. There was the dad he knew and loved. "They're supposed to taste like fish," Derrick reminded him. "Mom put tuna in the middle of them. That's what we used to get in our lunches."

"I'm sorry about that," his dad said, and judging by his serious tone, he meant it. "I knew she couldn't cook the first time she made me dinner forty–some-odd years ago. But once your mother decided I was the one she was going to marry, I didn't stand a chance."

Derrick decided not to tell him that Mom said the same thing about him.

"I like Jill," Dad said. "She seems intelligent and friendly. It's good to see you with someone who has some brains for once."

"Dad, we're not dating."

"She's the mother of your child. Of course, you're dating. Whether you like it or not, the two of you will be dating for the rest of your life."

Derrick glanced back at Jill and tried to picture the two of them together—forever. "I hardly know her."

"So what?"

"She's not my type."

"You mean you're not *her* type."

"What do you mean by that?"

"Look at her," Dad said. "She's perfect. She's got grace and manners and she has a singing voice."

Since when did his father care about grace and manners? The alien was back. "What do you mean a singing voice? Have you heard her sing?"

"Of course not. And so what if she's not 38, 26, 38? Your mother likes her."

As his dad sang Jill's praises, Derrick watched Jill's eyes light up as she laughed about something Mom said to her, which frightened him a little because that meant Mom was telling her about how shy he used to be when he was six and how he was the only kid that would hang onto her leg as if he'd die if she left him for two minutes. Mom loved that story. The truth was Connor had been the shy one. Mom probably had the two of them mixed up, but it was her story and she was sticking to it.

As Dad rambled on, Derrick reached over and flicked a crumb off of his dad's favorite T-shirt, the bright yellow one that read, *DAD IS RAD*. "Are you ever going to get rid of that ugly shirt?"

"Probably not."

"You wear it just to annoy us, don't you?"

"You got it, kiddo."

Lexi tugged at the hem of Derrick's shirt, and he obediently bent down to her level. "What is it, Lexi?"

"Mommy said you would give me a piggy-back ride if I was good."

Derrick knew he'd been set up. He looked over at Sandy and saw her quickly look away. Satan was a tricky one. He looked at Lexi. "Have you been a good girl today?"

Her eyes widened. "Very good. And I wike your house."

"It's not *W*ike, it's *L*ike," his dad explained to Lexi. "Put your tongue like this." Dad showed Lexi how to make the L sound and Derrick didn't try to stop him.

As Derrick watched his father try to show Lexi what to do, he couldn't help but wonder when he had become his dad? He shook his head at the thought.

Lexi curled her tongue and said, "Wike." And the two of them went back and forth until Dad finally just walked away.

Lexi quickly forgot all about Dad and turned back to Derrick. "I want to see the ponies."

"We'll ride the ponies after everyone eats, okay? Until then, you'll have to pretend I'm a pony." Derrick set his plate on the corner of the closest food table and then hunched down low so Lexi could climb onto his back.

With a running start, Lexi jumped instead of climbed, and then used the heels of both her feet to kick him in the ribs. "Faster, faster," she said. And he dutifully obeyed. If Maggie hadn't appeared through the side gate wearing a white cotton dress and looking like a million bucks, he might have lasted another five minutes, at least.

CHAPTER 14

"So you're not married and you're not dating anyone?"

Jill smiled at Grandma Dora and answered the same question for the third time in the past ten minutes. Derrick's sister, Rachel, gave Jill an I'm-so-sorry-you-have-to-go-through-this look.

Truthfully though, Grandma Dora was fun to be around and Jill was glad she'd come to the picnic to meet everyone. Derrick's family, whether she had planned it this way or not, was going to be a part of her and Ryan's life. Over the last few hours, Jill had managed to squeeze in a few questions of her own, but getting a word in edgewise was not an easy task around the Baylor family.

"I'm glad you're available," Grandma Dora said, "because I think you and my little monkey make a cute couple."

Rachel put a hand to her temple. "Oh, Grandma, please. We all have real-life names and Derrick is way too old to be called monkey any longer."

"Don't get your panties in a twist, my little Tinkerbell. It's just a name. Nothing to get worked up about."

"She is right," Derrick's mom chimed in. "Jill and Derrick definitely make gorgeous babies together. Just look at this sweet face. Is he the best baby in the whole wide world, or what?"

Rachel and Jill looked at one another and laughed.

An hour and a half ago Jill had given up trying to convince Derrick's mother, two dozen neighbors, and especially Grandma Dora, that she and Derrick weren't meant to be. They were not fate in the making or destiny at work. For starters she explained that Derrick loved football, while Jill had never watched a game in her life. According to some older articles she'd found on the Internet, Derrick tended to date curvy voluptuous women. Jill happened to be the opposite of voluptuous. She wore an A cup before Ryan was born, and she had no hips to speak of. According to his sisters, Derrick was a meat and potato guy. She preferred sushi. Derrick was one of ten; she was one of two. He liked action movies; she liked romantic comedies. He liked coffee; she liked tea. The list went on and on.

But, after getting to know Derrick over the past two weeks, she realized none of that mattered.

She liked Derrick Baylor.

She liked the way he looked into her eyes whenever they said hello. She liked the way he kissed, too, and the way she felt when he wrapped her in his arms and held her tight. She liked the way his mouth curved upward and his eyes twinkled when he smiled. He always smelled good, and he looked as good wearing a pair of sweats and a T-shirt as he did in slacks and a button-down shirt. She liked his positive and cheerful disposition. She liked the way he looked at Ryan as if his chest might burst from all the love he was feeling every time he cradled his son in his arms. And now, Jill realized, she liked his family too.

But although there was chemistry between them, and she knew there was because she had felt it more than once, there was also something missing. Something was holding Derrick back. And yet she couldn't put a finger on it.

Or could she?

Lexi had run off to join her mom, and Derrick, Jill noticed, was staring longingly at a young woman as she came through the back gate. It was Maggie, the attorney engaged to Derrick's brother, Aaron.

And that's when it struck her like a hammer to her head.

Derrick had feelings for Maggie. It was written all over his face. That's why he'd been looking out the window, searching for her when they had run into Aaron downtown. Derrick was in love with Maggie, the woman who was engaged to be married to Derrick's adopted brother, Aaron. A person would have to be blind not to see it.

At this very moment, across the yard, Derrick was fawning over Maggie like a starved dog finally getting a treat. If he had a tail, it would be wagging. His full attention was focused on Maggie as the pair headed her way.

"Maggie," Derrick said, his eyes never leaving Maggie's face. "I'd like you to meet Jill Garrison and my son, Ryan."

Maggie wore a summer dress with a pair of strappy sandals. Her hair was sleek and blonde and pulled back at the sides with clips, revealing high cheekbones, perfect bow-shaped lips, and eyes as blue as the cloudless sky above them.

"It's nice to meet you," Maggie said as they exchanged a friendly handshake. "And look at Ryan. Oh, my, he's beautiful," Maggie said when Derrick's mom pulled back the baby blanket so she could get a better look at him.

"He's precious." Maggie looked back at Derrick's mom and said, "Aaron told me to say hello to everyone and to tell you he'd stop by next week."

Jill watched Derrick watching Maggie. Her insides twisted.

Music started up in the distance, breaking her away from her thoughts. They all looked toward the barn where a medley of banjo and fiddle music could be heard. Derrick's youngest sister, Zoey, jumped to her feet. Her long dark hair hung in one thick braid and it swung over her shoulder as she grabbed a hold of Jill's hand. "Come on. You have to see this!"

Derrick's mom insisted Jill go with Zoey, promising to take good care of Ryan while she was gone. She overheard Mrs. Baylor telling Derrick to go to the barn, too.

As Zoey pulled Jill toward the barn, Lexi shouted her name, waving for all she was worth. Lexi was riding the tiniest Shetland pony she'd ever seen. Sandy stood on one side of the pony while

Jake stood on the other side. Jill knew that Sandy had hoped to see Connor today, but apparently he was a no show.

Inside the barn, bales of hay were stacked against the walls at different levels so guests could use the hay as seats. At the far wall was a live band that consisted of four men, all wearing overalls and playing instruments: two fiddlers, a guitar player, and a banjo player.

Jill felt as if she'd been transported to another time as Zoey dragged her to the middle of the barn. "Come on," Zoey said, "it's time to do a little square dancing."

Jill laughed. "The last time I square danced was in fourth grade."

The moment Derrick entered the barn, Zoey waved him over, telling him that Jill could use a lesson in square dancing. Before Jill could protest, Derrick placed his hands on Jill's waist. "It's easy," he said. "Just follow my lead."

Zoey went to stand before the band and shouted loud enough to be heard over the music. "Okay, people," she said, "let's dance."

Four more couples of assorted ages joined Jill and Derrick on the straw-littered dance floor.

"I've seen most of you here before," Zoey said into a microphone that somebody handed her, "so I'm not going to waste too much time explaining the Butterfly Whirl. Let's get started."

Derrick kept a firm hold of Jill's waist and then told her to put her arm around his waist, too. She tried not to think about everyone watching them, but heat rose to her cheeks all the same. The couples moved in a circle until the music changed. Derrick let go of her hand and gave her a little push to get her moving toward the middle of the circle with the other four ladies. The men did a little jig that was just a few kicks and a heel-toe movement as they circled the women. The dance moves were easy to follow and the whole thing was surprisingly fun.

Jill laughed every time Derrick passed by, wiggling his brows and square dancing with exaggerated arm and leg movements.

"Now things are going to get a little tougher," Zoey said. "It's time for the gentlemen to allemande left, and then scoop up their partner and whirl back to place. Let's go."

Squeals of delight escaped her when Derrick took her by the waist again and picked her up so high she felt as if she was flying through the air. He finally put her down and held her until she had her balance again.

"Okay, people, it's time for the do-si-do. Bow to your corner, bow to your own. Three hands up and 'round you go. Break it up with a do-si-do. Chicken in the bread pan kickin' out dough."

Everybody faced each other, moved clockwise and first passed shoulder to shoulder, and then back-to-back. Next their left shoulders passed, before they all ended up where they started.

They stuck with the do-si-do long enough for Derrick to add a spin while performing the move.

Jill couldn't help but smile. "Show off."

"You haven't seen anything yet."

"Somebody has a big head."

"Who?" He looked around.

She laughed at his silliness as she followed along with the group and hooked her arm around his elbow. He twirled her in a circle before he let go and she found herself face to face with his brother, Connor.

He bowed. She curtsied.

"Well, hello there," Connor said, his voice an octave deeper than Derrick's.

"Nice to see you again," she replied before they stepped shoulder to shoulder and then back again.

"Did your friend come with you today?" he asked.

Jill nodded. "She's with Lexi and the ponies."

They hooked arms at the elbows, twirled, and then changed partners. She did this three more times until she was paired with Derrick again.

"I missed you," he said.

"I doubt that."

"It's the truth." He picked her up by the waist, his eyes never leaving hers as he twirled her about, making her blush, something she seemed to be doing a lot of lately.

"Time for all you kind folk to make a basket," Zoey called out.

And before Jill could bow out, she found herself doing what all the other ladies were doing, raising her arms up and around her partner's neck. Derrick took hold of her waist and lifted her from the ground.

Pressed up against him, she felt every nerve ending in her body sizzle and crackle. For a fleeting moment in time, Jill thought he might kiss her, but then the music stopped and the dance was done.

~~~

"Look what the cat dragged home," Jake said, gesturing with his chin toward the house.

Sandy looked over her shoulder and tried not to look too obviously pleased by Connor's presence when she saw him approaching.

"Wook at me!" Lexi shouted, making Jake wince.

"It's *La La L*ook not *W*ook."

"Wa Wa Wook!" she shouted with glee.

Sandy had already explained to Jake that she'd taken Lexi to a speech therapist, who told her that once more teeth came in Lexi would be able to pronounce her Ls, but he and his brothers didn't appear to believe her.

"Hey," Connor said as he caught up to them. "How's it going?"

Jake had hold of the reins and he didn't slow down to wait for his brother.

Sandy held onto Lexi's leg and walked backwards so she could keep up with Jake and yet talk to Connor. "As you can see, we're all having fun." Connor had looked nice in a suit last week, but in jeans and a T-shirt, he took her breath away. His arms weren't as built as his brother Derrick's, but he definitely worked out on a regular basis. As he caught up to her, she noted that he smelled good too, like fresh hay mixed with a hint of spicy cologne.

Connor walked at her side and reached out to stroke the pony's wiry mane. "This is Peanuts. Peanuts used to be my pony," he told Lexi. "My brothers and I all used to play cowboys and Indians and Peanuts was the fastest of the bunch. Nobody could catch us."

"He's wrong," Jake told Lexi. "After Connor left for college, Mom said he was mine and Peanuts here has been my pony ever since."

"Okay children," Sandy teased, "enough."

Connor chuckled, but Jake didn't look happy about having Connor around.

About six inches taller than Jake, Connor towered over his brother, making it easy for him to reach over and rub his knuckles over the top of Jake's head. "You can have Peanuts, okay?"

"He's all yours," Jake said, handing him the reins. "I promised Sandy I would teach her to square dance. No time like the present."

Sandy didn't know what to say. She preferred to stay and talk to Connor, but she had expressed interest when Jake had mentioned square dancing earlier.

"I would love to," she told Jake, thinking fast, "but I better stay with Lexi."

"Don't worry, Connor will keep an eye on her, right Connor?"

Connor glanced from his brother to Sandy. "It would be my pleasure."

Sandy inwardly scolded herself for telling Jake she would dance with him. She'd been waiting for Connor to arrive all afternoon and now that he was finally here, she had to leave him. Sometimes life just wasn't fair. "Are you sure you don't mind?"

"Go have fun. Lexi and I will be fine."

"Lexi, you be a good girl for Connor, okay?"

Her curls bobbed when she nodded. "I wike him."

Connor laughed.

"I'll hurry back," Sandy said, but Jake grabbed her hand and pulled her along before she could add anything else, or gaze into his eyes for a few minutes longer, or think of an excuse to reach out and touch him. When she and Jake got as far as the barn, she looked over her shoulder and watched Connor lead Peanuts in another circle and at the same time laugh at something Lexi said.

Then he turned her way, as if he knew she'd be looking.

~~~

After her third dance, Sandy took a seat on a bale of hay next to Jill and wiped her brow. "Thank you, Jake. That was fun."

"I'll grab you both some punch and I'll be right back."

"I think Jake has a crush on you," Jill said. "What happened to Connor?"

"He's leading the pony around with Lexi. To tell you the truth, I wanted to dance with Connor, but by the time Jake had asked me to dance, I didn't think Connor was going to show up anyhow. I feel like I'm back in high school."

Jill laughed as she brushed hay from her pants.

Sandy gestured a hand toward Derrick and the woman he was talking to. "Is that his attorney?"

"Yes, it is. She's also his adopted brother's fiancée. Her name is Maggie."

They both watched Derrick as he chatted with the woman.

Sandy's eyes narrowed. "What's going on with the whole court thing, anyhow? Is he still going to try to get partial custody of Ryan?"

"I guess we'll be discussing all of that before a court assigned mediator in a few weeks."

"Maybe if you just agree to let him see Ryan four times a year that will satisfy him and you won't have to bother with mediation."

Jill chewed on her bottom lip. "I really don't know what to do at this point. I really should talk to Thomas about it."

"There are thousands of attorneys out there. You don't need to get Thomas involved."

Jill sighed as she continued to watch Derrick and Maggie. "What do you think about those two? I met Aaron, Derrick's adopted brother and Maggie's fiancé, the day Derrick and I took Ryan to his doctor appointment. There was some obvious animosity between the two brothers."

"Interesting."

"And then yesterday," Jill went on, "before my date with Ryan's pediatrician, Nate Lerner, I saw Maggie at Derrick's apartment. When I asked him about her visit, he played it off as if it was nothing, said she was just helping him decorate Ryan's room."

"I didn't know you went out with Ryan's pediatrician."

Jill nodded. "It was supposed to be dinner and a movie, but he was called away to be in the delivery room for an emergency c-section. Instead, I ended up watching a movie with Derrick—after he walked into my apartment unannounced and caught me half-dressed."

"This just keeps getting better and better." Sandy angled her head as she looked closely at Jill. "He's growing on you, isn't he?"

"I don't know. Maybe. Yes. Sometimes Derrick looks at me as if I'm the only woman in the world and other times he just looks confused."

"Men."

"Yeah."

"If God was a woman, she wouldn't have been so cruel."

Jake returned with a glass of punch for each of them, putting an end to any further talk of Derrick Baylor.

~~~

"Thanks so much for having me and Ryan at your house today," Jill told Phil Baylor. "I had a wonderful time."

"I should be thanking you for bringing Ryan. It meant a lot to all of us." He gave her a hug. "While you retrieve your son," he

148

told her, "I'll grab the rest of your things." He pointed to her left. "Ryan is asleep in Derrick's old bedroom down the hall to the left. I'll be right there."

"Thank you." As Jill headed down the hallway, she took her time looking at all the family pictures hanging on the walls. Apparently it wasn't easy squeezing ten kids into one picture because in most of the pictures someone's head or body was cut off by the frame. There were photos of Derrick playing football and of all the Baylor boys riding horses and ponies and swinging from ropes in the barn. A large section of the wall was devoted to ribbons and awards they had won at horse and pony shows.

Voices caught her attention as she neared the first bedroom. She recognized Derrick's voice and when she peeked through the partially open door, she saw Derrick and Maggie standing near the portable crib. Derrick's mother stood on the opposite side and was about to pick up Ryan when Maggie held up two pieces of paper and said, "I have some very good news." She jiggled the paper in her hand. "Guess what this is?"

"I have no idea," Derrick said.

Mrs. Baylor paid no attention as she scooped Ryan into her arms.

"Not only is it the letter you sent to CryoCorp," Maggie said excitedly, "but a copy of the check CryoCorp cashed, proving they received the letter and the check within days of the date you said you mailed it. Not only will CryoCorp be forced to admit to their part in this mess, the judge will have no choice but to give you half custody of Ryan."

Derrick's father had returned with Jill's things. He coughed to let everyone know he and Jill were standing at the door.

Everyone turned their way.

Jill's stomach churned and her eyes stung. She didn't know what to say; she only knew she needed to leave right this minute. She never should have come today. She had wanted to play fair, but now something stirred inside of her, something deep and dark and scary, something telling her she needed to be wary of Derrick and his family. Not because they might not be good people—her instincts told her they wanted only the best for her and Ryan—but because she needed to be the one who decided what was best for her and her son. Although she'd truly started to believe she might be able to handle Derrick being a part of Ryan's life, she wasn't ready to give Derrick half custody or any say at all when it came to Ryan.

Unsure of what to say, she stepped forward. Derrick's mom handed Ryan over. As Jill held her baby close to her chest, her gaze connected with Derrick's. "I should go. I need to get Ryan home."

"I'm sorry," Maggie said, and Jill wasn't sure if the apology was meant for her alone or for Derrick's family, too, but it didn't matter. If anything, Jill felt as if she should be thanking Maggie for making her see how quickly she'd reverted back to doing exactly what she'd been doing her entire life—trying to please everyone else. She had a son now and she needed to put his welfare above all else. Ryan was her son, and nobody, including Derrick Baylor and his family, was going to take him away from her.

The ride home was almost more than Jill could handle. Lexi and Ryan fell fast asleep when she needed the distraction most. Sandy had on her earphones and was listening to her iPod. Her eyes were closed.

"I'm sorry about the situation with the letter," Derrick said. "I know what you're thinking and I want you to know that nobody was trying to hide anything from you."

Jill's gaze was directed out the window. She watched the sunset behind row after row of houses and trees as it all swept by in a hazy blur. She didn't want to talk about this now. She needed to think, to plan, to decide what her next step was going to be.

"You're not going to talk to me?"

"I spent months enduring injections and medications," Jill blurted out, unrehearsed. "For eight and a half months I carried my baby inside of me. I ate right and exercised every day. Ryan belongs to me and nobody is going to take him away from me."

"I would never take him away from you."

"Then why are you proceeding with this mediation thing?"

"We haven't known each other very long. Doesn't it make sense that I would want some sort of formalized document stating your agreement that Ryan is also my son and I can spend time with him?"

She reached for her purse, rifled through it and pulled out a pen and paper. She scribbled the words: *Derrick Baylor is the father of my son, Ryan Michael Garrison.* Then she stared at the paper for a moment longer before she crumpled the paper and tossed it to the floor. "I think you should have blood tests taken."

He kept his eyes on the road. "Why?"

"What if you're not his father? How do we really know?"

"That's not necessary. CryoCorp sent me a letter with your designated number on it. That's how I found you in the first place."

"Companies are run by people. People make mistakes. I'm going to call the court and tell them I do not want to proceed until blood tests confirm paternity."

CHAPTER 15

Jill looked from the beautiful plaque to her two friends and co-workers, Sandy and Chelsey. "Up and Coming Food Magazine of the Year. We did it, girls."

The three of them gathered in her apartment where they usually met twice a month, but tonight was extra special. Jill stood and held up her champagne glass. "I want to make a toast."

Sandy and Chelsey held up their glasses too.

"I wanted to invite you here today to not only celebrate winning '*Up and Coming*,' but also for working endless hours to produce the best issue of *Food for All* yet. You both did an amazing job and I'm proud to have the honor to work with such dedicated and talented people."

The doorbell rang.

Jill went to the door and looked out the peephole before opening it.

"Flowers for Jill Garrison," he said.

"That would be me." She signed the paper on his clipboard and then took the flowers. They smelled heavenly. She knew who they were from and she knew he was probably watching, so she didn't dare look pleased by them. "Thank you," she said before shutting the door.

The flowers came in a vase with water, saving her from having to cut and arrange. The other bouquets Derrick had sent over the past three days had each been delivered at different times of the day and in different vases. She put the lilies on the kitchen counter next to the roses and tulips and avoided going near the kitchen sink since she figured Derrick would be watching from his apartment. The man would stop at nothing.

Chelsey joined her in the kitchen and took a long whiff. "They smell wonderful. I don't think I've ever seen such beautiful flowers."

"You can have them."

"Really? Thanks."

"So, let me get this straight," Chelsey said. "You're mad at Derrick Baylor because he wants half custody of his son?"

"I'm not mad at him. I just don't trust him or his family and I don't want him around. Not until everything is figured out legally."

Chelsey looked at Sandy. "I thought you said his family was amazing and that you both had a great time?"

"They seem like great people," Jill agreed. "It's just that they're—" She looked heavenward as she grasped for the right words to explain what she wanted to convey. "They're really, *really*, into family. You know what I mean? The Baylor family is crazy over-the-top, ridiculously loving and caring. I swear they would probably all jump off a bridge at once if it meant saving one of their own—" Jill stopped in mid-sentence when she realized she wasn't helping her position any. She waved a hand through the air. "Never mind—it's hard to explain."

"Jill doesn't want any help raising her son," Sandy said. "She's tired of people telling her what to do and how to do it. She wants to take control of her life."

Hearing it like that made Jill realize how silly it all sounded.

"Everything seemed to be going along so smoothly, though," Chelsey said. "What happened? Are you refusing to let him see his son because you're afraid that down the road Ryan will love his father more than you? I don't get it."

Jill was thankful when Sandy stepped in once again to answer the question for her.

"Here's the problem," Sandy explained. "Derrick Baylor was paid money to be a sperm donor. He wasn't paid to be a father. Donors sign papers and documents stating their agreement to remain anonymous. Women who use donors to have babies don't even have to put a face to the donor unless they want to."

Lexi was watching her favorite show on the television in her bedroom, but Jill lowered her voice when she added, "If Lexi's father walked through that door right now, would you want to give him half custody?"

"No."

"Why not?"

"Because giving him half custody would give him half a say on every decision I make when it comes to Lexi's well-being."

"Exactly," Jill said with a smile. *Case closed.*

~~~

Once the three of them had come to a decision on the next month's issue of *Food for All*, everyone left and the apartment was quiet again. After feeding Ryan, Jill placed him on her shoulder and began pacing the length of the room. She patted his back until he awarded her with a good-sized burp. "You're a good boy."

Chelsey, she noticed, had forgotten to take the flowers home with her and the scent of daylilies filled the apartment. Jill reached for the card poking out from the vase.

Give Ryan a kiss for me, Derrick

Jill kissed the top of Ryan's head and breathed in his baby smell. She glanced out the window above her sink. Derrick's kitchen light was on and she could see him moving around.

Her heart sank. She hadn't seen him in seventy-two hours and she already missed him—a man who wanted to take away the right to raise her son in a manner she saw fit—a man who had become a donor solely for selfish reasons, only to barge into her life with no thought for anyone but himself—a man who had managed to get under her skin by opening up to her and being a great listener. He'd taught her to do-si-do and charmed her with his crooked smiles and playful winks…and flowers.

Damn him.

~~~

The column for next month's issue kept Jill busy for the next few days. When the doorbell rang, she jumped. Once again she'd forgotten to tape the "don't ring the bell" sign over the doorbell. Maybe she'd call an electrician this afternoon and have it disconnected so people wouldn't ring the bell and wake the baby.

She opened the door, expecting to see the delivery boy with another flower arrangement. She was only half right. It wasn't the flower boy delivering a large bouquet of two dozen long-stemmed red roses. This time it was Derrick in the flesh.

"You need to stop with the flowers," she said.

"I can't."

"Why not?"

"I miss spending time with you and Ryan."

"I understand that you want to spend time with your son, but we need to get things sorted out legally before I can let you inside my apartment again."

He gestured a hand between the two of them. "I miss our time together," he said.

She tried not to notice the strain of his shirt around his biceps or his damp hair and newly shaved jaw. "Did you go to the doctor for a blood test?"

He nodded. "I'll let you know when the results are in."

"No need. Nate will let me know."

"Don't do this," Derrick said. "Don't shut me out."

"Frankly, Derrick, the truth is I don't know you that well and I don't trust you."

He took her hand in his before she could stop him. "We were having fun together, weren't we?"

She took her hand back. "That's not the point."

"You don't like flowers, is that it?"

"They're very nice, but please stop."

"Let me cook dinner for you tonight. Once you've tried my lasagna you'll be hard pressed not to put it on the cover of your magazine."

She dropped her gaze to the ground and shook her head.

"I'll do anything to change things between us. Anything at all."

He had no idea how difficult he was making this for her. He also had no idea that she was falling for him. Letting him into her apartment was one thing, but letting him into her heart was something else altogether. Apologizing for the kiss they had shared had been her first clue that he wasn't emotionally available. The way he'd looked at Maggie on two separate occasions was her second clue. She couldn't let Derrick come inside even if she wanted to—he was trouble with a capital T. The last thing she could handle right now was a broken heart.

She looked into his eyes. "We need to see this court thing through to the end before we talk about being friends. I want to go to sleep at night knowing Ryan belongs to me, and that nobody, not even his own father, can take him from me. I can't afford to be your friend and risk everything."

"So that's it?"

"I'm afraid so."

"I miss you both," he said. "I'll go, but I'm not going to give up easily."

She nodded and shut the door. And then she melted to the floor and cried.

~~~

That night Derrick found himself talking to his mom again, which told him he really did need to make some changes in his life. Holding his cell phone to his ear, he leaned his head back against the couch and used his free hand to hold a bag of ice to his knee.

"When will your father and I get to see Ryan again?" Mom asked.

"I have no idea. I already told you, I think you scared her off with those ham rolls. How many times do we all need to tell you that the ham roll recipe needs to be burned?"

"Grandma Dora gave me that recipe."

"Well, as soon as she kicks the bucket you need to throw that recipe in the grave with her."

A gasp sounded and then laughter. "She's going to get even with you when she hears about this."

Derrick smiled because he knew Mom was right. Grandma Dora would get even. He and Grandma teased one another about things most people didn't kid about, let alone talk about. But that's what made Grandma Dora special. She wasn't like any other grandma in the world.

Mom's long, ponderous sigh came through the receiver. "I could have sworn Jill enjoyed herself when she was here."

"She had a great time, Mom. But that's not the problem. Maggie never should have given me the letter or brought up anything to do with the custody case. It wasn't the time or the place."

"Maggie feels horrible about that. She was excited to give you the news. She's only trying to help you and she's doing it against Aaron's wishes."

Derrick stopped the bag of ice from slipping off of his sore knee. "What's wrong with Aaron anyhow? He's making a big deal about nothing." Derrick knew that wasn't really a fair assessment of Aaron's recent moodiness, but his mother didn't know the whole story and he wasn't ready to fill her in on the details.

"He's sensitive," she said. "He's always felt there was a competition between you and him. You should call him and tell him he has nothing to worry about. Tell him you're not in love with Maggie and that you would never try to come between them. That's all he needs to hear."

Derrick wasn't sure if he could ever do that. "Did he say that?"

"I'm a mother. I know these things."

A burnt smell and a haze of smoke reminded him he had put a frozen dinner in the oven. "I've gotta go, Mom. Dinner is calling."

She barely had time to say goodbye before he jumped to his feet, letting the bag of ice drop to the floor as he tossed his cell phone to the cushion. He grabbed a potholder, pulled the burnt TV dinner from the bottom rack, and tossed it into the sink.

Smoke curled upward and threatened to fill the room.

He hobbled to the front door and opened it. Then he rubbed his eyes and blinked a couple of times to make sure he wasn't seeing things. Jill stood right outside his door, her face pale and her eyes big and round, filled with worry.

"Jill? What's going on?"

She reached out and grabbed his hand, pulling him toward her apartment. "It's Ryan. He's had a fever for the past few hours and he's not crying like he usually does and Nate hasn't called back and I don't know what to do."

Leaving his door open, Derrick followed her into her apartment and to Ryan's room. Ryan's eyes were wide open. He kicked his feet and the corners of his mouth turned upward. "Look at that," Derrick said, "he smiled at me."

She reached her hand over the side of the crib and touched Ryan's forehead. "He's not smiling at you. He has gas."

Derrick didn't believe it for a moment, but he wasn't going to argue. He angled his head for a better look at his son. The little guy looked pretty much like he always did. He reached into the crib and touched Ryan's forehead just as Jill had done. "You're right. He does feel warm. How long has he felt that way?"

"He felt warm this morning. I didn't think much of it, though, until he slept through his late afternoon feeding. That's when I decided to take his temperature. At four o'clock it was one hundred and a little while ago I took it again and it was a tiny bit over one hundred. That's when I decided to call Nate."

"Did you read anything about temperatures in that baby book of yours?"

She nodded. "It said to make sure the baby is not dressed too warm—not too many blankets or too many layers of clothing."

"Is your computer still on?"

She nodded again.

"Mind if I use it to look up a few things?"

"It's on the coffee table in the other room."

Derrick headed that way and it wasn't long before Jill walked into the room holding Ryan. "Any luck?"

"It says here that you get the best reading by taking the temperature rectally."

"I used an ear thermometer."

"They recommend waiting twenty minutes if the baby has had a bath."

"Really? It says that?"

"Why, did you give him a bath?"

"Yes, and I don't have a rectal thermometer."

"I have one at my place."

"You did think of everything, didn't you?"

"The people at the store were really helpful." He went to the door, telling her he would be right back, which he was in record time. He slid the thermometer from its plastic casing and held it upward in the air. "Have you done this before?"

"No," Jill said. "The ear thermometer seemed like a better option at the time."

"I can see your point, but we might as well cover all bases before we panic." He gestured back toward Ryan's room. "Shall we?"

She followed him into the baby's room and placed Ryan on the changing table.

"We have to take off his diaper and then be careful to not insert the thermometer too far in."

"You go ahead and do it," Jill said. "I'll keep him distracted." Jill proceeded to kiss Ryan's face and talk to him about all the wonderful things they were going to do together someday.

Derrick didn't like the thought of not being a part of all that fun. He unfastened the diaper and examined the situation for a minute before he made any attempt to do anything with the thermometer.

"Are you finished?"

"I haven't even started. Give me a minute."

"Don't be surprised if he—"

"Too late. Nasty."

He ignored the smile on Jill's face. The thermometer beeped and he quickly removed it. "It's 99 degrees Fahrenheit, which is okay."

"Isn't it supposed to be 98.6?" She handed him a baby wipe.

"If the rectal temperature is 100.4 degrees or higher we have cause to worry. Why don't we wait and see what the doctor has to say."

The minutes ticked by as they sat quietly in the main room and waited for the phone to ring. Holding Ryan in his arms, he watched the little guy suck on a bottle of formula. Jill sat in the chair across from his. Her face was pale.

"Try not to worry," he told her. "There's nothing we can do until we know what's wrong, if anything. I have an idea. Why don't we do what my family does when we try not to get overly worked up about something?"

"What does your family do?"

"We talk about other things." He watched her twiddle her thumbs in her lap and bite her bottom lip. "Tell me what it was like growing up in New York City."

"I wouldn't know where to start."

"What were you like as a child?"

"I guess you could say I was a people pleaser."

He arched a questioning brow.

"I would do anything and everything to try and make my parents proud. Not an easy thing to do. It was easier to get their attention by doing something wrong, like leaving fingerprints on the glass table."

Derrick had wanted to get her mind off of Ryan, but he could see that she was agitated by the memories. His heart went out to her.

"Tell me more about your sister," he said.

"My father used to call Laura his Mona Lisa, perfect in every way. She always managed to do everything right, which pleased my father to no end. The Laura you met last week was not the same sister I grew up with. She told me she's joining a band and that she's the singer."

"Is she any good?"

"I have no idea. I've never heard my sister sing in my life. But I've never seen her look so happy either." She looked thoughtful for a moment before she said, "Those parents of mine, though. The people you met were definitely the real deal." She curled her feet beneath her.

"Do you think they will ever accept you and your sister for who you are?"

"In their own way, I think they're trying." Jill sighed. "In a nutshell, my parents are wealthy, sophisticated, powerful, and well-connected: the crème de la crème of New York society. My mother loves anything that glitters. She also loves money, expensive handbags, and financial scandals."

"And your father?"

"As you probably noticed, he's a very serious man who loves his law firm first and my sister second."

"I'm sorry."

"Don't be. I love them and each one of them loves me in their own special way. If it wasn't for my mother's love of fabulous cuisine, I never would have developed a taste for Cara cara lacquered chicken breast with watermelon radishes or chilled carrot soup topped with olive oil."

"Sounds delicious."

She smiled at his sarcasm.

"For someone who talks about their love of food the way you do," he added, "you sure don't eat much."

"I've had the best. I'm picky."

Ryan stopped sucking on the bottle, prompting Derrick to lift him to his shoulder where he'd already placed a clean towel. He patted Ryan on the back.

"You're getting good at that."

"I'm trying."

"Thanks for helping me out tonight, especially after the way I've treated you."

"I understand why you'd be upset. Maggie never should have brought those papers to the party."

"Speaking of which…what is the deal with you and Maggie?"

"Like I said before, we've been friends for a long time."

"I can't be friends with someone who can't be honest with me."

"It's the truth," he said.

She angled her head. "Are you in denial when it comes to your feelings for Maggie, or do you think everyone around you is blind?"

"What do you mean?"

"Aaron gave you a black eye—obviously it had to do with Maggie. Twice now I've seen you look at her with longing and desire. Your feelings for Maggie also explain why a friendly, good-looking guy like yourself is still single."

"So, you think I'm friendly and good-looking?"

He was definitely in denial, she decided. "I think you have an ego the size of Mount Everest. That's what I think."

~~~

Maggie followed Aaron to the closet in the spare bedroom and watched him dig through sleeping bags, extra pillows, and a pile of pending Goodwill donations until he found the duffel bag he was looking for.

She plunked her hands on her hips. "I cannot believe you're walking out on me."

"I cannot believe you helped Derrick decorate and then went to Mom's house knowing Derrick would be there."

She followed him down the hall and into their bedroom, where he tossed the duffel bag onto their bed. "I helped your brother Garrett decorate, too, when Bailey was born. I told you from the beginning that I was going to help Derrick and that's what I was doing. That letter from CryoCorp is going to give your brother a chance to have a relationship with his son. That should mean something to you."

Aaron's face turned beet red as he stabbed a finger through the air. "This is exactly why I didn't want to move back to Los Angeles. But you insisted. Because I trusted you and loved you, I went along with it."

He laughed. "The funniest part of this whole sordid affair is that Derrick's stupid little vow is beginning to make sense after all. Derrick, the football player who cared more about a stupid ball than homework or grades, turns out to be smarter than all of us. Who woulda thunk?"

Maggie sighed. "What are you talking about?"

"The vow I told you about. Derrick made us all poke our finger with a needle and let a drop of blood fall to the paper where he'd written the vow that we each had to repeat. 'I will never, under any circumstance, kiss Maggie Monroe, go on a date with Maggie Monroe, or have a relationship with Maggie Monroe for as long as I live because the brotherhood always comes first.'" He held up his pointy finger and said, "'I, Aaron William Baylor, will never allow a female, more specifically, Maggie Monroe, to come between us and break the bond I have with my brothers.'"

Nervous laughter escaped her, mostly because she couldn't believe what she was hearing or that Aaron would even bother bringing up the absurd vow at such a horrible time.

"Go ahead and laugh, Maggie. But it's true. Derrick has loved you since the beginning of time, and he must have known you loved him, too, but he wasn't willing to jeopardize his relationship with me, so he never went after you. It's clear to me now. He knew all along what would happen if one of us broke the vow."

"And what exactly would happen, Aaron?"

"Whoever broke the vow would ultimately have to give up one for the other."

"Funny," she said, "the only person I can see choosing one over the other is you."

Aaron went back to shoving clothes into the duffel bag.

"I don't love Derrick," she said as she touched his shoulder and felt his muscles tighten. "I never have. I only love you. I've never loved anyone but you. I always thought you knew that."

He pulled away and disappeared inside the bathroom to collect his toiletries. When he came back, he tossed his things inside the duffel bag with everything else. Then he turned to her and said, "You're the one who made me choose, Maggie. I asked you not to take on Derrick's problems, but you insisted." He tied the bag. "Because of our busy lives, we haven't had time to go to a movie or dinner, but as soon as Derrick has a problem, you're suddenly as free as a bird—nothing but time on your hands to meet with him in court and discuss his problems over the phone. You couldn't say no to him. Even after he kissed you in the courtroom, proving my point, you still couldn't say no."

She followed Aaron through the house and to the front door. "He's your brother. Did you ever stop to think that the Baylor family was my family, too? Did you ever wonder how that made me feel, knowing that all of you signed some silly piece of paper to keep me out of your silly little club? Made a stupid vow to keep me out of your lives?"

Aaron walked out the door.

She followed him to the car. "After your mother left you and your father, who do you think your father was telling all his sorrows to?"

He didn't look interested as he threw his bag into the trunk of his car.

"It was my mother whose creamy white breasts your father buried his head between and told his woes to."

Aaron didn't say a word.

"Once my father learned of the affair and finally had enough, he left without saying good-bye to *me*. I haven't seen him since. And I wasn't even the one who betrayed him."

Aaron finally looked at her, his eyes filled with shock.

"Did any of your brotherhood ever bother to check up on *me* and see that my life was turning to shit while you all bonded together and made blood vows?"

"I didn't know."

"Because none of you cared about anyone but yourselves. And through it all, before and after I left for college, I always knew that *you* were the one for me and that you would come for me. And that made everything bad in my life bearable. Because I knew you were the one who knew me best and loved me most." She crossed her arms. "But you're right. We never should have moved back to Los Angeles. It's turned out to be some sort of crazy, stupid test. A test we couldn't pass. But don't you worry about me because I don't need you, Aaron. I've been alone for most of my life. I don't need anyone."

CHAPTER 16

Jill stepped inside Sandy's apartment and looked around, stunned by the decorative changes her friend had made in the past few months. Sandy was usually the one coming to her place to cook and do business, especially since she liked to take Lexi to the park afterward. But now that Jill had caught a glimpse of handmade curtains and travertine floors, giving the place a light and airy feel, Jill knew it had been way too long since she'd visited. "I love what you've done to the place."

"Thanks." Sandy took the diaper bag out of her hands and set it to the side while Jill unbuckled Ryan from his carrier and lifted him into her arms.

"I'm having fun decorating."

Ryan let out a small cry and Sandy came up close and took a good long look at him. "He looks perfectly fine to me."

"He is fine. According to Nate it's normal for babies to get a little warm once in a while. If Ryan's temperature had gone over 100 degrees then he said I would have needed to bring him in for a closer look."

"That makes sense."

"You should have seen Derrick last night. He pretended to be calm as we waited for Nate to return my phone call, but any time Ryan so much as sneezed, the big tough quarterback was overcome with anxiety: pacing the floor and twiddling his fingers."

"So how did Derrick get involved last night?" Sandy asked. "I thought you were finished with him?"

"I panicked. After Nate failed to return my call, I ran to Derrick's place to get a second opinion."

"Who's Nate?"

"Ryan's pediatrician, the guy I told you about when we were in the barn."

"Let me get this straight," Sandy said. "You ran to Derrick because Ryan had a slight fever?"

"It wasn't just the fever," Jill said. "Ryan wasn't crying as much as he usually does and he slept through his feeding."

Sandy headed for the kitchen. "I see."

"According to Nate, he gets calls like mine all of the time."

Sandy stopped what she was doing and looked Jill square in the eyes. "It sounds to me like you were looking for an excuse to run to Derrick's place."

"Don't be ridiculous."

"Come on, Jill. I saw you and Derrick wrapped in each other's arms when your parents came to visit and then again when the two of you were doing the do-si-do in the barn. I could have fried an egg on the heat sizzling between the two of you."

Jill readjusted Ryan onto her shoulder and gently patted his back. "I thought there might be something sizzling between us, too, but after I kissed him in his apartment he backed off and even went so far as to apologize and then seal our friendship with a handshake."

Sandy selected two tall glasses from a cupboard and set them on the granite island between them. "What do you mean?"

Jill scrunched her nose at the memory. "It was the same day that you and my parents walked into Derrick's apartment and found us on the floor."

"Ahh. That's right. I never heard the full story."

"I had gone to Derrick's apartment to invite him to go with us to Ryan's doctor appointment. Derrick was icing his sore knee, but he wanted to go, so I gave him some ibuprofen and then helped him to his room so he could dress. It sounds silly, but we tripped over a backpack and fell onto his bed. He sort of fell on top of me, or maybe I fell on him, I can't remember—"

Sandy waved a frustrated hand through the air. "Forget about all that. Skip to the good part."

"The bed frame broke next—"

"Leave it to a bunch of guys to put a bed together." Sandy retrieved a pitcher of iced tea from the refrigerator and filled their glasses.

"Yes, well, the frame broke, we rolled across the mattress, and then I did what hundreds of females had surely done before me…I wrapped my arms around Derrick Baylor's neck and I kissed him."

"And then what?"

"Well, that's when you and my parents showed up."

"Oh."

"After everyone left, Derrick helped me to my feet. As I gazed into his eyes with 'do me, take me' scrawled across my forehead, hoping to finish the kiss, he took a step back and apologized."

Sandy set the pitcher down. "He didn't."

"He did."

"That's horrible."

"That's what I thought."

"What did you do next?"

"I grabbed my purse and got the heck out of his apartment before I did something really stupid, like jump his bones." Jill moaned. "You should have seen me. I went all hot and heavy on him. It was pathetic."

"You're not pathetic. I know you said that he had his eye on Maggie, but I would have sworn he only had eyes for you when we were all square dancing in the barn."

"Yeah, well, remember when Derrick first came to my apartment and he had a black eye?"

Sandy nodded.

"It was Maggie's husband-to-be, Aaron, who punched him."

"How do you know that?"

"Derrick and I ran into Aaron at an art festival after the doctor's appointment."

Sandy rubbed her temple, trying to take it all in.

"It's worse than that," Jill went on. "In the parking lot, before leaving for the doctor's appointment, Derrick pulled me aside and said the kiss was a mistake and that he takes full responsibility. He said if we're going to be friends then we need to keep things cordial between us. After that, he squished his big body into my tiny car. He looked ridiculously uncomfortable and I was glad."

Sandy sipped her iced tea. "This doesn't make sense. Men don't squish into tiny cars with a bad knee and send flowers every day just for the hell of it. I understand that he wants to be close to his son, but none of this adds up. Derrick must have it bad for you. Maybe he just doesn't realize it yet. Men are dense that way, you know."

"Well, he did seem sort of jealous after he found out that Nate—you know, the pediatrician—wanted to take me to dinner and a movie."

"I realize we have both been incredibly busy," Sandy said, "but why didn't I know any of this?"

Jill sipped her tea. "I thought I told you. Nate and I are old friends. He's handsome and sweet, and he'd be considered a fine catch by most, but I only agreed to go out with him because my pride had been shaken that same morning. He was called away for an emergency before the date ended, which was just as well since I couldn't get my mind off of Derrick."

"Derrick Baylor is turning out to be more than a puzzle. Maybe I'll ask Connor about his brother when I see him this Friday."

"Connor, as in Derrick's brother, Connor?"

Sandy smiled. "That's the one."

"He called you?"

"Not exactly. I called his office and made an appointment."

"He's a gynecologist."

"Exactly."

"Are you sure you want to do that?" Jill asked since Sandy had a tendency to do things she later regretted.

"I know what I'm doing."

Jill shook her head. "You are *bad*."

Sandy smiled. "I'm so bad, I'm good."

CHAPTER 17

Helen Baylor stared up at the ceiling and watched the moonlight filter in through the blinds. "Phil, are you awake?"

Her husband rolled from his side to his back. "I am now."

"I'm worried about Maggie and Aaron."

"They'll work things out. Just give them time."

He closed his eyes again and she listened to his deep, even breathing, hoping the sound would lull her to sleep.

No such luck.

"If Derrick would just talk to Aaron," she said, "tell him he wishes him and Maggie well, then Maggie and Aaron could move on with their lives. Why is Derrick being so stubborn?"

"Because he is his mother's son."

Helen smiled as she curled up next to her husband, something she always did when she had too much on her mind and couldn't sleep. "What do you think about Jill Garrison?"

He adjusted his arm so her head fit neatly in the crook of his arm. "I think she's a lovely girl. I told you that. We're lucky to have her as part of the family."

"Where were we when Derrick was off collecting money for his sperm? Why would he do such a thing? Where did we go wrong?"

Phil reached out a hand and brushed his fingers across her cheek. "Kids do funny and unpredictable things. I'm sure he had his reasons at the time, but he can't turn back the clock. And besides, Jill seems like a good woman and we got a fine looking grandson out of the deal. I can't complain."

"I think I should pay Jill a visit. Derrick sounded confused the last time I talked to him. He could probably use my help. What do you think?"

"I think you should remember what happened the last time you stuck your nose where it didn't belong."

She made a tsking sound. "Connor needed to know what his wife was up to. He deserved to know."

"Nothing good came of his knowing about her drug problem, though."

"I hope you're not blaming me for her overdose."

"Of course, I don't blame you. Don't be silly. I just think people need to figure things out for themselves—without others meddling into their private matters."

She pulled away from him.

"I'm sorry," he said. "I didn't mean to hurt your feelings. It's just that everything seemed to fall apart quickly after you told Connor."

"Once Connor knew what he was dealing with, he was able to get her help. Amanda would have conquered the drug problem, too, if that drug dealing monster had stayed away like the court had ordered."

"Addictions aren't easy...mostly because the monsters, in some form or another, are always there lurking in a corner, waiting for a weak moment." He reached for Helen and coaxed her back toward him until she rested her head on his chest once again.

"Do you think Connor will ever forgive me?"

"I think he already has. He just hasn't realized it yet."

"I hope you're right."

"We've been married for nearly forty years. You know I always am."

She pushed him gently and they both chuckled, but she knew she wouldn't get much sleep tonight. The wheels in her head were turning, making a racket as they went round and round, causing her to worry about Jill and Ryan and Derrick. Instinct told her that Jill and Derrick were meant to be together. Now if she could just get her son to open his eyes.

~~~

"Oh, my God! It's Derrick Baylor," a willowy blonde cried out from the other side of the grocery store.

Jill looked up from the cucumbers in the produce section and watched two women, one blonde and the other brunette, approach Derrick, one fawning over him while the other shuffled through her purse, looking for something for him to autograph.

Derrick had insisted he go to the store with Jill. Ever since he had helped her with Ryan when she thought he was sick, Derrick had been sticking to her like glue. She wasn't complaining, though. Between taking care of Ryan and keeping up with her editorial commitments, she needed all the help she could get. To make matters worse, her mother had called to tell her they were heading back from San Francisco and would be stopping by. Jill insisted on cooking them dinner. She hoped they could all bury any bad feelings and move on. She also hoped that a nice quiet dinner would give her parents a chance to hold their grandson.

The tall blonde gave up looking for a piece of paper and asked Derrick to sign the back of her shirt instead. She pushed her hair high on her head and turned about to give him access. He did as she asked, and then laughed at something she whispered into his ear. The brunette wasn't the sort of girl who liked to be outdone. She lifted her shirt high enough to show off her bellybutton ring and asked him to sign her flat-as-a-board stomach.

Derrick was in charge of the grocery cart and Ryan, who happened to be fastened to the carrier buckled to the front of the cart. Ryan was growing more restless by the minute. He cried out, letting Derrick know enough was enough.

"Sorry girls, but it looks like my son needs me."

"He's so cute," the woman said as she reluctantly pulled her shirt back into place. "I didn't know you had any kids."

The blonde slipped a business card into the front pocket of his jeans. "Let me know if you ever need a babysitter."

"Yeah, okay," Derrick said as he unbuckled Ryan from the carrier and held him close to his chest.

Jill left the cucumbers and got as far as the broccoli when she saw the women walk off. Derrick was smiling at Ryan, and he lifted him high enough in the air so he could kiss the tip of his nose.

How many years, Jill wondered, had she longed for exactly this sort of moment with Thomas? She and Thomas had been introduced by her parents when she was eighteen and a freshman at NYU. The attraction between the two of them had been instantaneous and they were engaged before she turned nineteen. After Thomas graduated from law school, her father hired him as an in-house attorney at his law firm in New York. She'd spent many hours dreaming of someday having Thomas's baby. She'd always wanted a large family and she'd always imagined sharing the joys of parenting with someone she loved.

With one hand holding his son, Derrick used the other hand to push the cart her way. "I think I've got this whole baby thing down to a—"

A long burp cut him off in mid-sentence.

Jill laughed at the wide-eyed surprise on Derrick's face as they merged together in the aisle. Whenever they spent time together, she found herself laughing. "It's a good idea to always put a cloth on your shoulder before you burp him."

"You don't say?"

She helped him place Ryan back in the carrier. When that was done, she used baby wipes to clean the spit-up from his shirt. "There. You're good to go."

He pushed the cart while she followed at his side. "Is it always this difficult for you to grocery shop?" she asked him.

"What do you mean?"

"All the fans stopping you every few minutes and asking for autographs."

"Oh, that. Sure, it takes time, but as far as I'm concerned, handing out autographs goes with the territory." He pulled the business card from his pants pocket and shoved it into her baby bag. "In case you ever need a babysitter."

Once again Jill found herself staring into expressive brown eyes. Judging by the lines crinkling the corners of his eyes when he smiled, he'd spent a lot of time outdoors and even more time laughing. She liked this man, Ryan's father, a man she had no business liking. Her parents would never approve. They had a habit of pigeonholing people. They considered athletes to be overpaid and pampered. They would not approve of his jeans or untucked button-down shirt. They would not care for his tousled hair or his brawniness, a sign of arrogance in their eyes. No, they would never learn to like anything about Derrick Baylor. And although she knew it wasn't fair or right, the realization made her like him even more.

"So what are we going to cook for your parents?" he asked.

"We?"

He followed behind as she pushed the cart to the meat section. "I'm not invited?"

She picked out a pork tenderloin and placed it in the cart. "Well, it's just that—"

"You don't think I stand a chance in hell of ever gaining their approval, do you?"

"Where were you when they took us out to dinner last week? They aren't regular people, Derrick. They're judgmental and—"

He laughed as he threw an arm around her shoulder and drew her in close. "Lighten up. I was only teasing. I have no intention of barging in on your dinner. You and Ryan need to spend some time with your family alone."

"I think somebody wants to talk to you." She gestured with her chin toward a man standing behind him, a handsome, slightly older man with striking blue eyes.

Derrick turned about. "Max!" he said.

The two men shook hands, clearly excited to see one another.

"Jill, this is Max Dutton, one of the best linebackers in NFL history."

"Well, I don't know about that," Max said, "but I appreciate the compliment."

Max stepped forward and shook Jill's hand. He wasn't as tall as Derrick, but what he lost in height, he made up in width—all muscle and brawn. "And who is this little guy?"

"This is our son, Ryan," Derrick told him.

"I hadn't heard." Max slapped Derrick on the back. "Congratulations."

"How many kids do you have these days?" Derrick asked Max. "Every time I see you in the paper, it seems Kari and you are having another baby."

Max grinned. "Our oldest, Molly, graduated from USC a few years ago and now she and her mother are busy writing a mother-daughter nutrition book together. The youngest, Austin, will be a year next month. I finally got myself a boy. Not that I wasn't fine with all girls, because I was. Girls are fun. I should know since I now have four of them."

"You *have* been busy."

"I better let you two lovebirds go," Max said. "I just ran inside to grab milk, but then I saw the two of you looking into one another's eyes as if time had stopped and that's when I realized it was somebody I knew. We'll all have to get together sometime. Kari would love to meet Ryan and your lovely wife, Jill."

"Sounds like a plan," Derrick said as he shook Max's hand.

Max wrapped his arms around Jill and gave her a friendly hug before he slipped away and disappeared down the nearest aisle.

Jill felt her cell phone vibrating at the bottom of her purse, but chose to ignore it. "Well, that was interesting," she said. "I believe I just met a human tornado."

Derrick laughed as he followed her down the aisle with all the spices and teas. "I hope you don't mind that I didn't correct him when he referred to you as my wife."

"No problem," she said over her shoulder. "I've been called worse."

"Very funny," he said.

She stopped in front of the spices and tried to remember what she had needed. "How's your knee feeling?"

"It's better." He shifted his weight from one foot to the other. "I try not to think about it, especially since I'm not going to let it slow me down when training camp starts in a few weeks."

"What does the doctor say about that?"

"Nobody but Connor knows about my knee. I plan on keeping it that way."

"Isn't that dangerous?"

"Football players play with injuries all of the time."

"No game is worth losing a limb over," she said. When he didn't answer right away, she looked at him and noticed him studying her closely.

"What?" She lifted her fingers to her face, feeling for crumbs or something wet and sticky. "Do I have something on my face?"

The expression on his face confused her. The man was one big contradiction. When he reached out a hand and moved some hair out of her face, she didn't stop him.

"There's something about you, Jill Garrison, that makes me feel good inside, something that makes me want to reach out and touch you to see if you're for real." He brushed the pad of his thumb over her chin and then leaned forward to kiss her.

She put her hand on his chest to stop him. "Don't do this, Derrick."

"Do what?"

"Pretend like this thing between us, whatever it is, is something more than a simple friendship. Every time you touch me like this, or gaze into my eyes like that, you confuse me. Please don't fool me into thinking you have something more to offer than you really do."

He seemed to think about what she said before he straightened. "You're right. I'm sorry."

A part of her had hoped he would tell her she was wrong about him having feelings for Maggie, maybe even tell her he was falling for her, and he couldn't stop himself from kissing her any more than he could stop the earth from rotating on its axis. But he didn't say another word.

Ignoring the kick in the gut, she forced a smile and said, "Help me find the allspice and let's get out of here before that photographer takes another picture of us."

He looked over his shoulder and the saw the flash of a camera.

This was the last time she was ever going to go shopping with him. Between his fans, friends, and photographers, what should have taken thirty minutes had taken well over an hour. At this rate, she was never going to get anything done today.

~ ~ ~

They were five minutes from home when Derrick was forced to put a firm foot on the brakes of his SUV in order to miss hitting a stray dog.

A car coming from the opposite direction was approaching fast.

"That poor dog is going to get hit," Jill said.

The dog stood squarely in the middle of the road. Jill squeezed her eyes shut, unable to watch.

The car swerved and honked as it passed, but the dog hardly flinched.

"That does it." Derrick pulled his car to the side of the road, shut off the engine, and put on the hazard lights.

"Be careful. This is a dangerous road."

He shut the door and headed straight for the dog, but the animal ran, making its way down the middle of the road. Derrick stuck a hand out as if he were a traffic cop and tried to stop the next car, but the car swerved around him and the dog and whizzed by in a blur.

"Are you crazy? Slow down," he called after the car.

The dog was confused. From the looks of it, the poor thing hadn't eaten in days. Its fur was matted and one of its eyes was swollen shut. When it wasn't running, it walked with an uneven step. A kindred spirit, Derrick thought.

"Derrick," Jill called from the car. "You're going to get yourself killed out there."

This was the second time in less than an hour that Jill worried over him: first his leg and now this. "Don't worry, darling," he called back. "I promise to return unharmed."

She rolled her eyes at him and then pulled her head back into the car.

It took him twenty minutes to get his hands on the mutt. With the ugly beast in his arms, he waited for traffic to pass so he could cross the street safely and get back to his car.

The windows were rolled down and Jill was sitting in the back seat feeding Ryan.

Standing on the safe side of the road and looking into the open window, he let Jill take a look at the dog. "I never should have wasted my time, let alone risked my life, to save the mutt. Look at him, would you?"

The dog angled its head. One ear stuck straight up, the other ear flopped to the side. One eye was swollen shut. A thick scar cut through the right side of the dog's mouth, causing its yellow crooked teeth to show and making it look as if the animal was smiling. The upper part of its body was bald while the rest of the dog's body had random patches of wiry, coarse grayish fur that looked more like human hair than fur.

Jill wrinkled her nose. "What kind of dog is it?"

"Good question. At this point, I'm not even sure if it is a dog."

She laughed.

"I don't see any houses nearby and it doesn't have a collar. I guess I'll have to take him home and make a few calls to the local vets in the area and see if anyone is missing a dog that looks like a cross between a Siamese cat and a giant Chihuahua."

Jill climbed out of the car with Ryan in her arms and shut the door behind her.

"Why don't we put Ryan's carrier in the front for the rest of the ride home?" Derrick asked.

"That's too dangerous," Jill said. "I'll sit in the front with the dog to keep him from jumping on Ryan."

Once the baby was buckled into his car seat in the back and Jill was in buckled in the passenger seat, Derrick set the dog on her lap. She wrapped her arms around the ugly thing, her nose wrinkling when she got a whiff of skunk and who knew what else.

He watched the dog for a moment, making sure it wasn't going to try and escape or bite his way out of her arms. "Are you all right?" he asked. "The dog seems friendly enough."

"I've never seen a scarier looking animal," Jill said. The dog tried to escape from her lap, but she held tight. Every once in a while the dog would stop and sniff Jill and then go back to sniffing the dashboard.

Derrick climbed in behind the wheel. "Are we good to go?"

"If you want to make a quick trip to the dentist for a cleaning, I'm sure I've got another few hours left in me."

He looked at her and grinned. "Is that sarcasm I'm detecting?"

The smile she gave him in return made his heart beat a little faster. *What the hell was wrong with him? Did he have feelings for Jill? How could that be?* He was confused, he told himself. Maggie was the only woman for him.

Jill's phone rang. Keeping one arm around the dog, she somehow managed to answer her cell phone by the second ring. By the time she hung up, he was pulling the car into the parking lot of their apartment building.

"Another problem with the magazine?" he asked.

"It's always something," she said. "Every month we test some of the main recipes, but this month we're scheduled to have a cook off featuring three busy stay-at-home moms. The restaurant we were planning to use fell through. As you already know, our tester chef quit and I haven't had time to find someone to replace her."

"Anything I can do to help?"

"Not unless you have a restaurant-size kitchen I can use."

The dog was excited at the prospect of getting out of the car. Jill struggled to hang on while he pawed at the window. "Calm down," she said, giving the animal a gentle pat on the back. The dog looked at her with one ear pointed forward.

Derrick jumped out of the car and came around the front so he could grab hold of the dog. "I've got the beast," he told her. "I also happened to have a restaurant-size kitchen you can use."

CHAPTER 18

Sandy straightened her newly-fitted pencil skirt, retrieved her compact mirror from her purse and checked her lipstick. Then she took a deep breath and headed inside the office building. The click of her three-inch heels made a racket as she walked across polished slate. She made her way to the directory where she searched for Connor's name. Her newly manicured nail followed the list of names until she came to Dr. Connor Baylor, Suite 300.

Perfect.

She'd had a pap smear three months ago, but she wasn't the squeamish sort, and she figured an extra examination never hurt anyone. The elevator doors opened. She stepped inside and pushed the number three button. The ride up was smooth and uneventful, but once she stepped into the hallway and saw Suite 300 looming ahead of her, her heart rate kicked into high gear.

Pull it together, girlfriend. Sandy hadn't felt this out of sorts since her date two years ago with Glenn Price, a semi-famous singer from Britain. She walked into the lobby, signed in, and took a seat with the other women waiting their turn. After filling out the paperwork, she picked up *Sports Illustrated* and rifled through the pages, trying to get her mind off of what she was doing…and what she would say to Connor when he opened the door and saw her sitting on his examination table.

She didn't have to wait long.

The nurse led her down the hallway and to the third room on the right. Dr. Connor Baylor was nowhere in sight. The nurse had her stand on the scale. Next, she took Sandy's blood pressure and temperature. "Go ahead and put this gown on, top and bottom. Dr. Baylor will be in shortly to see you."

Sandy stripped down to her thong underwear and push-up bra. She then took her time folding her clothes and setting them neatly on the chair in the corner of the room. A knock sounded on the door. Only a minute had passed since the nurse left the room. She figured the nurse had forgotten something. "Come in."

When she turned to the door, she noticed Connor's broad shoulders filling the opening.

The nurse stood directly behind him and tried to get a peek at whatever had stopped him in his tracks, but he kept her at bay. "Sorry," he said. "I thought you were—Sandy—what are you doing here?"

"Hi, Connor." She reached for the paper gown. "You were so quick I figured it was the nurse again."

His gaze started at her feet and quickly worked its way upward, settling on her face.

His expression, Sandy realized, was unreadable. If anything, she would have to guess that he was not pleased. "I'll leave you alone while you get the gown on and then we'll talk."

"Whatever you say, doc."

He gave her a tight smile and backed away, shutting the door behind him.

Man, oh, man. Connor Baylor needed to lighten up. He acted as if he hadn't seen it all a thousand times before. She took off her undergarments and put on the paper gown as instructed. She took a seat on the edge of the examination table and swung her legs straight out in front of her so she could admire her pedicure. Her nails had been painted a deep red, matching her lipstick.

Endless minutes ticked by before a knock finally sounded on the door. This time the nurse came in first and then assured Dr.

Baylor that the patient was ready for him. Connor Baylor was obviously a stickler for rules.

He took a couple of long strides into the room. He wore a crisp white lab coat over a polo shirt and a pair of wrinkle free khaki-colored slacks. He was tall and broad shouldered and his demeanor bordered on stiff and unyielding. His square jaw was cleanly shaven, revealing a healthy tan. All of the Baylor brothers were good-looking but this particular one took her breath away. No wonder the waiting room was packed with females waiting to be seen by Dr. Baylor. His hair was thick and neatly cut around the ears. He was dashing and debonair, a man who would stand out in a crowd of George Clooney look-alikes.

It was quiet while he read whatever was attached to the clipboard. "So, you're not pregnant?"

"Nope. Not pregnant. Not unless it was a case of immaculate conception."

He didn't laugh; in fact, he hardly flinched. Nurse Ratched, his sidekick, was just as unflappable.

"It says here that you haven't had a pap smear in two years. Why is that?"

She lifted her shoulders and said, "I've been a very bad girl."

He looked at the nurse. The two of them were speaking some sort of sign language that didn't require the use of their hands. He turned back to her once again and looked her square in the eyes. "The last doctor you saw was Dr. Bricca?"

She nodded.

"You've decided to change doctors?"

Duh. She nodded again.

"Why is that?"

"I guess you could say I'm impulsive."

"I see."

"After meeting you, I thought you seemed like the type of doctor who would take extra good care of his patients."

"I think I know what the problem is," he said. "I want you to get dressed and meet me in my office when you're done."

Without waiting for a response, he headed out the door.

She looked at the nurse. "Is he serious?"

The nurse picked up the clipboard and made a note. She leaned back against the counter and said, "He's a busy man. You don't really think you're the first woman to come in here looking for more than a quick examination, do you?"

"You're not implying what I think you're implying, are you?"

"Go ahead, play your little game," the nurse said as she headed for the door, "but you should be aware that you're not the first female to come into Dr. Baylor's office to flaunt your goods. And you won't be the last."

Sandy stared at the closed door after Nurse Ratched left.

Suddenly, she felt painfully self-conscious.

What was she doing here?

What a fool she was. She dressed in record time before quietly stepping out of the office and heading for the back door, where she slipped out of the building unnoticed.

CHAPTER 19

It was early on Saturday morning when Jill jumped at the sound of a high-pitched screech. "I'll call you right back," she told Chelsey before clicking her cell phone shut and running outside her apartment. She saw Derrick rushing down the stairs with the dog. He had made a leash out of strips of cloth. "What was that noise?" she asked. "Was that you or the dog?"

He stopped three steps from the bottom. "Very funny," he said, looking over his shoulder at her. "Hank and I have been kicked out of the apartment building by the manager."

"Hank?"

"Yeah, I thought that was a good name for the beast."

"You can't leave me," Jill said.

He grinned. "I'm pretty sure that's the sweetest thing you've ever said to me. I didn't know you cared."

She raked her fingers through tangled morning hair. "You know what I mean. My parents are coming tomorrow and you promised to do a taste test after I cook a trial dinner today." He was also going to watch Ryan while she finished an article for the magazine and returned some calls, but she kept that to herself. Her shoulders fell in defeat. "I need you."

He looked at his watch. "I'm taking Hank to my place in Malibu. I'll be back before you can say, 'What would I do without Derrick Baylor in my life?'"

"What would I do without Derrick Baylor in my life?" she said.

He winked. "Now say—"

She cut him off with a huff and headed back inside her apartment.

Jill shut the door behind her and looked around at the mess: There were boxes of diapers stacked in the corner of the room. Formula and bottles covered the kitchen counter. Dishes filled the sink and papers were scattered across the coffee table. The portable crib took up most of her small living area. She had set it up there so she could keep an eye on Ryan while she got things done. She looked at Ryan and watched him kick his legs and stare wide-eyed at the toys that dangled from a plastic band tied from one end of the crib to the other, high enough that he couldn't hurt himself.

She smiled at her son. "Did you hear what your mother just said to your father? She said she needed him." Straightening, she moaned as she found herself looking into the mirror on the wall directly across from where she stood. "What are you doing to yourself?" she asked her reflection. "What do you want?"

"I want him," her reflection answered.

"Well, that's too bad," she told herself, "because he's taken."

We always gave up too easily. Her sister's words came back to haunt her. Laura was right. She never stuck up for herself. She never fought her parents for her independence and she never fought for Thomas. Hell, she never told Thomas what she wanted either. Their relationship had been a farce. She'd always felt more alone when she was with Thomas than when she was without him. She had never once been honest with herself. It was time to grow up.

The truth was she liked Derrick and he liked her.

She needed to develop a backbone and see if what they shared could grow into something more. A broken heart never killed anyone, she told herself.

The remainder of the day flew by. It was amazing what one person could accomplish with the right motivation. She had dressed in a pair of dark jeans and a green halter top that made her green eyes pop. The vitamins she'd been taking had given her hair more shine and her skin looked better than ever.

Not only was Ryan asleep in his room, she'd already returned phone calls, written a first draft of this month's column, and dinner was in the oven. The phone rang. It was Chelsey. No more calls tonight, she decided. She clicked the phone to Off and set it on the kitchen counter. All she needed to do now was set the table. After that, she planned to concentrate on making Derrick forget all about Maggie Monroe.

~ ~ ~

Derrick called Jill for the third time, but there was still no answer.

The day had been endless.

Upon arriving at his Malibu home, his sister's car broke down, so he had dropped off the dog and then drove Zoey to Mom's house so she could borrow their car. Then Grandma Dora showed up and insisted he stay and eat lunch with all of them. By the time he finished visiting, ran to the store for dog food, dropped off the food and then left his house in Malibu for the second time, his other sister called and blurted out that Aaron had left Maggie.

He tried to call Jill hours ago, to tell her he would be late, but she hadn't answered her phone. Next, he drove to Maggie's house, where he sat waiting for Maggie to return home. It was now dark outside.

Relieved to see Maggie's car finally pull up the gravelly driveway, he stood and headed that way.

"Derrick," she said the moment she climbed out of her car and spotted him. "What are you doing here?"

"I heard about Aaron leaving," he told her. "I thought maybe you could use some company." Damn, he thought, the minute the words left his lips. It was too early. Too early to offer her the world and see what she thought about that. Heavy lidded, bloodshot eyes told him Maggie wasn't ready to discuss her future with him or anyone else.

"You need to leave," she said, shaking her head.

He followed her up the walkway leading to the front entrance.

After she unlocked the door, she turned to him and said goodnight. He put his arms around her and held her close, but she pushed him away. She went inside and shut the door behind her without a glance back or another word spoken.

For a long moment Derrick stood in silence. He felt empty and hollow, his chest tight.

It was midnight by the time a taxi dropped Derrick off and he trudged up the stairs leading to his apartment. The bartender at Murphy's had cut him off after a few hours and called him a taxi. The stars were out and the crickets were chirping as a cool wind blew in from the Pacific.

The lights in Jill's apartment were on. He was surprised to see her door come open. Jill stood beneath the door frame, looking worried. "Is everything okay?"

He nodded.

"Is Hank okay?"

"Hank is good."

"Are you okay? You look pale. Is it your leg?"

He looked past her, into her apartment, and saw that the table was perfectly set with a white table cloth and fine china, crystal wine glasses, and candles waiting to be lit. He was a fool to have let her down when she had told him she needed him. "You look amazing."

"Thanks."

"Is Ryan awake?" His legs felt unsteady as he approached. He put a hand on the doorframe to help keep his balance.

"I put him to bed a while ago."

She looked beautiful tonight. "I'm sorry about today," he began, aware of the mere inches of air between them. He could smell her soapy clean hair. She was a cool breeze on a warm day.

"Did you eat?" she asked him.

He shook his head, but the truth was he couldn't remember. "You've been drinking."

She was looking up at him, her eyes adoring, her full lips beckoning him and making him forget everything else.

"Do you want to come inside?"

He nodded and said, "I thought you'd never ask."

She opened the door wider and somehow he managed to step inside without falling on his face. The room did a little spin and then stopped. Whiskey never did sit well with him. He followed her into the kitchen.

"I made a chocolate soufflé," she said. She dipped her finger into the creamy middle and then turned and held her finger up. "Do you want to try it?"

He took her finger into his mouth and licked it clean.

And that was that.

He couldn't stop himself from kissing her if he tried. With the palm of his hand on the back of her head, he brushed his mouth over hers and was instantly consumed by the sweet taste of her. She didn't push him away and for that he was thankful. He deepened the kiss. Her tongue met with his. Need, desire, and lust took over and he lifted her high until she was sitting on the counter near the sink.

She surprised him when she pulled her top over her head, revealing creamy white breasts spilling over a sexy pink bra.

He followed suit and pulled his shirt off, and then pushed the soufflé aside, but not before dipping his finger into the middle of it. He made a path of chocolate from her mouth, downward over her neck and lower until he met with creamy mounds of flesh. Lowering his mouth to the bottom of the chocolaty trail, he slowly worked his way back up to her mouth.

Her fingers made a trail of their own through his hair, bringing his mouth impossibly closer to hers. Her lips were sweet and hot and he realized in that moment that he needed her more than ever. Everything around him was a blur, but he knew that was because his world had literally just been flipped over on its ass.

Jill's pent up desire was obvious, and he was going to be the one to set her free. He would see to that. She needed him as much as he needed her.

She pulled her mouth from his and made a downward trail of kisses over his jaw and down his neck. When she pulled away, he lifted her into his arms and carried her to her bedroom.

After stripping off each other's clothes, all bets were off. They were on the bed, and he hovered over her. Jill was no longer the reserved mother of his son. She was a siren. Her hands and mouth explored, slowly at first, and then building in intensity until her breathing was uneven. Her enthusiasm was contagious and it seemed neither of them could get enough of one another until he entered her. Her body melded into his and every movement she made felt like a well-rehearsed dance…as if she had been made for him alone. Her warm lips no longer caressed his flesh, but her eyes met his as they moved in a rhythm all their own.

He was breathing hard, his mouth hovering over hers, and in that moment as they both exploded together into unprecedented rapture, he possessed absolute clarity, a lucidity that threatened to turn his life, his world, upside down. It struck him quick, like the flash of a shooting star, or like being hit over the head by a hammer. Cupid had shot him right where it counted.

Suddenly nobody existed in this world but Jill.

The emotions that ran through his body were alien, like setting foot on foreign lands for the first time. Derrick was somewhere he'd never been and he wasn't sure how he felt about it. The air was no longer just for breathing. Every molecule inside of him was alive, pumping vigorously through his veins like blood that had been given oxygen after a long draught.

Her head now rested in the crook of his arm, her breathing even against his chest.

No awkwardness in the silence, just a quiet peacefulness in the aftermath of bliss.

~~~

After making love to Derrick Baylor, Jill had awoken at three in the morning to Ryan's crying. She was surprised to see that Derrick was gone, since she hadn't heard him leave the apartment and he hadn't said goodbye. At six Jill showered and dressed and then gathered the courage to walk over to Derrick's apartment and see what was going on. He wasn't home but there was a note taped to his door.

Jill, I'm sorry I had to leave so abruptly. Things to do, places to go. I'll see you in Malibu.

Also included in the note was his address and gate code.

She read the note once again. He was obviously having regrets. Why else would he run away like that? Jill knew that she had nobody to blame for last night but herself. He'd been drinking. That should have been her first clue that it was not a good idea to sleep with him.

But he had been so damn charming.

One kiss. One lick of his chocolaty covered finger, she thought. That's all it had taken to get her all worked up. *Sheesh.*

She was everything her parents accused her of being: irresponsible, immature, and impulsive. A lot of "I" words. She could think of a few more to add to the list, like idiot and insane.

By eight o'clock, the beautiful cloudless Saturday contrasted greatly with Jill's mood as she, Sandy, Lexi, and Ryan drove down Highway 101 toward Malibu.

The windows were rolled down and the warm air lifted Jill's hair from her shoulders. Feeling sick to her stomach, she tried to sound cheerful as she spoke to Sandy, who was unusually quiet this morning. "So tell me," Jill said, keeping her eyes on the road, "how was your appointment with Connor the other day?"

Sandy huffed. "Oh, no you don't. You first. It's obvious that something is going on with you and I won't hesitate to bet that it has something to do with you and Derrick."

"I saw him last night," Jill said. "End of story."

"Pshhh. Don't be ridiculous. I'm not so easily fooled. What happened?"

Jill glanced in the rearview mirror and saw Lexi examining Ryan's toes.

"Go ahead," Sandy said, "give me a few hints."

"Okay, let's see…there was chocolate soufflé involved."

"I WUV chocolate!" Lexi shouted.

"Not too loud," Sandy cautioned Lexi. "We don't want to wake the baby." Sandy pursed her lips as she tried to think. "Give me another clue."

"There was licking involved."

"I WUV wicking popsicles."

Sandy laughed. "I don't think she was licking popsicles, honey, but thanks for—" Sandy's eyes bulged when she finally got a hint of what Jill might be getting at. "Oh, my God! If you weren't licking popsicles, then—"

"Wowipops!"

They both laughed before Sandy leaned between the seats and handed Lexi her cassette player with the earphones. "Do you want to listen to your favorite song?"

"Yay! Old McDonald had a farm!"

Once Sandy had Lexi situated with her earphones, she straightened in her seat and turned back to Jill. "And I thought I was the wild one."

"Needless to say, I would be singing a different tune right now if he hadn't made a quick exit in the middle of the night."

"No goodbye?"

Jill shook her head. "Just a note on the door to his apartment."

"What are you going to do?"

"I have no idea."

"I don't get it. What does all of this kissing and licking going on mean? You told me the other day that you thought Derrick liked someone else."

Jill sighed. "He'd been drinking last night."

"Oh, no."

"Yep. And I still let him inside my door and into my bedroom." Jill let out a long drawn out moan before she made a confession. "He does something to me, Sandy. He makes me feel things I haven't ever felt before. Despite everything that has happened, I think I'm just going to take things one day at a time.

If not for the note he left on his door this morning, I would have thought I was making a big deal about nothing."

"What did the note say?"

"'*Sorry I had to leave. Things to do, places to go.*' Something along those lines."

"I tried to warn you about him from the start. I hate the idea of you getting hurt."

"Love hurts."

Sandy pretended to faint against her seat. "Did you just say what I think you said?"

"I know. It's crazy. I've known the man for what—three weeks? But it is what it is. I can't stop myself from feeling what I feel, can I?"

"I guess not."

"Don't worry about me," Jill said. "I'll figure things out before I fall so hard I can't lift myself up again. Now tell me about your appointment with the other Mr. Baylor."

"Let's just say that it certainly didn't go as expected," Sandy began. "No chocolate or licking involved. There I was, sitting on the table looking sexy in my paper gown, when Dr. Connor Baylor came in and got all stiff and bothered. Before I could say 'boo' he told me to get dressed and meet him in his office."

"No way."

"Way."

"So what did Connor say once you were in his office?"

"I never made it that far. After he left the examination room, Nurse Ratched informed me that I wasn't the first woman to make a fool out of myself when it came to the good doctor, and I wouldn't be the last."

"And you let that stop you?"

Sandy shrugged. "I know; it's not like me to be so easily swayed, but the whole thing was strange. After he walked out of the room, I felt foolish and desperate. I mean, it would have been one thing if he'd handled the situation as I expected him to, but—"

"What did you expect exactly?"

"I expected him to excuse Nurse Ratched from the room and then proceed to help me into the stirrups."

"Are you serious?"

"Perfectly. Isn't that what everyone fantasizes about when they get their yearly check-up with a hot physician?"

"No."

"Whatever. You don't have to get all bent out of shape over it, especially since nothing happened. The way he looked at me before walking out and leaving me sitting there, made me feel…well, stupid."

"I'm sorry."

Sandy sighed. "Don't be. Lesson learned. I realize most of my relationships don't last very long, but I think I now have a new record."

For the next twenty minutes they talked about the magazine and Jill couldn't help but think how great it was to have a friend, a true friend, who understood her.

After making a right on Franklin and then another left after that, Jill drove her Jetta up close to an iron gate leading to a steep driveway. The house sitting at the top of the hill was a sprawling mansion taken right out of ancient times. It had a balanced, symmetrical façade and smooth stone walls. The roof, topped with balustrade, and the amazing decorative pillars reminiscent of ancient Greece, added a magnificent touch to the entrance.

"Are you sure this is the right place?" Sandy asked. "This looks more like a hotel than a house."

"I wike this house," Lexi said from her big girl car seat in the back.

"This is it," Jill said. "Four-twenty one Gladiola." Jill leaned out the window and entered the gate code Derrick had jotted down for her.

The wrought iron gate opened and she drove up the driveway between two rows of giant imported palms. She parked the car near the wide stairs leading to the entrance of the house and even Lexi was quiet as they watched a fountain of water rise high into two wide arcs before cascading into a surrounding pond.

"I had no idea," Sandy said.

"You and me both."

"He's done well for himself."

"Apparently."

Speaking of the devil.

Upon seeing Derrick, Jill couldn't seem to stop her heart from pounding against her chest. Before they had a chance to climb out of the car, he was headed their way, taking the stairs two at a time.

As Sandy helped Lexi out of her car seat, Derrick opened the back door and unstrapped Ryan. "Chelsey is already inside taking pictures," he said.

"Great," Sandy said while Jill tried to collect herself.

Ryan made a gurgling noise.

"Did you hear that?" Derrick asked. "I think he said Da-Da."

Sandy laughed. "Nice try," she said. "He won't be talking for a few more months."

"Hey, Lexi," Derrick said, patting the top of her head as she came around the back of the car and latched onto his leg, a routine the two of them shared every time they saw one another.

"Your house is amazing," Sandy said. "An elegant stone structure. Grand and overdone—like its owner," Sandy told him as she moved to the back of the car to grab some things from the trunk.

"Thank you," he said. "I'll take that as a compliment. I designed the monstrosity myself," he added proudly.

Sandy used her hand to shield her eyes from the morning sun as she looked toward the house again. "Amazing. Do you mind if Lexi and I go on ahead and take a look around, or do we need a tour guide?"

"Make yourselves at home," he said, ignoring her tour guide comment.

Lexi and Sandy ran off before Jill could stop them. A quiet moment stretched into two while Jill wondered what was going through his head. She couldn't help but feel as if he was avoiding making eye contact with her as he fiddled with getting Ryan out of the back seat.

"Thanks again for letting us use your house and for getting here extra early to let Chelsey set up."

"Any time," he said.

"About last night—" Jill said after swallowing a lump in her throat. "I hope things won't be—you know—"

"Jill! Where are you? I need you," Chelsey yelled from the top of the stairs. "Do you need help carrying something?"

"I'll be right there," Jill said.

She looked at Derrick, and almost it seemed, by accident, he looked at her for the first time since last night, and in that instant, she knew the answer to her question. Not only did he regret making love to her, he was going to pretend it never happened. Her heart sank as if there was a heavy chain wrapped around her aorta, twisting and pulling.

Ryan cried out, prompting Derrick to jump into action. He took Ryan from his car seat and held him close to his chest. Then he grabbed the baby bag and as Jill followed him toward the stairs leading to the house he said, "We couldn't have asked for better weather today."

Instead of answering him, she stopped where she was and put her face toward the sun and breathed in some fresh ocean air. Last night Derrick Baylor had wrapped his arms around her and held her tight. They had made love more than once. For the first time in her life, she had experienced what lovemaking was all about. Giving and taking, laughing and loving. Every moment had been special. She had never been able to experience anything like that with Thomas. Thomas had what the doctors referred to as psychological impotence. His thoughts or feelings prevented him from a full erection. She had done everything in her power to help him…them…so the two of them could have that special intimacy between two people. She went to the doctor with Thomas and she tried everything: sexy lingerie, a strip tease, two weeks one-on-one with a sex therapist after he insinuated that she might be the problem. Hell, she would have had a pole installed in their bedroom if he had asked, but Thomas never seemed all that interested.

Derrick, on the other hand, had taken interest in every part of her body last night, waking something dormant inside of her and making her aware of all she'd been missing. In one night, he had made her feel as if she had climbed to the top of Kilimanjaro blindfolded. He had taken her to new heights, to a place she had no idea existed. Holding her, looking into her eyes, they had climaxed together and she was pretty sure she had been reborn.

Until now.

"Is anything wrong?" he asked her, bringing her out of her trance.

She put on a happy face. "Don't be silly," she lied. "Everything is hunky dory."

CHAPTER 20

For the last two hours Derrick's insides curdled and twisted every time he glanced Jill's way. He knew damn well leaving her place in the dark of night without a word said had been uncouth. But he hadn't known what else to do. He knew he needed to talk to her, but what would he say? *Last night was the most incredible night of my life. You're an incredible woman and you are beautiful.*

Every morning when I awake, my first thoughts are of you. Sunset, sunrise...I think of you. I look at my son...I see you. Right now, across the room, I hear you...and I find myself wanting to feel you wrapped in my arms again. And yet, I can't say with conviction that you're the only woman on my mind.

Is it possible to love two women?

"Okay, ladies, you know the rules," Jill said.

His house was filled to the brim with people.

He noticed that Jill kept glancing toward the entryway. Tonight she would be cooking dinner for her parents, but before dinner, her parents had promised to come to Malibu to meet Derrick's family and to see their daughter in action.

The three women selected to be a part of the *Everyday Woman Cook Off* had arrived twenty minutes ago. Chelsey had brought everything they needed to prepare the kitchen for the cook off.

Also joining the fun were Derrick's mother and father, who had arrived shortly after Jill and Sandy; same with Derrick's two sisters and his twin brothers, Brad and Cliff. A day spent with the Baylor family was always like attending a reunion, everybody acting as if years had passed since they saw each other last.

Chelsey was already taking pictures and also showing a young photographer-in-training how things were done.

The women who had come to cook were all over fifty and all wearing matching red aprons with *Food For All* printed in big block letters. They stood ready and waiting in Derrick's restaurant-size kitchen.

"You have twenty minutes to make your appetizers," Jill told the ladies. "The judges will include myself; my mother, the lovely Mrs. Garrison who has come all the way from New York City," she grinned and gestured toward her mother who had just walked in the door, looking agitated, "and the charming Mrs. Baylor, mother of NFL star Derrick Baylor, whom most of you have already had the pleasure of meeting. As you know, the winner of this cook off will be featured on the cover of next month's issue of *Food For All*."

One of the cooks held up a hand. "I have a question."

"Go ahead, Mrs. Murnane."

"There are only two ovens and three of us."

"Because of the sudden change in venue," Jill said, "cooking time will not be included in the twenty minute prep time you've been given."

"Who gets to use the oven first?" Mrs. Murnane wanted to know.

Jill tried to ignore the dull throbbing working its way toward the front of her skull. "After the twenty minutes are up," Jill said, "time will not be a factor. But if it will make you feel better, you can put your cooking sheet in the oven first."

One of the ladies wore a tall white European chef hat, and she shook her head, causing the hat to tilt to the right. "Sorry," she said. "I already called it."

Jill frowned. "Called what?"

"This oven right here."

"All right then, Mrs. Murnane will use the one on the other side."

The woman with the braided silvery hair shook her head exactly as the lady with the hat had done. "Nope. Sorry. It's taken."

Derrick handed Ryan to his mother and came to stand at Jill's side. He pointed outside toward the pool. "There's another kitchen in the guest house. I'll take Mrs. Murnane's tray over there when she's ready."

Mrs. Murnane didn't look satisfied.

"The kitchen includes a state-of-the-art oven," Derrick added, "one of those high-performance Bosch ovens all the women in town are raving about."

Jill wondered if he'd just made that up or if he was a connoisseur of kitchen appliances.

"Fine," Mrs. Murnane said, her lips pursed. "Please run over there now," she told Derrick, "and preset the temperature to 350 degrees."

The silver-haired woman frowned before bending low to take a closer look at her oven. "Is that fair?" she asked. "My oven isn't a Bosch."

"Are you going to strangle her, or am I?" Derrick whispered into Jill's ear.

Jill smiled. "I think I'll let you do the honors."

"All three of the ovens," Derrick told the ladies, "are state-of-the-art appliances with speed convection. The previous owner was a chef for a five-star restaurant."

"I thought you designed this house?" Jill said under her breath.

"I did."

Jill shook her head since he was obviously making up a story, but she let it go. The only thing that mattered was that the women were suddenly satisfied with the equipment they had to work with. All three women looked at Jill and waited for further instruction.

Jill glanced at the clock. "Okay, ladies. Let's start cooking."

Pans and utensils clinked as the three cooks worked their magic, everyone around them talking at once. Out of the corner of her eye, Jill caught her mother motioning for her to come talk to her.

"Mom," Jill said as she headed for the entry where her mother stood. "Come into the kitchen and meet everyone."

"Not now. Your father's waiting in the car and I only came here to tell you that we won't be able to stay after all. Your father has been called back to the office—some sort of emergency that only he can resolve."

Jill shouldn't have been surprised, but the truth was, deep down, she'd thought that if her parents showed up, she would place Ryan in her mother's arms and her mother would instantly realize that there was more to life than fashion shows and five-star hotels.

"Would you look at that?" Derrick said from across the room. "Ryan has your mother's mouth."

Before Jill could stop him, Derrick had crossed the room and placed Ryan in her mother's arms. Almost instantly her mother's features softened as she gazed upon her grandson.

"The same green eyes, too," Derrick's sister said.

It wasn't long before everybody except the cooks were huddled around her mother, everyone commenting at once on the amazing likeness between Ryan and Jill's mother.

A honk sounded from outside and her mother looked up at Jill with watery eyes.

"It's okay," Jill told her. "I know you wouldn't leave so soon if you didn't have to."

Derrick took Ryan from her mother and Jill walked her outside, down the stairs, and to the driveway where her father waited impatiently in their rental car.

For the first time in many years her mother turned to her with open arms and they held each other for a short time. Surprised by her mother's frailness, Jill found herself wanting to tell her how much she loved her, and then beg her to stay for a few days or at least a few hours and just hold her and talk to her about babies and life, but no words came.

"Come back with us," her father said through the open window, interrupting the first *real* moment she'd had with her mother in years, if ever. "Thomas has hired an investigator in the area and he has some information on the Baylor family. If you are serious about protecting your son's interests, give Thomas a call."

"Derrick is a good man," Jill said. "Ryan will be fine."

"Thomas is worried about you."

Her mother's pale, slender fingers touched Jill's forearm as if in understanding.

"Tell Thomas I'm fine," Jill answered. "More importantly, tell him I'm happy."

Her mother patted her arm one last time before she climbed into the car.

Jill stood in the driveway for a moment after their car disappeared through the gates and down the road. She tried to recall being a small child wrapped in her mother's arms, tried to remember even one time that just the two of them had spent quality time together, but no memories came forth.

A gentle hand came to rest upon her shoulder and when she turned about she was greeted by Derrick's mom.

"Is everything all right?" Mrs. Baylor asked.

"Everything's fine," Jill said. "Thanks for asking."

"I'm sorry they had to return to New York so soon. I was hoping to invite your parents over for a real hoedown— something bigger and better than the little get-together you experienced last week."

The woman was like sunshine, Jill thought, and if Derrick's mom could be bottled and sold, she'd be worth millions. "How did you do it?" Jill asked.

"Do what?"

"Raise all of those kids. Everybody seems to get along and they genuinely seem to like one another."

"I had Phil to help me. Even so, there were days when I had to chase a few kids around the house with a broom."

Jill laughed.

"And if Ryan turns out to be anything like his father," she added, "you'll have your work cut out for you."

"Why? What was Derrick like as a child?"

"Ask his siblings and they'll all say the same thing. He was bossy." A twinkle set in her eye. "He was also my most sensitive child—even more so than the girls."

Jill couldn't imagine it. "Really?"

"That boy cried at the drop of a hat. If somebody took his toy, he cried. If his dinner wasn't hot enough, he cried. If his sister looked at him funny, he cried."

They both laughed.

"I never would have guessed him to be the football player out of the bunch." Mrs. Baylor shook her head in wonderment. "You just never really know how they're going to turn out. Mostly, you just pray they'll be good people."

"Hey, you two," Derrick called from the doorway. He held Ryan on one broad shoulder and patted him gently with his free hand. "The ladies are finished with their appetizers and they're waiting none too patiently for the judges to make a decision. If you don't get up here, spatulas are going to start flying."

"Who's going to be the third judge?" Mrs. Baylor asked.

"Not me," Derrick said. "There's not one appetizer in there that has chocolate in it."

"You don't like chocolate," his mother reminded him.

"I do now."

Jill looked at Derrick and for the first time all day, their gazes met and held. Seconds felt like minutes until screams broke out from inside the house, followed by the sound of pans and utensils clattering to the floor.

Lexi greeted them at the entryway, appearing out of nowhere. She was out of breath and her eyes were big and round. Speaking in her usual high-pitched voice, she said something about a pig running loose in the house.

By the time Jill reached the kitchen, she noticed both of Derrick's sisters outside the French-style patio doors looking in. Two of the ladies had climbed up onto the granite counter for safety. The silver-haired woman was armed and dangerous, holding a colander and a spatula out in front of her, ready to strike.

Bruschetta and gyoza and pieces of sausage and scallions were everywhere. Trays had fallen, and red and yellow sauces dotted the wood cabinets.

Derrick's brothers and his father were playing basketball in the indoor court, oblivious to everything going on in the main house. Sandy and Mrs. Murnane had disappeared. Chelsey's new photographer-in-training snapped away as if he were paparazzi instead of a photographer for a cooking magazine.

The cook off was turning into a disaster.

"Where's your mother?" Jill asked Lexi.

"She's chasing the pig."

"A pig? Really? Are you sure?"

Lexi nodded, making her curls bob. "It says oink oink."

Derrick opened the French doors and frowned at his sisters. "What are you two doing?"

"Hiding," Zoey said.

"From the pig?"

Rachel nodded. "It was the ugliest thing I've ever seen. It had patches of white hair and a limp."

Derrick burst out laughing. Then he turned about and looked at the mess. "Did Hank do this?"

"Who's Hank?" Mrs. Baylor asked as she picked up pieces of bruschetta and melon balls and tossed it all into the garbage under the sink.

"It's a dog," Jill told her, relieved to know there wasn't a pig running around loose. "The dog was in the middle of the road and sure to be run over until Derrick saved him."

Zoey snorted. "Was that thing here in this house all night?"

"I left him food and water in the pool room," Derrick said, "but he must have found a way out."

The pitter-patter of feet could be heard just before Hank made another appearance. Derrick handed Ryan off to his mother again while his sisters screamed and ran back outside. Hank had a clump of hair in his mouth. Derrick ran toward the front entry and grabbed the dog as he ran by, stopping Hank from wreaking more havoc. "Looks like Hank got a hold of somebody's wig."

Sandy and Mrs. Murnane came around the corner just as Derrick's older brother, Connor, came through the front door and joined the party.

Mrs. Murnane looked as if she'd just returned from running a twenty mile marathon. Not only was she huffing and puffing, she was as bald as an eagle—maybe balder.

Derrick finally managed to dislodge the wig from Hank's mouth and quickly handed it to the poor woman.

Globs of white lumpy sauce dripped from the collar of Sandy's blouse.

Connor angled his head as he took a good look at Sandy's blouse and even took a whiff. "Is that Brie cheese?"

"As a matter of fact, it is," Sandy said. "What are you doing here?"

"I heard that you might be here and I was hoping we could talk."

"I'm busy."

"I'll wait."

They all moved into kitchen area to let everyone know they were now safe from the wild beast. The silver-haired woman sitting atop the granite counter saw that the animal had been detained and quickly dropped the colander and spatula so that she could grab hold of her plate of appetizers, the only appetizers that hadn't been ruined. "It looks like I'm the only one with an appetizer left. Does that mean I win?"

"Over my dead body," Mrs. Murnane said, shaking her wig at her.

"Everybody wins," Chelsey said in defeat. "I was the only one who had the opportunity to taste the appetizers before they were destroyed. They were all delicious."

"Who's going to be on the cover?" one of the women asked.

"All three of you." Chelsey turned toward Mrs. Murnane. "The bathroom is down the hall to the right. Why don't all three of you get yourselves fixed up and we'll take pictures of all of you together by the pool."

Sandy looked at Jill. "What do you think?"

"I think Chelsey is a genius."

~~~

As Chelsey and her intern took pictures of the women posing by the pool, Sandy watched the photo shoot from a few feet away. It wasn't easy staying focused, though, with Connor following her every move. She looked over her shoulder at him. "Are you still here?"

"I'm not leaving until you talk to me."

"Okay, fine. What is it?"

Before he could get a word out, Lexi came running toward them and wedged her small body between them. "Where's the pig?"

"It was a dog, Lexi. He's in the pool house for now."

"He's ugwy."

"Looks aren't everything," Sandy told her. "He's a nice dog with a good heart and that's all that matters, right?"

Lexi nodded and then shoved a finger up her nose before she ran off.

"What did I tell you about putting fingers up your nose?"

"Cute kid," he said.

"Thanks," she said without looking his way. She wanted to ignore him, mostly because she was embarrassed about the other day, but it wasn't easy ignoring a man who looked like Connor Baylor. He wore a suit and tie and she was beginning to think he just liked making everyone around him feel underdressed. His hair was neatly cut. He wore a Rolex around his wrist and Ferragamos on his feet. His cologne smelled provocative and woodsy.

"Do you mind telling me why you left without saying goodbye the other day?" he asked.

She turned on him then. "Why did you leave me sitting on that exam table looking like a fool? The least you could have done is shove one of those little rubber lights in my ear and look inside."

"I'm an ob-gyn. I don't stick anything in anyone's ears."

She crossed her arms. "That figures."

"Besides," he said, "you didn't need an exam."

"How would you know?"

"I could see it in your eyes."

"Ridiculous."

"Did you need an exam?" he asked.

"No, but that's not the point."

"The point is," he told her, "I figured if I was going to give you an exam it wasn't going to be in my office."

She lifted her chin. "Where would it be?"

"Your bed, my bed, outside under the stars, anywhere but there."

Her cheeks heated, mostly because he'd caught her completely off guard. He was clean cut, a little on the stiff side, a man of few words. He didn't curse and there was no way this man made love outside under the stars, let alone in the backseat of his car. *Or did he?*

He stepped so close she could feel the heat of his body. "Cat got your tongue?"

"You could say that."

"So, what do you think?"

"About which part?"

"If you had known I was going to ask you out when you came into my office, would you have come to my office or would you have snuck out the back door?"

"I'd have to think about it."

His fingers jangled the change in his pockets. "Playing hard to get now?"

"You could say that."

"How hard?"

She smiled. "Very hard."

"I have a conference next week, but the Friday after next."

"That's a long way off. I might be busy."

"I'll make it worth the wait. Seven o'clock sharp. Be ready."

"You don't know where I live."

"I know where you live."

"What about Lexi?"

He grabbed hold of Derrick's arm as he passed by. "Derrick, could you watch Lexi Friday after next, seven o'clock?"

"Sure." Derrick looked at Sandy and said, "Drop her off at my apartment any time after six. I'll be there."

"Thanks."

"Not a problem," Derrick said before heading onward.

Sandy tried to ignore the hot blood pulsing through her veins as she looked up into Connor's eyes. "I wouldn't know what to wear."

"Something short, something black, and a pair of three-inch heels."

"I'll think about it."

"You do that."

And then he walked off, confident and carefree.

Sandy rubbed her arms and wondered if she should forget everything he just said—teach him a lesson—make him see that he couldn't just march up to her any old time and snap his fingers and make her jump. But even as that particular thought swished through her mind, she shivered in anticipation of what he might have planned.

CHAPTER 21

After everyone had left, including Sandy and Lexi, since Connor had offered to take them home, Derrick invited Jill to sit for a while. More than anything he wanted to take her into his arms and hold her tight, but he also knew she might have questions, and he wasn't sure if he was ready to tell her everything.

He had set up the portable crib in the living area and Ryan was asleep after a long day of being worshipped by his aunts and grandmother. Derrick and Jill sat poolside overlooking the private beach. Together they watched the changing colors of the sunset on the horizon. Hank wandered over and Derrick scratched the top of his head. In the distance, he heard the waves crashing against the shore. The air smelled salty and refreshing.

"A lot has happened in the past three and a half weeks," he said, hoping to get a dialogue going. He could tell by Jill's actions all day that she was either embarrassed about last night or disappointed in him, or both.

Jill nodded, her gaze focused on the view. "Ryan's growing fast," she agreed.

Ryan was a good baby, he thought. And Jill was right, he was growing fast. When he looked at his son these days, he saw recognition in Ryan's eyes. Ryan was a smart boy, an amazing boy. Having a child did something to a person. Changed them in ways they never imagined. Being a father made him want to be a better man.

He wondered if he and Jill would have met under different circumstances, and yet he already knew the answer. No. They were from different worlds. They hung out with different crowds and they had different interests. He'd had a string of women in his lifetime, only a few whose names he could remember. He also had many women friends. He thought Jill would fit neatly into the friend category when he first met her, but now he knew otherwise. Jill was different. She was intelligent and complicated, stubborn and caring to a fault. And cold.

"You're shivering," he said, stating the obvious.

Jill kept her gaze on the horizon and dismissed his statement with a wave of her hand. "You're supposed to be watching the sunset."

The French doors leading into the house had been left open so they would be able to hear Ryan if he woke up. Derrick disappeared inside and returned with a blanket. They were sitting on a double recliner, but this time when he took a seat, he wrapped the blanket along with his arm around her shoulders and said, "Better?"

"Much," she said, resting in the crook of his arm, her gaze on the lavender hues painted across the sky, a sight he enjoyed night after night when he was home. Together they watched the end of a long day fade away. After the sky turned a dark crimson, he said, "I'm sorry you didn't get to visit with your parents. You put a lot of work and preparation into the dinner you had planned for them."

"It's no big deal. I'm the one that didn't even want them to visit, remember? Karma gets the best of you every time." She released a long sigh and then turned her head so she could look up at him. "Thanks for everything today. I couldn't have pulled it off without you. At this point, I don't know what I'm going to do when you're off to training camp."

"I'll always find time for you and Ryan."

Derrick found himself wishing life could always feel so simple and nice. "I should be thanking you for putting up with my family today," he told her. "I never invited them, story of my life, but they always seem to show up anyhow."

She smiled. "I love your family."

He breathed in the sweet scent of her hair.

"I probably smell like bruschetta and Brie," she said with a chuckle.

"I like bruschetta and Brie." He was tempted to nibble on her neck.

Hank was lying on a blanket nearby and he made a yipping noise. Apparently Hank was dreaming. Tomorrow Derrick would put an ad in the paper and see if anyone claimed the dog as their own.

"I don't think any of those ladies will cause a problem or think of suing the magazine now that they'll all be on the cover together," Jill said.

"I think you're right." All day, Derrick realized, the two of them had made nothing but small talk. It was his fault. He needed to apologize for leaving her in the middle of the night without saying goodbye. He needed to tell her exactly how he was feeling, no matter how complicated.

"I hope Mrs. Murnane can find a wig she likes as much as Hank liked that one."

To hell with it. He couldn't take it anymore. He adjusted himself so that he was on his side and they were face to face and then he brushed his lips over hers. Her eyes glistened in the moonlight. She was beautiful and she tasted like heaven.

"I should check on Ryan," she said, her actions contradicting her words as she angled her head so he had no choice but to kiss her neck.

She tried to get up from the recliner, but he used his body to keep her from going anywhere.

She laughed and he nibbled on her neck, working his way up to her ear. His body hummed with life as it often did when he was around her. He couldn't seem to get enough of Jill Garrison, hadn't been able to get his mind off of her since the first day they met. Everything inside of him zipped and zapped like electrical charges going off. She was the real deal. She said what she meant and meant what she said. There were no guessing games when it came to Jill and he found that maddeningly refreshing.

His mouth found hers again and he kissed her long and hard and when he pulled away for a mere heartbeat she said, "Do you think maybe this is all happening too fast?"

He raised his body, using his arms to prop himself upward. "No. I think it's happening too slow." He kissed the tip of her chin.

"That's because you're a man."

He smiled. "And it doesn't hurt that you're a woman."

"You know what I mean." She reached up a hand and smoothed her fingers over his stubbled jaw.

"Actually, I don't think I do know what you mean," she said. She met his gaze square on. "I'm not sure my heart can handle being broken again so soon."

His gut tightened, but he said nothing—only listened.

"You might not want to or mean to, but it's different with guys. Men aren't afraid of losing a part of themselves in a mere kiss."

"That's not true," he said. "I lose a piece of myself every time I kiss you. It's downright frightening."

"Then why risk it?"

"Because the magnet on my refrigerator says I should do something that scares me every single day."

"Now you're just making fun."

"I know that every moment I'm not with you, I'm thinking about being with you."

"The truth is we have very little in common."

"That's not true," he said. "I like dogs."

"Exactly my point, since I prefer cats."

"What about football?" he asked.

"I've never been fond of sports."

"Many women don't like sports. I like to sleep in," he added. "Everyone likes to sleep in."

She sighed. "I've been an early riser since the day I was born."

His mouth dropped open in mock terror. "What about movies? I like horror films...thrillers...action packed films."

"Romantic comedies are nice. I like romance."

He maneuvered his body to make sure he wasn't squishing her, and then he kissed her again and once more just for the hell of it. He finally pulled away and said, "I like romance, too."

"You come from a big family."

"I do."

"And mine is small."

"That it is."

"You like lasagna. I like sushi."

He nibbled on her ear.

"The list goes on," she said in defeat.

He dragged his mouth across her cheek. "Yeah...it's never-ending."

"That feels good."

"Hmmm."

"Derrick," she said. "I don't mean to ruin the moment, but why did you leave last night? How do you really feel about me, about us?"

Looking down at her, he took in every single detail. Her small nose, creamy skin, and heart-shaped face would inspire any painter to grab his brush and canvas. Her eyes were bright, filled with something he couldn't put his finger on.

She brushed a hand over his forearm. "What are you thinking?"

"I'm thinking you're beautiful beneath the moonlight. And I thought of something we have in common...Ryan...we both love Ryan."

"True."

She reached forward and played with the hair swirling about his ear and that small insignificant action made him want nothing more than to carry her to the beach and make love to her beneath the stars, but first he needed to man-up and come clean. "Listen to me, Jill." He kept his gaze on hers. "I don't wear my emotions on my sleeve. In fact, I don't usually get emotional. At least, I didn't until Ryan was born. I'm not sure how I feel about that...but I'm getting completely off subject here." He exhaled. "Let me start again. Last night was a night I will remember for the rest of my life. Cliché, I know, but it's true." He stopped again. He inhaled, glanced up at the stars, and then started again. "What I'm trying to say is that...I want you to know that...I can't remember the last time that I've wanted to kiss anyone the way I want to kiss you. And that scares the hell out of me. But I've never let fear control me. Never have, never will."

"Derrick," she said. "What are you trying to tell me?"

"I'm trying to be absolutely truthful with my feelings for you. From the start, you've been upfront and real with me. I want to do the same."

She watched him for a moment before she said, "Is this about Maggie?"

"No," he said shaking his head, "not really. This is about us."

He felt her stiffen, her eyes unblinking as she waited for him to spit it all out.

"I'm just trying to be straight with you," he said. "I like you and I want to be with you."

"You have feelings for both us, Maggie and I, and you're confused."

She was right. That was the problem. "Yes," he said as he leaned his head back against the lounge chair and looked up at a star-filled sky, feeling as if a thousand pounds had just been lifted from his shoulders. She was absolutely right.

Jill slid her legs to the side of the chair and came to her feet.

He lifted his head. "Where are you going?"

"It's late. I need to get going."

"You're not going to stay tonight?"

"Here? With you?"

He nodded before he realized that in one-tenth of a second everything changed between them. *Did he do something wrong?* He jumped to his feet and nearly tripped over the lounge chair to get to her side. He took her hands in his and said, "I'm falling for you, Jill. I'm falling so hard and fast my head is spinning."

"But you also have feelings for Maggie."

He wanted nothing more than to deny it, take everything he'd just said right back, wind the clock backwards a few short minutes and start over. This whole forthright truth crap wasn't working like it was supposed to. "I was trying to be real with you."

"And I can't tell you how much I appreciate it," she said without emotion.

"I was hoping that what we've shared and my being truthful would be the beginning of something incredible."

She angled her head as her gaze delved deeply into his, looking at him as if he was a moron or something worse. He hoped beyond hope that in the end, meaning in the next two minutes, she would be willing to give the two of them a shot. Forget about any feelings he might have for Maggie because more than anything he was sort of hoping those particular feelings would just disappear, go "poof" into thin air.

Jill straightened and looked about as if she had been about to say something but changed her mind. She tried to pull her hand away, but he wouldn't let go.

"Don't go," he said.

She looked at him. "I was also hoping this was the beginning of something wonderful, but it is what it is. You can't help feeling what you feel. I'm grateful that you opened up to me and told me the truth. And I hope you understand when I tell you that I can't do this thing with you anymore...be your friend...grocery shopping, chocolate...stars. I can't do any of it with you because I'll never know in any given moment whether you're thinking about me or her."

Derrick was at a complete loss as to what to do, so he just stood there like a fool and watched her walk back into the house, gather her things and leave. He wanted to run to the front of the house and stop her before she left, convince her that he had it all wrong and she was the only girl for him, but his legs were glued to the ground. He wasn't a moron. He was an idiot and a moron.

CHAPTER 22

Jill looked around the ballroom, wondering when Thomas was going to arrive.

Her gaze swept toward the entrance, past the woman with the French twist who was talking to a statuesque brunette wearing to-the-elbow black silk gloves. Jill hardly noticed the tall blonde dripping in diamonds as her gaze locked on the newest arrival standing at the top of the staircase.

Instead of Thomas, it was Derrick who walked into the Grand Ballroom dressed to the hilt in top hat and tails. He'd gone all out and all eyes were on him, watching his every move as the music changed tempo and he moved to the music, gyrating his hips and making the women swoon as he danced his way down the wide set of stairs and across the marble floor until he stood before her.

A sly smile covered Jill's face as she snapped her fingers, prompting the waiter to bring them a large glass bowl filled with a creamy ganache used for tarts, truffles, and for filling soufflés.

Derrick didn't bother dipping just one finger. He took a whole handful of the chocolate filling whipped up by none other than Wolfgang Puck, who stood in the foreground holding a chocolate covered whisk. Fireworks exploded, lighting up the sky outside. Bells rang in the distance; Derrick winked and she laughed as tiny chocolate truffles rained down around them.

Jill jolted upward in bed and opened her eyes.

She looked about her bedroom, everything in its place. Her heart pounded against her chest. She had done it again.

~~~

Today they were celebrating.

Chelsey, Jill, and Sandy drank champagne while they looked through dozens of pictures and tried to decide which picture from the cook off would be used as the cover for next month's issue of *Food For All.*

It didn't take Jill long to select her favorite eight-by-ten glossy. "This one is perfect."

Chelsey popped the cork from a bottle of champagne and then ducked as the cork bounced off the ceiling and hit the refrigerator before rolling around on the floor. "Who wants champagne?" she asked.

"Just a tiny bit for me," Sandy said.

Chelsey filled the fluted glasses with champagne and set two of them on the coffee table.

Sandy examined the picture Jill held up and wrinkled her nose. "I don't know if Mrs. Murnane is going to like that one. If you look closely, you can see that her wig isn't quite centered on her head."

"You're right," Jill said. She put the picture in the reject pile and looked back at the remaining pictures.

Chelsey picked up a picture and held it up for all to see. "How about this one? All three women look good."

Jill crossed her arms. "But the silver-haired woman—"

"Fiona," Sandy said. "That's her name."

"Fiona isn't smiling," Jill finished.

"But it is the most flattering," Sandy said. "If it were you, would you want the one where you're smiling or the picture with the most flattering angles?"

"The most flattering angles," they all said in unison.

"Okay, that's the one." Jill moved the rest of the pictures into the reject pile and then lifted her glass. "Cheers to our amazing photographer and another successful cover."

Sandy held up her glass and the other two picked up their champagne glasses and clinked them together before drinking.

"Who made the lasagna?" Chelsey asked. "It's delicious."

"When Derrick saw me heading up the stairs this morning," Sandy replied, "he insisted I take the lasagna he'd made. In exchange, I gave him Lexi and Ryan for a few hours."

Jill hadn't been happy about the exchange but she'd stayed in her bedroom while Sandy gathered everything Derrick would need and then after he'd left, she'd given Sandy a piece of her mind.

"The man cooks and changes diapers," Chelsey said with a shake of her head. "The last time I was here he was sending flowers every five minutes. Are you going to propose to him," she asked Jill, "or am I?"

Jill tried not to groan.

"Some girls have all the luck," Chelsey went on. "Of all the sperm in all the sperm banks around the world and you pick his."

"He has a lot of brothers," Sandy said just as the doorbell rang.

Chelsey jumped to her feet and opened the door. "More flowers. Who would have guessed?" She signed the receipt and then handed the delivery boy his clipboard. "Thanks," she said, before closing the door and handing Jill the card that came with the flowers.

Jill read the card. "They're not from Derrick. The flowers are from Dr. Nathaniel Lerner." Although she was grateful that Derrick had told her the truth about his feelings for her, she couldn't help but feel sick to her stomach every time she thought of him. Derrick Baylor had needled his way into her life. Not only was he the father to her son, he was a genuinely good guy. Her instincts told her he meant well. She knew he cared about her, but she didn't want to be second best. She deserved better, she thought.

A couple of knocks on the door caused Jill's heart to skip a beat.

This time Sandy got the door. As Jill suspected, it was Derrick who stood on the other side, holding Ryan in his arms while Lexi held onto his leg.

"Mom," Lexi said. "Look what Rine is wearing."

Derrick smiled as he held Ryan up for all to see.

Her son was dressed in a sailor outfit, complete with navy trim and buttons, a navy bow at the collar, and an anchor image on the hat.

"Ahoy, mate," Derrick said in a cheerful voice.

"Ahoy!" Lexi shouted as she jumped over the threshold and skipped across the room to where Jill sat.

Sandy glanced over her shoulder at the clock hanging on the kitchen wall. "You're twenty-five minutes late."

"Life at sea isn't easy and this is the welcome we get?" Derrick looked at Ryan and said, "What do you think about that, mate?"

"Batten down all hatches!" Lexi said.

Sandy smiled. "Is that what he's been teaching you all day?"

Lexi nodded.

Ryan kicked his legs and made a gurgling noise.

"Ryan is wondering why he hasn't been kissed yet." Jill had already come to her feet. She scooped Ryan out of his arms and kissed his pudgy face.

"Aren't you eating with us?" Chelsey asked Derrick.

"Unfortunately," he said, "I can't. It's Wednesday and I promised Mom I would make a showing for dinner this week."

"I'll forgive you," Chelsey said, "if you get me passes into the Condor's locker room this season."

Sandy thought that was a fair deal. Sandy and Chelsey chatted amongst themselves about football and how much they didn't know about the game, but how they both enjoyed the uniforms and especially the way the pants molded to the players' thighs and butt.

Derrick's gaze settled on the flowers on the counter behind Jill. "Looks like you need to have a talk with the pediatrician."

Jill lowered her voice. "Which part of 'I don't want to be your friend' did you not understand?"

"I don't want to lose you," he said.

"You never had me to lose. And I don't want to talk about this right now," she whispered.

"Tell the doctor that you're taken."

She angled her head. "Are you for real?"

"You told me you had feelings for me."

"That was before you made it clear that you still have feelings for Maggie."

He frowned, but didn't refute what she was saying.

"You're confused," she said.

Once again his large frame filled the doorway. His close proximity made her feel weak in the knees. "There's something really great happening between the two of us," he said. "It's way too soon to call it quits."

She shook her head at his audacity. "I can't talk about this now."

"Fine," he said before she could shut the door in his face. "I'll be here," he glanced at his watch, "by eight o'clock tonight. We'll talk then."

~~~

Derrick didn't bother knocking. Instead, he opened the front door to his parents' house and led Hank inside on a leash. The dog's tail wagged, hitting the door with a *thump, thump, thump*. He quietly shut the door behind him, hoping to surprise his mom. Although he'd told her he was coming, he was pretty sure she hadn't believed him.

A cacophony of voices and sounds traveled from the dining room and kitchen, reminding him of his childhood when all of his sisters and brothers and a few neighborhood stragglers would come together in Mom's kitchen and set the table or help with dinner, everyone always talking at once.

"Look what the cat dragged in," Jake said the moment Derrick stepped into view.

"Did you have to bring that dog?" Rachel asked.

Derrick patted Hank on the rump and held tight to his leash. "He's a good dog and he's lonely at the big house now that Zoey moved back to her place."

"I can't believe you'll let Hank into your house, but not Jim Jensen." Rachel shook her head. "It makes no sense at all."

His mom tossed a salad in the kitchen. "Did you call the local veterinarians to see if anyone has lost their dog?"

Rachel snorted. "Look at the animal, Mom. Would you want Hank back if you lost him?"

Jake came to Derrick's side and pet the dog on the head while Mom looked adoringly at Hank. "Of course I would want him back. What's not to love?"

Hank wagged his tail.

"I've called at least a dozen vets," Derrick said. "I was hoping all of you could help me make flyers."

When no one responded, Derrick figured he was on his own.

Dad gave the dog a biscuit and then took the leash from him and led Hank outside. "Let me introduce Hank to Lucky and Princess and see if they all get along."

"Thanks. I appreciate that, Dad. Where's the Rad Dad T-shirt?"

"If I had known you were actually going to show up, I would have worn it."

Derrick laughed as he headed for Mom and gave her a hug. "Something smells good."

"Pork chops with maple sauce, salmon potato salad, and banana cream cheesecake."

"Sounds like a winning combo."

"How's your knee?" she asked, ignoring his teasing.

He frowned. "Who told you I was having problems with my knee?"

"I'm your mother. I know these things."

Brad sat at the booth in the kitchen. "We've all noticed you limping around in pain at some point or another. Have you talked to your coach about it?"

Frustrated, Derrick raked his fingers through his hair. "I'm back on the field next week. Nobody will ever know."

"You can't play football forever," Jake reminded him.

"I appreciate everyone's concern," Derrick said, which was a big fat lie since he plainly did not like them nosing in on his business, "but I've got it taken care of." He did a little dance. "See? The leg is as good as new."

His brother Cliff came in from outside, followed by Dad. Derrick was thankful for the interruption.

"Hey, bro, how's it going?" Cliff asked. "Good looking dog you found yourself."

They hugged and patted one another on the back and Derrick actually found himself wondering why it had taken him so long to join them on Wednesday night for dinner.

"I hear congratulations are in order," Zoey added as she appeared from down the hall.

"For what?" Derrick asked.

"Mom told us you and Jill finally hooked up."

Derrick looked at Mom, who merely waved a dismissive hand and went on with whatever she was doing now. And then he remembered why he rarely came to these get-togethers.

"I like Jill very much," Rachel said as she placed a fork next to every plate on the table in the dining room.

Dad handed him the salt and pepper shakers. "Put those on the table, would you?"

Derrick did as he was told and then he glanced at his watch.

"Don't even think about it," Mom said as she patted his forearm.

Damn. She was on to him.

"So when are you going to move back into your house in Malibu?" Dad asked.

"And more importantly," Zoey said, "when are Jill and Ryan going to move in with you?"

"First comes love," Mom told his sister as she passed the glass bowl filled with potato salad, gesturing for his sister to set it on the table. "After the love part, we can all discuss the moving in part."

"*We?*" Derrick asked. "*We* don't discuss my love life or decide what's best for me. Jill and I will discuss our love lives and our future together without any help from the likes of you all." *Were they all insane?*

"A little testy, aren't we?" Jake asked.

"He's sensitive," Mom corrected.

Of course they were all insane. Why was he even questioning it?

"He's obviously in love," Rachel chimed in as if he wasn't in the same room.

His dad came up close to Derrick for a better look. "How can you tell?"

"He just talked about discussing his love life with Jill," Rachel said. "Why would anyone discuss their love life if they didn't have one?"

"You're a clever child," Dad said, tweaking her nose as if she was five-years old.

Derrick winced. "Dad smells like cigars again, Mom."

"Phil. You didn't?"

His dad narrowed his eyes at Derrick in warning. "I want to hear more about this falling in love stuff," Dad said to get him back for tattling, "and how *WE* are all going to figure out what you and Jill—"

"Hey," Derrick said, cutting him off, "did you all hear Connor's taking Sandy out this Friday night? What about that!"

His mother's eyes widened and his sister motioned for him to be quiet by slicing a hand across her throat. "What?" Derrick asked, truly baffled.

Jake's face reddened just before he headed out the sliding glass door, shutting it firmly behind him.

Zoey sighed. "Jake has a crush on Sandy and ever since he discovered Connor had an eye on her, too, he's been upset."

"And you call me the sensitive one?" Derrick shook his head.

The click of the front door told him they had more company. When Maggie walked into the kitchen, all conversation came to a halt.

Derrick wasn't sure if everyone stopped talking because they were waiting to see if Aaron was going to walk in behind her, or if they just didn't know what to say to her since Aaron had up and left her.

The last time he'd seen Maggie she'd been red-nosed and puffy-eyed from too much crying. Tonight though, she looked back to normal: all creamy skinned and beautiful—pint-sized and bright-eyed.

Derrick approached her first and took her hand in his. "How are you holding up?"

"I'm glad you're here," she said. "I wanted to apologize for the way I acted the last time I saw you. You came all that way to offer me support and I treated you rudely and I'm sorry. You didn't deserve that."

"You never have to apologize to me. You know that. You're going through some tough times and I want you to know I'll always be here for you. Anytime of the day or night just give me a call and I'll be there."

As she smiled at him, the family surrounded them, everyone wanting to give Maggie their love and support.

By the time they sat for dinner and the food was passed around the table, Jake had reappeared and had taken a seat between his sisters. His brothers, Garrett and Lucas and, of course, Aaron, were the only people missing, and for the next few hours, everybody laughed and reminisced, talking about everything from sports to ebooks, and a splash of politics without the bickering.

Maggie sat next to him and when he talked about the adoring way in which his son looked at him, she reached out and touched his arm in a gentle and loving manner, just a simple brush of the fingers across his wrist.

Derek felt something very strange happening.

In that very moment, instantaneously, something bubbled and awakened inside of him. It was almost as if a part of his childhood flashed before him, showing him what he'd failed to see all the years before, revealing the truth, the answer to the question that had been nagging him for all the days of his life.

It was the strangest thing.

Such a small thing. One touch of his wrist—crazy really, the light brush of her fingertips against his skin—that's all it took. He saw green eyes and a small nose. He saw a big smile and a cute little dent. He saw ridiculously large pink slippers. It was Jill he saw in his mind's eye. Maggie was touching him and yet he only saw Jill.

He needed to see Jill, in the flesh. Not tomorrow, not tonight, but right now.

He pushed his chair away from the table and stood. "I have to go."

Maggie did the same. "I'll get my things."

He lifted a puzzled brow.

Mom happened to be looking his way and she filled in the blanks. "Maggie had a friend drop her off. I told her you'd give her a ride home if you came since the apartments where you're staying are the closest to Maggie's place."

Maggie touched his shoulder. He felt it again. Clarity.

"I hope you don't mind?" she asked.

"Not at all. And I'm sure Mom and Dad won't mind if I leave Hank with them for a few days."

Dad opened his mouth to protest, but Mom was quicker to the draw and she said, "Make it a week. He's such a lovely dog."

Derrick pointed a finger at Dad and grinned.

By the time he and Maggie said their goodbyes to his family, Grandma Dora and her new boyfriend had made an appearance. *Didn't they understand that he was in a hurry?*

He felt the minutes and then hours ticking by at a snail's pace. It was just almost eight o'clock by the time they arrived at Maggie's house. If he hurried, he would only be a few minutes late to Jill's.

He pulled up to the curb and shut off the engine.

Derrick climbed out of the car and came around to open the door for Maggie.

"I can't thank you enough for the ride," she said as she stepped out. "Sorry about the extra stop. You're a godsend."

"No more apologizing, Maggie. I'm the one who should be saying I'm sorry. If I had left you alone when you asked me to,

Aaron would still be here. I had so much I wanted to tell you on the way here, but I couldn't seem to find the right words. It's the strangest thing, but tonight, when you—"

"You just can't leave well enough alone, can you?" a deep voice came from the shadowed porch.

The voice was slurred, but familiar. Derrick turned to see Aaron heading toward them.

Maggie stepped past Derrick and grabbed hold of Aaron's arm. "Aaron, what are you doing here?"

"Surprised?"

"Under the circumstances—yes. You're drunk."

"I'm still conscious, which means I'm tipsy at best."

"I better go," Derrick told Maggie, ignoring Aaron.

Aaron pulled away from Maggie. "Don't you move."

Derrick put his hands up in surrender. "This isn't what you think. Maggie and I both happened to show up for dinner tonight at Mom's and I brought Maggie home because Mom asked me to."

Aaron laughed. "Do you know how many times I've gone to dinner on Wednesday night?"

Derrick shook his head.

"Too many times to count. And guess what? You were never there. Not once. But suddenly this *one* time I'm not there and I'm supposed to believe that lo and behold it's just a coincidence that you happened to show up. Did you two sit next to one another at the dinner table?"

Maggie touched Aaron's shoulder. "That's not important—"

"It's important to me." Aaron shrugged her hand off of him and stepped toward Derrick. "I saw you sitting here the other day—last week—waiting for Maggie. I had come for the same reason, to talk to her, but once again you beat me to the punch."

"You should have told me you were here," Maggie said.

He gave her a tight smile. "And then what?

"I'll tell you what," Aaron continued before Maggie could respond. "If I had moved back in with you, it never could have worked because every time you walked out that door," he said to Maggie as he pointed to the entrance to their house, "I would have wondered where you were and if Derrick was with you. I can't trust him."

"But you can trust me," she said, clearly exasperated.

"I just can't do this anymore." Aaron shook his head. "Seeing him here the other night and then again right here, right now—" He slapped the side of his head with the palm of his hand. "What's it going to take for me to finally get it?"

"What *is it* going to take?" Derrick asked him, his voice calm. "Because I get it...I do...I finally get it, Aaron. I'll stay away from both of you for as long as it takes. I'll get a new lawyer. I'll go to court and get a restraining order against myself and I'll sign it, Aaron. I'll do whatever it takes because I didn't figure it out until tonight, but everybody was right all along...I'm not in love with Maggie."

Aaron's left fist connected with Derrick's jaw and then a quick right hook connected with his nose.

Maggie cried out, "Stop it!"

One minute he was making a life-changing confession, and in the next he was kissing the gravelly driveway. Derrick spit out a few pebbles and dirt and tasted blood. Maggie came toward him, but Derrick stopped her from coming any closer. "I think it's best if we stay away from one another."

"There's a hospital down the street. Your nose looks bad." She turned on Aaron. "I'm going to go inside my house and you're going to leave me alone. Do you hear me?"

Derrick brushed dirt from his pants and then used the sleeve of his shirt to wipe his bloody nose as he waited for Maggie to get inside the house and lock the door. "I'm sorry," he told Aaron, figuring he owed him that much. "I screwed up."

Aaron grunted. "You're an asshole."

"I know."

"You've been getting into the middle of my business since I was ten."

Derrick's head throbbed. "That long?"

"Probably longer," Aaron said, "but the first time I can remember is the time we were both saving up for that shiny red bike. We were pretty even until you started selling kisses to all the neighborhood girls for a quarter."

Despite the bloody face, Derrick grinned. "I remember that." His smile disappeared when he saw the pain on Aaron's face. "You're right. I am an asshole."

"Yeah, I gave up competing with you about fifteen years ago."

"You were the one who talked me into playing football," Derrick said as the memory hit him.

Aaron nodded. "I didn't like the game and I figured I would enjoy watching you get beat up. The whole plan sort of backfired on me, of course, because you excelled at the sport and became more popular than ever."

Derrick gave up worrying about his nose. Instead he jangled the keys in his pocket. "I never meant to make your life miserable. I just have a knack for doing that to people."

"Yeah, you do."

Derrick gestured with his chin toward the house. "I think she's mad at both of us."

"She should be. I wouldn't blame her if she decided to never talk to me again. I've been a jerk. And that goes double for you."

"Well, if there's one thing I know for sure after all of this, it's that Maggie Monroe loves you and always has. It's taken me too many years to see that I can't always have my way. Jill figured that out about me within weeks of meeting me."

"Smart girl. I like her already."

Derrick opened the car door and gestured toward the passenger seat. "Need a ride?"

"It's the least you could do," Aaron said. "I'm staying at the hotel three blocks down the road." Aaron walked toward the car, opened the passenger door and climbed in. "After you drop me off you might want to visit a med center. That nose looks bad."

CHAPTER 23

Derrick limped up the stairs. Jill's apartment was dark. He unlocked the door to his place, turned on the lights, and went straight to the bathroom to take a look at the damage to his face. He put a finger to his upper lip and tried to get a look at his teeth.

The doctor at the med center had said he'd chipped a tooth. At least his front teeth appeared to be okay. A gash through his left eyebrow was held together with a small butterfly bandage. His eye was black and blue and swollen. *Great. Just great.*

He went to his bedroom next and changed into a pair of sweats and a clean T-shirt. He tossed his blood-streaked clothes into the garbage.

Tonight was turning out to be more bitter than sweet, but still bittersweet all the same.

More than anything he'd wanted to see Jill tonight—talk to her and see how she was doing. Since making love to her, she'd been in his every thought. He'd never felt this way about anyone before—not even Maggie, and that's what he'd realized at dinner tonight. He'd wanted to rush home to Jill and lift her into his arms and look her square in the eyes when he told her he'd missed her, and more importantly, that he loved her—only her—nobody else. He only had a week left before training camp began.

He planned to make the most of it by spending every minute with Jill and Ryan. He would do whatever he had to in order to convince her that she was the only woman for him.

The harder he had tried to get back to Jill tonight, the more difficult the task had become. For the first time since he'd moved into the apartment, he felt cold and lonely. He grabbed a bag of frozen peas and placed it on his eye. With one good eye, he glanced out the window over his kitchen sink to see if Jill's light had come on yet. Ryan usually woke up for a feeding about now. Finally, he swallowed a couple of ibuprofen and then made his way to the couch. Propping his head on a decorative pillow, he shut his eyes.

Despite the pain, he felt as if a heavy weight had lifted from his heart. All these years he'd thought he was in love with Maggie. Now he realized he'd been obsessed with the *idea* of being in love with her. Loving Maggie was synonymous to competing and "winning" her in the end. That's all it was—a competition. He'd deserved everything that came to him tonight. He had a lot of groveling to do before either Aaron or Maggie could forgive him. No wonder his family hadn't understood him, especially these past few months. Hell, he hadn't understood himself.

~~~

Derrick jerked to an upright position. The sun shot through the window, heating his face and blinding him. It took a moment to figure out he'd fallen asleep on the couch. He rubbed the back of his neck and slid his feet to the floor. He felt like hell. There wasn't a muscle that didn't ache.

It was already noon.

He looked out the window toward Jill's apartment and realized that she'd probably left for Ryan's doctor appointment hours ago.

Careful not to make any jarring movements, he made his way to the bathroom. He brushed his teeth, which was no easy feat considering his swollen lip. Then he splashed cold water on his face and looked at his reflection in the mirror. His eye looked a little better than his lip today.

A knock sounded at his door and he headed that way, excited by the prospect of finally having the chance to talk to Jill.

But it was Maggie who stood on the other side of the door, looking fresh and summery in a pair of jean shorts and a pink shirt. Trying to hide his disappointment at seeing her standing there instead of Jill, he welcomed her into his apartment with a crooked smile.

"Oh, you poor thing," Maggie said, squeezing her way inside and then shutting the door behind her.

"What are you doing here?" he asked.

"We need to talk."

For some reason, that particular statement made him nervous.

"It's okay," she said, obviously noting the apprehension he was feeling. "I came because I won't be able to rest until I talk to you once and for all. I have some important questions to ask you."

"Okay," he said, swallowing the knot in his throat. "Shoot."

"You look horrible."

"Thanks."

"Aaron has a mean right hook, doesn't he?"

"That he does."

"Who would have guessed?"

"Not me."

She put a hand to his jaw. He stood there stiffly and let her touch him since he figured she obviously had something very serious she wanted to say. Then he noticed a strange look in her eyes and it struck him. "Don't say it," he said.

"Don't say what?"

"Don't tell me you're sorry because I'm the only one who should be apologizing. We could both say we're sorry until we're blue in the face, but it isn't going to do either of us a bit of good."

"You're right."

He kept looking out the window toward Jill's apartment. It felt as if months had passed by since he'd seen her. "So, what is it, Maggie?"

She dropped her arm to her side, resting her hand on the purse dangling from her shoulder. "It's about me and you."

He didn't like where this conversation was going. Two weeks ago, hell, two days ago, he would have given his right arm to spend time alone with her, but now all he could think about was Jill. He looked over Maggie's head again toward Jill's apartment. She should be home by now.

Where was she?

Suddenly he felt very uncomfortable having Maggie standing here before him, alone—just the two of them. "What is it, Maggie?"

"I've had a lot of time recently to think about things…to think about us."

A long uncomfortable pause settled between them. He went to the kitchen and poured himself a glass of water. The pain in his head had become intolerable. He took two more ibuprofen. "Can I get you anything?"

"No, thanks."

"Okay," he said. "Spit it out, Maggie. The suspense is killing me. What exactly are you trying to tell me?"

"I love you," she blurted. "I want to be with you forever. Runaway with me, Derrick. Today. Now."

A throaty guffaw escaped him and water threatened to shoot out of his nose.

Maggie huffed. "Are you laughing?"

"I'm sorry. It's just that your timing is impeccable. I don't love you, Maggie."

"So you weren't just saying that because Aaron was standing there last night?"

"No. I was telling the truth. I guess I just needed some sense knocked into me to make me realize I didn't like losing you to Aaron."

She put the palms of her hands to his chest and shoved him hard.

"Hey…what are you doing?"

She shoved him again and then hit him on the shoulder with her fist.

She was a tiny thing and he felt nothing, of course, but he took a couple of backward steps just in case she decided to pick up the coffee table and hurl it his way.

Her face was all shades of red now. "So you're telling me that you got in my face every chance you could, you ruined my relationship, you did it all just for the hell of it…all because you're a big tough guy who's used to getting his way? Because you like to win?"

She marched across the room and opened the door. He followed her outside. "I know it's bad, Maggie." He moved as close as he could, but not close enough for her to take an eyeball. "I wish I could take it all back," he said. "I wish I had seen what everyone else saw a long time ago. I love you like a sister, but the truth is, I love Jill. I didn't know what love was until I met her."

Maggie didn't look convinced.

"It's crazy, but it's true. I think I've loved Jill since the very first moment I laid eyes on her."

Maggie lifted her arms, prompting him to take another step back. She smiled and took a step forward, and then cupped her hands around his face, stood on the tips of her toes, and gave him a peck on the cheek. Before he knew what she was up to, she dropped her hands from his face and simply hugged him, squeezing him so tight he thought he might break in half. When she was done with him, she merely hitched her purse up higher on her shoulder, looking happy and maybe even amused, as if she'd never expected him to run off into the sunset with her in the first place. "Thank you, Derrick. I'll see you in the courtroom on Monday."

He scratched his head. "You're going to be there? After everything I've put you through?" Nothing made sense anymore.

"That's right," she said. "I wouldn't miss it for the world."

Maggie headed down the stairs and Derrick, sensing someone watching, looked over his shoulder toward Jill's apartment and saw her through the kitchen window.

~~~

On the drive home from Ryan's appointment with Dr. Lerner, Jill rolled down the window and let the warm Los Angeles air swoosh through her hair as she passed by the Warner Brothers Studio and NBC.

Dr. Nate Lerner had expressed pleasure at seeing how well her son was progressing. After Nate finished the exam, she thanked him for the flowers and then proceeded to tell him that her life was chaotic right now and she needed to get things in order before she dated him or anyone else. He had been more than gracious, telling her to let him know when she was ready for another date. He promised to make it a night when he wasn't on call.

Jill hated to admit it, but she had hoped Derrick would appear at her door last night at eight o'clock as he said he would so they could talk. She had definitely fallen in love with him. How and why, she could only guess. Despite Derrick being a no-show, she'd managed to sleep through the night. Ryan was over a month old now and he'd slept until five this morning. She felt rested and eager to start the day.

Today was Thursday. The mediation was scheduled for Monday morning. Once that was over with, everything would be spelled out in black and white, and she would be able to move on. There would be no more guessing games. Knowing she wouldn't have to worry about Ryan being taken from her would be a tremendous weight off of her shoulders.

Jill pulled into the parking space and saw that Derrick's car was still there. Her heart raced at the thought of seeing him. She couldn't help it.

With Ryan in the carrier and the baby bag thrown over her shoulder, she made her way up the stairs. A light breeze cooled her face. A hummingbird drank from the feeder outside her neighbor's window.

Once she was inside her apartment, she took Ryan out of his carrier and carried him to his room, smiling at his wiggling form as he kicked his legs and stretched his arms. Leaving him in his crib, she headed for the kitchen to get his bottle. As she filled a pan with an inch of water to heat the bottle, she saw the door to Derrick's apartment open wide.

It was Derrick and Maggie. They were talking, both of them looking serious until Maggie grabbed his face and kissed him. After the kiss ended, they embraced for what felt like an eternity.

Her heart dropped. Her breathing stilled. Yesterday, she'd begun to think that maybe she was being too hard on Derrick. Maybe, despite everything she'd seen with her own two eyes, the two of them stood a chance.

God, how dense could she be? She'd been such a fool. She'd tried to get past his obvious infatuation with the woman, but now something told her there was much more to the story. As if he sensed her watching, Derrick looked up and saw her through the window. He wasted no time heading for Jill's apartment.

Jill opened the door before he could knock. Her jaw dropped the moment she saw his face at closer view. "What happened to you?"

"It's a long story."

He tried to come inside but she blocked the entrance. "Answer a few questions and then we'll talk."

"Okay. If it's about what you just saw—"

"Last week when you took Hank to your Malibu house," she began, cutting him off without apology, "and then didn't return until midnight—where were you?"

His hands sank deep into the front pockets of his sweats. "Everywhere," he said. "If I recall correctly, that was a crazy day." His eyes narrowed and his lips pressed together as if that might help jog his memory. "My sister's car broke down," he said. "I remember that much."

"Did you see Maggie that night—you know—before you came here?" Before the kiss, she thought. Before you kissed me madly and heatedly and then made love to me and turned my world upside down.

He nodded. "I believe I might have."

"Yes or no."

"Yes."

"And then again last night—"

"It was a coincidence. Nothing more."

"Did you see Maggie at her house last night?"

He nodded.

Exactly what she was afraid of. "I'll see you in court Monday morning."

She tried to shut the door, but he kept a hand on the door frame.

He frowned. "You said we could talk."

"That was before you answered my questions."

Again, she tried to shut the door.

He refused to budge. "Don't do this, Jill. It's not what it seems."

"You don't understand," she said. "I'm not angry with you. I'm only disappointed. You don't owe me anything and I don't owe you anything. When it comes right down to it, we hardly know one another."

"That's not true. I know you're responsible and hard working. You're a terrific mother and a loving person. I know you like sushi and chocolate soufflé with a firm crust and a soft middle. *The Notebook* is one of your all-time favorite movies, you prefer cats over dogs, and you're the best thing that's come into my life in a very long time."

He looked and sounded sincere, but none of that mattered. She didn't want to be with a man who might be looking at her, but instead be thinking of another. She knew he was confused and that her reaction to seeing him with Maggie might be unfair, but he didn't love her and she deserved that much, at least. After all she'd been through, she deserved that much.

"And you're beautiful," he continued, his voice hoarse, his tone bordering on desperate. "What you see is what you get. You don't ever pretend to be someone you're not. That's one of the things I like most about you."

There was that word again. *Like. He liked her. He really liked her.* She sighed. Exactly why she couldn't let him in the door. This had nothing to do with Maggie and everything to do with how she wanted to be treated. After seven years, Thomas hadn't known what he wanted either. She sure knew how to pick'em. "I'm sorry, but I don't want a man who can't figure out what he wants. I'm no longer the naïve young woman I used to be. I deserve better."

~~~

The last time Jill saw Derrick was three days ago. Tomorrow she would see him in the courtroom. She sighed. That wasn't the whole truth. The last time she'd seen him was an hour ago when she'd peeked through a slit in the blinds covering her front window and watched him head for the parking lot. As always, he had looked devastatingly handsome in a white-button down shirt with rolled up sleeves and slacks that fit him snug around the thighs. She wondered where he was going and what he was doing.

Hoping to get her mind off of him, she took Ryan to the other room to give him a bath. Once the water temperature was just right, she set him in the tub.

"You are the sweetest boy in the world, aren't you?" Such a miracle he was. Ryan no longer cried every time she held him. In fact, Nate had suggested the reason he might have cried so much in the beginning was because he could sense Jill's apprehension. In a short time, though, she'd become confident with her ability to take care of him. Apparently babies sensed when their mothers were nervous.

She cupped warm water from the tub into the palm of her hand and rinsed him off, and then toweled him dry and wrapped him in a warm blanket. As she headed to the main room, she caught a glimpse of a shadow through the blinds. Someone was standing outside her front door. Sandy had said she might stop by with a couple of articles she'd written for this month's issue of *Food for All*. The magazine did well last month, and next month they were hoping to double the sales. Chelsey credited Derrick Baylor with the upward spike in sales, but Jill chose to believe it was the great recipes and informative articles that had done the trick.

She opened the door. Never in a millions years had she expected to see Thomas standing on her welcome mat.

"Hello, Jill."

No words came forth. Instead, she took a moment to look him over. She'd always liked his dark suits, crisp white shirts and perfectly combed hair, but for some reason the rigid look no longer suited him—or perhaps the look no longer suited her tastes, she wasn't sure. He looked tall, but not nearly as broad shouldered as she'd recalled him being in the strange dreams she'd been having lately. Judging by the paleness of his face, he'd been spending too many hours in the office instead of outdoors playing golf.

He tried handing her a bouquet of bright red tulips, but her hands were full so she gestured with her free hand toward the kitchen, and then followed him that way. Daylilies were her favorite flower, but Thomas was never one to remember details—even after seven years together. "Thank you," she said. "They're beautiful."

"Not nearly as beautiful as you."

She watched him closely, wondering what he might be up to. He'd never been big on compliments.

"Here," she said, handing Ryan over to him so she could put the flowers in a vase.

"Oh, no, I don't think that's a good idea."

Too late. He was already holding Ryan. His nose wrinkled, as if he was holding a skunk instead of a baby. She ignored Thomas's look of horror and took her time finding a vase.

The thought that Thomas was standing inside her apartment holding Ryan boggled the mind. Although her parents had mentioned Thomas more than once, she'd never really thought she'd see him again. She glanced at him again, wondering if he'd made the decision to visit on his own. She busied herself with cutting the stems and took her time arranging the flowers in the vase as she tried to wrap her mind around his being here.

When she turned about, she was surprised to find him so close. "What is it you wanted to talk to me about?"

"Isn't it obvious?"

The familiar puppy-dog-eyed look he gave her used to work every time, but now he just looked ridiculous. She had to stop herself from chuckling. "You've hardly said two words to me since leaving me at the church to fend for myself. Truthfully, I have no idea why you're here."

"I've never stopped loving you, Jill."

Her jaw dropped. "Are you kidding me? You didn't call for months after I moved. If you ever loved me, you would have come to California months ago."

"Your parents told me to give you time. They said you would be back before the summer was over. The next time I asked about you, I learned you were pregnant."

She wagged a finger at him.

He held Ryan closer to his chest for protection.

"Why did you leave me at the church, Thomas? How could you do that to me?"

"Because I'm a fool."

"Give me my baby." She scooped Ryan out of his arms.

Thomas looked down at the wet spot on his shirt.

"Looks like he peed on you. I'm going to put his diaper on and I'll be right back."

She returned moments later holding a newly diapered baby in her arms. Thomas stood in front of the sink and used a paper towel to dab cold water at the wet spot on his shirt.

"Do you have a crib or some place you can set him while we talk?"

"No. It's not his nap time and he likes to be held."

Thomas gestured toward the couch. "Shall we?"

Reluctantly, she took a seat in the chair across from the couch.

He sat on the couch and rubbed his hands over his knees, something he always used to do when he was nervous. No matter how many times she looked at him, she couldn't believe he was here, after all this time, sitting across from her.

He'd finally come.

She'd spent months dreaming of this moment and now here he was, and she wasn't sure she liked him being here at all.

"Remember the fight we had the night before our wedding?" he asked.

She nodded, although she had no idea what they had actually fought about that night. They were both nervous and stressed out from months of planning for the big day.

"After I left your house, I jumped in my car and I drove. I drove for miles until I no longer knew what city I was in. Once I found a hotel, I made my way to the hotel bar and drank my way into oblivion." Pausing, he looked at her. He looked teary-eyed. "You know I'm not a drinker. By the time I awoke the next morning, it was too late. The wedding was over. By the time I arrived at your house, you refused to talk to me."

She waited for something to happen inside of her, figuring she would feel the flutter of butterfly wings low in her belly or pangs of desire somewhere within, but she felt nothing.

He left the couch, came to stand before her and dropped to one knee. He placed a hand on her leg since her hands were busy with the baby. "I never stopped loving you, Jill. Come back to New York with me. I beg of you."

She only wished Sandy was here with a video camera. For over a year she'd fantasized about this very moment, about Thomas begging for her to come back to him. In her dreams they had embraced and cried before he whisked her to a chapel where they would finally become man and wife. Despite what he'd done, she still had feelings for him — brotherly love sort of feelings. For the first time in many months, she knew without a doubt that she'd done the right thing by moving to California.

She smiled; she couldn't help it.

For the first time in her life she was doing all of the things she'd dreamt about. She was in charge of her own magazine. She had a child, a son to call her own. She liked her apartment, and she had no doubt whatsoever that she would be a good mother to Ryan. Despite being burnt by love, she'd opened herself up again and would never regret the time she'd spent with Derrick.

For the first time in her life, she felt as if she could make decisions on her own without first asking friends and family what they thought. Not only was she using her instincts, she was following her dreams and it felt good.

Thomas must have taken the smile on her face as a positive sign because his eyes brightened with hope. "Remember the house I told you I had picked out for the two of us?"

She nodded.

"I bought it. Wait until you see what I've done with the office. It's all yours. You can hire a nanny and write articles for your little magazine if you have time. More importantly, I want you to edit the book that I've been writing. I'll include your name in the acknowledgement page."

It took everything she had not to roll her eyes and groan.

"Things are going to be different this time, Jill. Just give me a chance."

She held Ryan up for Thomas to see. "This is my life now, Thomas. Look at him. Look at him closely. He's my life, my love, my everything."

Thomas sighed. "It's not healthy for a child to be smothered in love, you know."

"I know, but I can't help it." She smiled again. "Look at him. He's irresistible, don't you think?"

Thomas took another long look and scratched the back of his neck.

"Do you want to hold him again? He's covered now."

"I'll pass. Thanks."

Her smile widened because she'd known exactly what he'd say. "I could never live with a man who didn't love Ryan as much as I do."

"I'm certain that over time I would come to feel whatever it is you feel for the baby."

"I'm sure you wouldn't, but that's not the reason I'm going to have to turn down your offer. I don't love you." She held Ryan close to her chest. "Wow, this is incredible."

"What is?"

"My being able to sit here, look you in the eye, and tell you with one-hundred-percent certainty that I don't love you. It's freeing, Thomas, and oh, so liberating!"

Thomas pushed himself to his feet and fiddled with his tie. "I guess I should be going."

She came to her feet and for a moment they just stood there looking at one another. But then she had an idea. She tilted her chin upward, closed her eyes and puckered up.

"What are you doing, Jill?"

"Kiss me." Holding Ryan with one hand, she used her free hand to tap a finger on her lips. "Quickly, Thomas, before it's too late."

He leaned down and kissed her. He lingered overly long, and she gently pushed him away. "Nothing. I feel absolutely nothing!"

Shaking his head, Thomas headed for the door.

"I'm sorry," she said, following close at his heels. "But I do appreciate you coming all this way."

"I'm sure you do." He opened the door and then turned back to her. "I'll be in court tomorrow. Your mother and father will be there, too. Your father has sent two of his best lawyers with me. By the time we're finished, you'll have full custody of your son."

So, her father *had* sent Thomas. "How do you intend to do that?"

"A piece of cake, really," he said. "It'll be an open and shut case. Trust me."

"Well, I don't want to hurt anybody's feelings. No need to get nasty."

"Do you want full custody of your son, or not?"

She chewed on her bottom lip. "Well, yes, but—"

"Just leave it me, Jill. Don't worry your little head about any of it."

Ignoring the "little head" statement, she clearly remembered why he used to get on her nerves. "I'm just asking you and your friends not to get carried away," she told him. "I know how malicious Dad's lawyers can get, like a frenzy of sharks. There's no need."

"I'll be so nice you might change your mind about coming home with me."

"Goodbye, Thomas. I'll see you in the courtroom."

CHAPTER 24

All hope Derrick had for an easy resolution concerning his son disappeared the moment Jill walked through the double doors with not only her parents at her side, but three attorneys. All three men wore matching double-breasted dark-blue suits with white button-down shirts and solid color silk ties. The lawyers hovered over Jill as if their lives depended on making her happy.

Jill's parents did not make eye contact as they passed by the long rectangular table surrounded by high-backed chairs. They were told to take a seat in the first row of chairs offered to the general public had this been a real trial.

The meeting today was taking place in an actual courtroom. The table at which Derrick and Jill would assemble had been set up between the bench where the judge would usually sit and the seats where Jill's parents were sitting now.

The mediator for today was a woman. She sat at the end of the long conference table wearing a wrinkled suit. The woman looked like she could use a good night's rest. She gestured for the foursome to take a seat across the table from Derrick.

Derrick came to his feet, leaned over the table and shook each attorney's hand. When he got to Jill, he held her gaze along with her hand and smiled. She looked nervous. Too many days had passed since he'd talked to her last. It had taken every ounce of will power he had not to knock on her door and try to get her to talk to him. His sisters had made him promise to stay away; give her some time they said, telling him he would only come across as desperate if he continued to knock on her door after she'd told him to stay away.

But today was the last day he was going to stay away.

No matter what happened in this courtroom today, win or lose, he wasn't going to stop knocking on her door until she let him inside. And when she did finally break down and open the door he was going to tell her the whole truth and nothing but the truth. He was in love with her and madly so.

It wouldn't be easy convincing her, but he wouldn't give up.

No way.

He'd made a mess of things, but he planned to set things straight between them.

Jill pulled her hand from his. "Are you all right?"

He nodded. "You didn't tell me you were going to bring an army."

"You didn't ask."

"So this is how it's going to be?"

"This is how it has to be. Ryan is my son. I want what's best for him."

"We want the same thing. Our situation doesn't need to be complicated."

The attorney next to her touched her arm as if to tell her not to say another word. Jill ignored him. "I agree with you. None of this need be complicated. That's why I plan to have this sticky situation resolved by the end of the day."

"That's what this is to you? A sticky situation?"

She lifted her chin a notch. "What would you call it, Mr. Baylor?"

Back to Mr. Baylor. Where was the woman who had invited him into her home and given him the gift of holding his son, the woman he'd talked with and laughed with, made love to? "I would call it what it is," Derrick said. "A man and a woman who were pulled together under unusual circumstances. Two people who love their son and want the best for him. Two people who a month ago didn't know the other existed but who were joined together by one innocent baby boy who needs them both."

"Many children are raised by one parent."

He held her gaze, intent on breaking through the invisible barrier she'd recently built just for him. "It doesn't need to be that way for Ryan. He has two parents who love him."

The door opened, breaking into their exchange. He looked toward the door and watched a young man enter with a message for the mediator.

Where was Maggie? She'd said she would come. From the looks of things, he needed her more than he first thought.

"It seems my time here needs to be kept to a minimum," the mediator informed everyone in the room. "We need to get started. Would you like to petition to postpone the meeting until you can hire an attorney to sit with you during the proceedings, Mr. Baylor?"

He glanced at his watch and sat back down. "No." He touched the file on the table in front of him. "I'll wing it."

The door swung open again and this time it was Maggie. He breathed a sigh of relief.

"I'm sorry I'm late," she said to everyone in the room. She set her briefcase on the floor next to Derrick.

He stood and held out a chair for her. "Thanks for coming. I appreciate it more than you know."

"A team of wild horses couldn't keep me away. You know that. Your face is healing nicely."

"Thanks. Maggie," Derrick said, "I'm sure you remember Jill Garrison from the barbeque at Mom's."

"Of course." The two women shook hands.

The man next to Jill stood and reached over the table to shake Maggie's hand too. "Thomas Fletcher," he said before turning and introducing the other lawyers.

Derrick looked from Thomas to Jill and wondered if this was the same Thomas she'd mentioned after kissing him in the backseat of his car—the same Thomas who had left her at the altar. Judging by the way she avoided his gaze, it was definitely the same Thomas.

"If it's okay with you," Maggie said to the mediator, "I would like to invite Derrick Baylor's family to sit in on the proceedings." She gestured toward the three lawyers and Jill. "Of course, only if Ms. Garrison agrees."

Thomas spoke for her. "I don't think it's appropriate to have family members sit in on the proceedings."

Jill shook her head, overriding her lawyer's wishes. "My parents are here. Of course, they can come in."

The mediator looked at Jill. "Unless you'd like to ask the people you brought along to step outside with his family. It's highly unusual to have family members attend these proceedings."

"I don't have any problem with Mr. Baylor's family sitting in on the proceedings," Jill told her.

Maggie went and opened the door, and then gestured for Derrick's family to enter. His parents were followed by Zoey, Rachel, Cliff, Lucas, Brad, Jake, and then Aaron, who gave Derrick a supportive nod. They all sat on the side opposite of Jill's parents.

"Let's get started," the mediator said. After explaining the mediation process and the ground rules, she pushed her glasses higher on her nose, looked from one side of the table to the other. "Under the circumstances," she said, referring to family members and lawyers, "I would like to keep the atmosphere non-threatening. I've read Mr. Baylor's account of what has happened and to get things rolling I'd like to start by asking Mr. Baylor to tell us exactly what he'd like to have happen with regard to Ryan Michael Garrison."

Everyone looked at Derrick and waited.

The quiet in the room was downright stifling. He looked at Jill. "As the papers confirm, the DNA testing confirms my parentage. What I want is a chance to get to know my son. I have a loving family that includes two parents, seven brothers, and two sisters. We're all especially close. Family is important to me. After Ryan was born, Jill Garrison gave me the chance to hold my son, a chance to take care of him and see what a miracle our son truly is. Jill didn't want me in her life, but she allowed me into her home despite any apprehension she had in the beginning. I'm grateful for that and I'm hoping she can find it in her heart to allow me to see Ryan on a regular basis."

"And what do you consider a 'regular basis'?"

"Best scenario," Derrick said, "would be a certain period of time each day." Every day, twenty-four-seven is what he wanted to say, but Jill looked so distant and cold he figured he would keep things formal and take it one step at a time until he could talk to her alone and tell her how he really felt about her and Ryan and this ridiculous court proceeding. "After training camp begins, I'm hoping Jill will consider letting me see my son whenever possible, especially before the season begins."

All three of her attorneys scribbled in their notebooks.

The mediator clasped her hands together. "What do you expect to happen when you travel to other cities to play football?"

"I'm usually home between games. I would hope we could work something out that would fit both of our schedules. You never know," he added with a wink at Jill because he couldn't resist, "you might like football." He looked back at the mediator. "She could travel with me and I could watch Ryan at night while Jill took phone calls and wrote articles, all of the business she takes care of on a daily basis to keep her magazine running smoothly."

"Absurd," Thomas said aloud.

The mediator rifled through her papers. "You live an hour away from Ms. Garrison's residence. Would you expect Ms. Garrison to drive Ryan to see you?"

"Absolutely not. I'm renting an apartment at the Four Seasons Apartments where Ms. Garrison resides. We're neighbors and I plan to keep it that way for as long as is necessary."

"He's your neighbor?" Thomas asked.

Jill hushed him.

"Is there anything else you would like to add?" the mediator asked Derrick.

Derrick looked at Maggie, who slid her notebook in front of him and used her pencil to point at the line she wanted him to read. "Yes," Derrick said. "I would like to ask for at least one day a month to take Ryan for the day to see my parents and siblings in Arcadia."

Jill grabbed Thomas's arm and whispered in his ear. Although Derrick preferred Jill in sweats and a T-shirt, she looked amazing in the dark sleeveless dress she had on. With her hair slicked back and wearing dark lipstick, she had a sophisticated look to her.

"Is that all?" the mediator asked.

Maggie pointed at the last line on her notebook.

Derrick read it, and then looked at Maggie to make sure this was really necessary. The expression on Maggie's face told him to continue. What choice did he have? Maggie had come today despite all the trouble he'd caused for her. He now felt obligated to follow her advice. "There is one more thing," Derrick said loud enough for everyone to hear. He kept his eyes on the paper as he read. "When I am forced to be away, I would like a weekly update of what is going on in Ryan's life, including pictures. I'll be happy to purchase a state-of-the-art digital camera for Jill's use."

"That's ridiculous," Thomas said.

Derrick looked at Jill.

"Let him finish," Jill said, her hand resting on Thomas's arm.

Derrick didn't like seeing her touch the guy. "That's it," Derrick said. "I'm done."

Thomas smiled, and then squeezed Jill's arm. "Wonderful," he said. "Since Ms. Garrison is visibly upset, I will speak for her if that's all right with our esteemed mediator."

The mediator took the bait, blushing and batting her eyelashes at the man Derrick already decided he didn't like.

"Against my advice," Thomas said, "Ms. Garrison came here today hoping we could settle this uncomfortable situation by providing Mr. Baylor with a signed agreement assuring him he would be provided with a yearly update of Ryan Michael's progress...pictures included."

Thomas flashed an irritating smile his way, making Derrick wish he could wipe the smirk clean off the man's face. Instead, Derrick gritted his teeth while Thomas Fletcher rambled on.

Next, Thomas slid a contract across the table toward the mediator. "Sources tell me Mr. Baylor has been taking prescription drugs for at least six months."

Derrick laughed. "That's absolutely not true. In fact, I still have the same bottle of pills my doctor prescribed six months ago." Derrick looked at Jill. "I'd like to know who your so-called 'sources' are."

She looked away.

"According to public record," Thomas went on, "Mr. Baylor's brother, Jake, had his driver's license taken away on two separate occasions."

Derrick looked at Maggie and then back at Tommy Boy. "What does that have to do with Ryan?"

"Everything," Thomas said.

"His brother, Jake, was also taken to small claims two years ago for aggravated assault."

"That's ridiculous. Jake was cleared. He can be a hothead at times, everyone knows that, but it was simply a misunderstanding."

Thomas looked Derrick square in the eyes. "Shall I go on?"

"By all means, please do. I have nothing to hide."

"Your sister-in-law received two DUI's and—"

The mediator interrupted with a raised hand.

"And now she's dead," Derrick said. "Are you happy?" Derrick looked at Jill. Her face was drained of all color, but she remained silent. "What happened to you?" he asked her. "One minute you're all apple pie and open arms and then this man comes back into your life, the same man who left you at the church to stare into the eyes of humiliation, and suddenly you forget you have a voice?"

She was obviously uncomfortable. She closed her eyes, but still said nothing.

His heart was racing, the blood in his veins pulsing at the idea of his family being dragged into this attempt to publicly humiliate him. Derrick turned to the mediator. "I don't see how my brother or my dead sister-in-law's actions are relevant to my seeing Ryan."

The mediator picked up her gavel and hit the sound block, but it fell to deaf ears.

Thomas's lips curled upward. "What kind of man makes passes at his brother's fiancée without remorse or shame? Is that the sort of man you would want taking your child for the day? A man without morals? A man who donates sperm for money and then lies on his application? A man whose relatives are continuously willing to risk the life of another human being because they can't seem to comprehend the difference between right and—"

Derrick stood so fast his chair toppled over behind him. His hands curled into fists at his sides.

Thomas stood, too. "Go ahead, show the court what sort of man you are...the kind of father you would be to Ryan."

"Stop it!" Jill said. She looked at Derrick. "I never gave him the permission to question your character or that of your family members. I asked him not to do this."

Derrick looked over his shoulder and saw the confusion in his mother's eyes. He'd had enough, so he turned and headed for the door. He couldn't do this to them, couldn't stand the idea of Jill and her pals putting his family through more of the same if he were to bring the case to trial.

"Leaving already?" Thomas asked. "We haven't even broken the ice yet, Mr. Baylor."

Maggie followed Derrick to the door. "Don't let him get to you," she said low enough that no one else could hear. "He's trying to intimidate you, the oldest trick in the book. Clearly they're not interested in bringing this case before a judge. He's playing hardball."

"I'm finished. No more."

"But Derrick—"

"I'm sorry. It's done. We tried." The door opened and then clicked shut behind him.

Maggie returned to her place at the table. She closed her notebook and tucked it inside her briefcase.

"We'd like to set a date to take this to trial," Thomas said.

"That won't be necessary," Maggie told him. "Mr. Baylor is prepared to sign whatever Ms. Garrison and her attorneys have brought for us today. You won."

~~~

Jill felt sick to her stomach. This wasn't how things were supposed to unfold.

"If it will do any good," Derrick's father said as he approached the table, "I would like to leave these with the court." He held up a thick packet. "These are letters and emails we collected from hundreds of people who can attest to our son's good character."

Jill wanted to explain to Derrick's father that this was not her doing, but she couldn't find the words to undo the hurt Thomas had already caused.

The mediator took the papers from Derrick's father and placed them on top of her file.

Thomas picked up the contract he'd meticulously prepared, but before handing the contract off to Maggie, Jill snatched it from him and ripped it in half.

"What are you doing?" Thomas asked. "Don't be childish."

"I want the court to know," Jill said to the mediator, ignoring Thomas, "that Derrick Baylor is a good man and a wonderful father. Every member of his family welcomed me into their lives without judgment or question." She turned toward Derrick's family. "I never intended for this to happen." She swept a hand toward Thomas. "I had no idea Mr. Fletcher and his lawyers would stoop so low. I'm so sorry."

"Jill!" her father said. "You do not need to apologize for wanting what's best for your son…our grandson."

"You're wrong," Jill told her father. "I was wrong. Being a part of the Baylor family is what's best for Ryan. My son would be lucky to have such a compassionate and caring family to call his own. These people already love Ryan as much as they love one another. I don't know what I was thinking in coming here today." Tears slid down both sides of her face. "I want Ryan to have the support and love of both our families." She looked at her mom, who looked torn between siding with her daughter or her own husband. Her father stood, wanting no part of Jill's heartfelt speech. "For some reason," Jill went on, "fate stepped in and brought these loving people into my life and, more importantly, into Ryan's life. I only hope Derrick's family can forgive me for making them listen to such a distasteful and unnecessary attack." She straightened, and then turned back to face Thomas. "I'd like you and your lawyer friends to leave now."

Less than ten minutes later, outside the Burbank courtroom with traffic on East Olive keeping a steady pace, Maggie approached Jill, stopping her before she entered the parking garage.

"Nice speech," Maggie said.

Jill answered with a tight, uncomfortable smile.

Maggie reached inside her purse, pulled out a tape recorder and pushed play.

Jill had no idea what Maggie was up to, but then she heard Maggie's voice emit from the recorder: "I *love you. I want to be with you forever. Runaway with me, Derrick. Today. Now.*"

Jill could hear Derrick laughing on the recorder.

"*Are you laughing?*" Maggie asked.

"*I'm sorry. It's just that your timing is impeccable. I don't love you, Maggie.*"

"*So you weren't just saying that because Aaron was standing there last night?*"

"*No. I was telling the truth. I guess I just needed some sense knocked into me to make me realize I didn't like losing to Aaron.*"

"*Hey…what are you doing?*"

There was some strange sounds in the background and then Maggie's voice again: "*So you're telling me you got in my face every chance you could, you ruined my relationship with Aaron, you did it all just for the hell of it…all because you're a big tough guy who's used to getting his way? Because you like to win?*"

"*I know it looks bad, Maggie. I wish I could take it all back. I wish I had seen what everyone else saw a long time ago. I love you like a sister, but the truth is, I love Jill. I didn't know what love was until I met her.*"

Maggie clicked the Off button. "For the record," she told Jill, "I didn't want to run off and marry Derrick, but I knew Derrick was falling for you way before he knew it himself. I also knew that the only way to make him see the truth was to offer him what he thought he wanted. It was a low blow, but I taped the conversation." She held up the recorder. "I did it because I wanted proof for Aaron. I didn't want to spend the rest of my life trying to convince Aaron that Derrick didn't love me the same way Aaron loves me. I love Aaron. I always have." She dropped the recorder into her purse. "You must think I'm nuts for stooping so low." Maggie sighed. "I just needed everyone to know that truth once and for all."

"I don't think you're nuts," Jill said. "I appreciate everything you've done." She shook her head. "I will say that I'm at a loss for words."

"That's understandable," Maggie said, "but there's one more thing."

Jill waited.

"Derrick wasn't ready to tell everyone in the courtroom, but he talked to his coach yesterday. He won't be playing football any longer. I guess his knee is worse than we all realized. He's retiring from the NFL."

"What's he going to do?"

"I'm not sure. I just thought you might want to know."

Jill wasn't sure exactly what Maggie expected from her, but she had a feeling she was trying to play matchmaker. "Thanks for telling me…and for allowing me to listen to the tape."

"No problem." Maggie reached into her purse again and this time she handed Jill a business card. "If you ever need a good lawyer, or just a friend, give me a call."

CHAPTER 25

Derrick had landed at LAX forty-five minutes ago, and he was glad to be home. It was Friday. He set the flowers he'd bought in the terminal on the passenger seat, put the key in the ignition, and headed for Burbank. Four days had passed since he'd left Jill and her lawyers in the courtroom. All four of those days were spent in New York City interviewing for a job.

After the mediation fiasco, he'd driven straight to his Malibu home. He'd allowed himself twenty-four hours to release his frustrations by swimming and shooting hoops. He'd been angry at the tactics Jill's lawyers had used and frustrated by Jill's refusal to see that it was best if he was in his son's life. He was also aggravated with himself for causing his family so much pain, first by coming between Aaron and Maggie and then by having their private lives thrown to the wolves. His parents had been through enough. And yet he'd continuously caused them trouble, and what did they do to punish him? Within hours of returning to his Malibu home from mediation, they smothered him with cards and phone calls and more love than any one man deserved.

It hadn't helped matters that his football career was over. But it didn't take him long to focus on the good, remember how lucky he was, and to once again feel grateful for all he had. By the time Gary Chamberlain called, asking him to fly back East to interview for a television commentator job, he was done with his pity-party and ready to tackle life head on.

Although the sharp pain pulsing through his knee was nothing compared to the pain he felt in his chest, a bottomless ache he knew wouldn't go away until he saw Jill again, he needed to take care of business first. He'd wanted to have something more than his heart to offer Jill when he returned home. He wanted to offer her a future.

And now that he was home again, he was ready.

~~~

Jill reviewed the list of articles they had planned for next month's issue and then moved on to the advertising and marketing they had planned. Sandy had done a superb job of getting advertisers excited about this month's issue.

Chelsey had already discussed her plans for the layout. Now she stood in the kitchen and looked out the window over Jill's sink. "So, Derrick moved out of the building?"

"I don't think he moved," Sandy said. "I peeked through his window and everything looks the same."

"You should call him," Chelsey told Jill.

"I tried, but he never returned my call. What does it matter anyhow? I'm beginning to think there's not a man in the world who truly knows what he wants out of life."

Chelsey sat on the chair across from Jill. Her brow puckered. "I thought you said you heard a tape recording of Derrick's voice telling his lawyer he loved you."

"That's right, I did."

"Maybe you should go after him."

"Why? He knows where to find me."

"Well, you did show up at mediation with three lawyers and then proceed to destroy his family, one member at a time. I mean, come on. We all know his family means everything to him. And if *you* really loved *him*, then you would go to him."

Jill frowned. "I told him right then and there that I had no idea Thomas was going to pull such a stunt." Jill didn't like the painful tug she felt inside, so she did her best to ignore it. "Derrick knows I was only trying to protect Ryan. Besides, I'm sure his family has told him I tore up the contract and kicked Thomas and his lawyer friends out of there. What else could I have done?"

Sandy exhaled. "Nothing. You did everything you could."

"I don't want to talk about this anymore," Jill said. "I have a date with Nate tonight and I don't want to feel depressed when he picks me up."

Chelsey raised a brow. "You have a date with the doctor?"

"It's no big deal," Jill assured her. "Nate knows I have a lot to deal with right now. We're just friends."

~~~

For what seemed like the hundredth time, Derrick stood in front of Jill's door.

He was dressed in a suit and tie of all things and he was holding two dozen red roses. Tucked inside his jacket pocket was a diamond ring, a two-carat flawless emerald cut antique that he'd splurged on after he'd turned down the job in New York and taken the broadcasting job in Los Angeles instead.

When he knocked, he noticed that his hands were trembling. He tried to laugh off the nerves. Believing it couldn't get any worse, Sandy opened the door.

Lexi screamed with joy when she saw him, latching onto his leg with such a loving fierceness, he thought his heart would melt. The kid was growing on him...literally.

He looked over Sandy's shoulder, trying to see into the apartment. "Is Jill home?"

"No, she's not." She leaned forward, close to his ear, so Lexi wouldn't overhear. "What the hell took you so long?"

"I just got off a plane from New York a few hours ago. I came as fast as I could."

"You were in New York? Connor didn't tell me you went to New York."

"Nobody knew."

Sandy crossed her arms. "She called you the day after the whole mediation mess."

He raked his fingers through his hair. "That must have been the restricted call I didn't pick up."

"What were you thinking not picking up the phone?"

"At the time, I'd had a couple of crappy days."

"Well, you snooze, you lose. She's on a date with Nate."

"I thought she told him to take a hike?"

"Apparently they're just friends."

"Great. Just great."

"Howiewood," Lexi said, tugging on his pants, determined to get his attention.

He patted the top of her head. "What is it, Lexi?"

"Wanna pway Barbies?"

He looked at Sandy and she moved to the side so he could come inside.

"Sure," he told Lexi. "Is Ryan in his room?"

Sandy nodded. "He should be waking up any time now."

"Why don't you let me watch Ryan until she gets home?" Derrick asked.

"Oh, I don't know." Sandy angled her head. "Unless—"

"Unless what?"

"I was supposed to go out with your brother tonight and you were supposed to be my babysitter."

"It's Friday. You're right. I'm sorry. It completely slipped my mind."

"Here, let me take those." Sandy took the flowers from him and headed for the kitchen.

While Lexi ran off to collect dolls, Sandy searched for a vase for the flowers. "If you watch Lexi," Sandy said, "I'll still have time to run home, get dressed, and surprise Connor."

"I don't know—"

"I'm not leaving Ryan and risking my friendship for nothing. As far as I'm concerned, you owe me."

He wanted, make that needed, to spend time with Jill alone. He wanted to make her an offer he prayed she wouldn't refuse. "Fine," he said. "I'll do it."

Lexi came running into the room with a backpack filled with dolls. Legs and arms stuck out of every crevice, making him realize he'd truly just struck a deal with the devil.

"Great." Sandy dropped the flowers to the counter, forgetting all about looking for a vase. She kneeled down so she was at eye level with her daughter. "Derrick is going to watch you until Jill returns home. How does that sound?"

"Yay!"

"But no more ice cream, okay?"

"Boo!"

It took Sandy under two minutes to gather her coat and purse and get to the door. She gave Derrick the once over. "You look nice by the way."

"Thanks."

She didn't open the door to leave. Instead, she stood there with her hand on the knob.

"What is it?"

"A part of me really wants to stay and see what happens between you and Jill."

He frowned. "Why? What do you think will happen?"

"I have no idea. That's why I'm so curious."

For the first time since he'd told Sandy he would watch Lexi, she stopped smiling and that worried him. "How angry is she?"

"I don't think Jill was ever angry, maybe just a little sad because she's never been loved the way she wants to be loved. She certainly doesn't believe you would ever come for her."

"She's not exactly waiting by the phone."

"No, she couldn't do that again. She didn't want to go tonight, but she had to go. Self-preservation and all that jazz."

His heart dropped to his stomach. He felt warm. He took his jacket off and hung it over his arm. "I had to go for the interview otherwise I would have had nothing to offer her and Ryan when I returned."

"She only wants you."

"I don't think she'd mind a little help putting Ryan through college later." He exhaled. "What time is Jill supposed to be home?"

"She didn't say."

"What time are you going to be home?"

"It depends on how things go."

Derrick couldn't remember the last time Connor went out with a woman. It was going to be a long night. "Why am I getting the sinking feeling this might not go as well as I thought?"

She laughed at his expense, said goodbye to Lexi one more time, and then headed out the door. Before he could close it, she whispered, "Did you bring a ring?"

He nodded.

Her eyes brightened. "Well, good luck then. You're going to need it."

"Thanks."

~~~

Not long after Sandy left, Derrick moved Ryan, Lexi, and all of her toys over to his apartment so he could get out of his suit and into something more comfortable. For over an hour he'd been watching Lexi hang onto the back of his couch as she jumped up and down. The girl refused to run out of energy. He'd never seen anything like it. Just watching Lexi from his seat on the couch made him tired.

It was nine o'clock.

Where was Jill?

If she and Nate were only friends, she would have been home by now.

"Howiewood?"

"Yes, Lexi?"

"Can I have more ice cream yet?"

"No way. You already had some and your mom said no ice cream."

She stopped jumping long enough to turn toward him. She pointed an accusing finger at him and her eyes narrowed. "You are in wots of trouble, mister."

"Story of my life."

She turned back toward the window and started jumping again.

"Is Jill home yet?" he asked her.

"Nope," Lexi said. "Wanna pway more Barbies?"

"No. Ken's tired. He went on vacation, remember?"

She stopped moving again and looked toward the ceiling. "I think I hear him coming back."

Derrick followed suit and looked toward the ceiling too. "I don't think so. He's in Hawaii right now. I'm pretty sure he rented once of those underwater cages so he could watch the sharks swim by."

She grinned, a Cheshire cat grin. Then she jumped off the couch and ran down the hall. Fifteen seconds later, she was back with Barbie and Ken. This time she handed him Barbie and kept Ken for herself. She pressed Ken's face against Barbie's plastic face and said, "Pweaze marry me."

He did his best imitation of a high girly voice. "No way, Jose."

"Why not? I wuv you."

"For starters, you're too skinny. I think you eat too many vegetables."

"I wike brocowi," she said in Ken's voice.

"I can tell."

"I'm Ken," Lexi reminded Barbie next. "I'm perfect."

"Nobody's perfect."

"If you don't marry me I'm going to eat more ice cream."

"If I give you more ice cream, Ken," he squeaked as he moved Barbie's arms, "then will you go back on vacation and stop asking me to marry you?"

"Yes," Lexi said.

"It's a deal." They both threw down their dolls and ran to the kitchen laughing.

~~~

It was after midnight when Derrick finally heard Jill's voice outside her apartment. He moved closer to the window, disappointed to see that Nate had decided to walk her to the door.

His window was partially open and he heard Nate say something.

He cringed when Jill laughed and laid a hand on his arm. Nate leaned forward.

Derrick jumped to his feet and ran to the door. The man was going in for the kill.

He opened the door in time to see Nate pick something up from the ground.

"Look at that," Nate said. "Find a penny, pick it up, and all that day you'll have good luck." He looked toward Derrick's open door. "He's back." He tossed the penny back on the ground.

Derrick ignored him. "It's cold out there," he said to Jill. "Where's your coat?"

Jill peered into the dark toward his apartment. "Is that you, Derrick?"

"Of course it's me. It's after midnight," he told her in case she didn't know.

Jill stood on tiptoes and whispered something into Nate's ear.

Nate kissed her cheek, sighed, and headed back the way he came, walking quietly down the stairs before disappearing into the night.

Jill turned toward him. Even in the dark he could see her eyes glowing like a wild beast in the night. "You just ruined my date," she said.

"According to Sandy, the two of you are just friends."

"God, she has a big mouth." She shuffled around inside her purse for her keys.

"Ryan and Lexi are asleep in my apartment. They're in Ryan's room."

"Where's Sandy?"

"I bribed her to leave Ryan with me. If you're going to get angry with anyone, it should be at me."

"Okay, I'm mad at you then. You have no right to just pop in whenever you feel like it and take my son. I don't like that."

"It won't happen again."

She crossed the hall and walked toward him.

He was inside. She was outside. They stood there for a moment, face to face, nobody saying a word.

"What do you want, Derrick?"

He raised a hand to the doorframe. "I'll tell you what I don't want."

"I'm listening."

"Life has a way of passing you by if you don't take charge and make every moment count. I don't want my son to knock on my door eighteen years from now and ask me why the hell I didn't care enough to be a part of his life. I don't want my son to think his father didn't love him enough to fight for him. I don't want to fight you, Jill. I love you. I'm glad you're Ryan's mother. He's lucky to have you. Mostly, I don't want to go to court—I won't go to court—not because I don't want Ryan just as much as you do or because of the money or the time it would take, but because I love my family, you and Ryan included, and I don't want to see anybody get hurt."

"Haven't you talked to your family since you left the courtroom?"

"I haven't had time. I've been in New York interviewing for a job."

Her chin came up a notch. She ducked under his arm and made her way into his apartment. Without another word she began to gather Ryan's things.

He shut the door, locked it, and then watched her pack up to go. "Where have you been?" he asked.

She grabbed the diaper bag and shoved empty baby bottles, towelettes, and a pacifier inside. Leaving the diaper bag on the floor, she walked toward the coffee table. "What do you mean?"

"Your date. Where did you go?"

She picked up the bronzed figurine sitting in the middle of the table. It had a red bow on it. "What's this?"

"I knew you liked it when you spotted it at the art festival in town so I looked the woman up when I was in New York."

"You bought this for me?"

He nodded.

"You remembered the artist's name and then you went out of your way to find her?"

Judging by the serious expression on her face, he wasn't sure what the correct answer was, but he decided to just go with his instincts. "Yes."

She moved around the coffee table and marched toward him like a tiger newly escaped from the zoo. For every step he took backward, she took one forward until his back was against the wall. "Did you just say you loved me somewhere in that speech of yours?"

"I believe I did."

"Then why didn't you call me or come see me before you flew off to New York?"

"I needed to take care of a few things first. If I could do it all over again, I would have come to see you before I left. I'm a slow learner."

"You smell like ice cream and Ryan."

"Thanks."

It was silent again. Silence at a time like this made him nervous. "What do you want me to do, Jill? I want to make things right between us. I do love you. In fact, if you had come home a little earlier I was going to ask you to marry me. I was wearing a suit and tie, carrying red roses, the whole nine yards."

"I want a man who knows exactly what he wants. A man who walks into a room and can't stop himself from wrapping his arms around me and kissing me the moment he sees me. That's what I want. I want to be kissed for no reason at all." She poked a finger into his chest. "I deserve to be kissed."

"I know you do." He gently moved the hair out of her face so he could get a good long look at her. Her face was flushed, her eyes fiery, her movements restless.

"It's been too long since you held me in your arms."

"Much too long." His hand made a path over her shoulder and down her bare arm. He leaned forward and kissed her neck. "You're beautiful." He wasn't thinking or analyzing or planning. He was just doing. Her skin felt soft beneath his lips.

"I want to feel desired and loved and all those things a woman should feel," she said.

"I want you to feel that, too." His lips made a trail upward over her chin and to the side of her mouth. They had a lot to talk about. He should stop kissing her so they could discuss what happened. They should talk about Ryan's future and myriad other things, but he couldn't stop, wouldn't stop, didn't want to stop. The way she shivered in his arms made him crazy. The way her skin heated beneath his lips made him hunger for more.

"That feels nice," she said.

His mouth covered hers and he kissed her again, longer and deeper this time, the palm of his hand cupping the back of her head. Then he pulled away and looked into her eyes. "Do you love me, too, Jill?"

"You know I do."

"Are you going to answer my question?"

"We went to dinner at Yang Chow's, you know, the Chinese restaurant and then he was called into the hospital and I sat in the cafeteria until he was finished."

"Not that question, the other one."

"I don't know what you're talking about."

"The will you marry me question." He grabbed the black box from the kitchen counter and opened it.

"That's quite a ring."

"You're quite a woman. I would get down on one knee if I could."

"The whole bended knee thing is over-rated anyhow. You really want to get married?"

He slipped the ring on her finger before she could answer. "More than anything in the world, I want to marry you. Will you marry me?"

She looked at the ring for a long while, and then looked up into his eyes.

"It's too late now, Jill. The ring's on your finger."

She laughed.

He lifted her into his arms. She felt weightless. Even with his bad knee, he knew he could carry her for miles if he needed to, but he didn't carry her any further than his bedroom. After setting her on the mattress, he took his time removing her clothes, one piece at a time, until she had nothing else for him to take off, leaving only flawless milky skin surrounded by silky sheets and moonlight.

"I do love you," she said as she helped him pull his shirt off.

"I love you too. Only you. Nobody else."

"That's good to know."

He smiled at her as he discarded the rest of his clothes. He locked the door and then climbed onto the bed next to her and held her close. He needed Jill much more than she needed him, but he decided to save that small tidbit for later. No need to confess all at this very moment. He could wait until tomorrow to tell her he'd be lost without her. For right now, he decided, he was just going to enjoy the moment and relish in the feel of having her arms wrapped around him, knowing she loved him for who he was, hoping she would love him for years to come.

He and Jill and Ryan would go on many adventures together.

He needed to take Jill skinny-dipping before Ryan was old enough to know that his parents were up to no good. He would spend the rest of his life testing her recipes and learning to like chocolate soufflé.

Life couldn't get any sweeter than that.

EPILOGUE

Nine Months Later

Jill and Derrick could not have asked for a more beautiful day to get married.

The sun was out, the clouds were few, and although it was unusually warm for May, a nice breeze kept their guests from getting too warm. The pastoral setting of the Baylor Pony Farm provided a relaxed, carefree atmosphere. As Jill made her way up the grassy aisle wearing a to-the-knee strapless chiffon wedding dress, she held tight to Phil Baylor's arm. She was thankful to have him at her side, glad to know she could call him Dad. Her parents, devastated by Laura's decision to join a band, still blamed Jill and thus declined any and all invitations to attend. A quick glance at Phil before he handed her off to his son revealed misty eyes and features softened from decades of love.

She kissed his fatherly cheek and thanked him for everything. Then she turned to Derrick. Although it was not part of the plan and had not been rehearsed this way, he wrapped her in his arms and kissed her as his father took a seat next to his mother.

Before joining Sandy and Aaron, who stood waiting with the family priest beneath the vine-covered trellis, Derrick gazed into her eyes and said, "How is it that you look more beautiful every day?"

She answered with a smile and then cupped his face between her palms. "You didn't run away," she half teased. "Thank you for that."

"All of those ponies you see over there in the pasture couldn't have dragged me away."

She smiled. "No cold feet or wobbly knees?"

"My knee has never been better," he lied, since she'd already heard that he was icing his knee all morning. "How about you?" he asked. "Feeling jittery? Are you going to faint and make me carry you the rest of the way?"

"Could you two move it along?" Zoey shouted from one of many fold-out seats facing the trellis where they would say their vows.

"Let them do their thing," Jake said, trying to quiet his sister.

"Are you kidding me? We could be here all day."

"Just ignore them," Derrick told her. "I think we should take our time."

"Just to bother your siblings?"

"No. I think we should take our time so that I can savor every moment of this day. When you look around, what do you see, Jill?"

She looked toward the pasture where ponies grazed, to Hank who was not happy about being tied up for the day, and then to all the guests before her gaze settled on his. "I see love."

"What do you smell?"

She closed her eyes and breathed in. "I smell fresh hay and warm skies."

He took a whiff. "I smell ponies and I think Mom snuck some of her ham rolls onto the food tables."

Jill laughed, and he squeezed her hands, maybe because he was nervous, but she didn't think that was it. Derrick Baylor seemed to be truly relishing the moment.

"We can't hear you two!" Zoey said right before somebody muffled her.

Derrick's gaze never left hers and Jill had to pinch herself to make sure she wasn't dreaming. Her husband-to-be looked dashing in his fitted suit, although she knew he couldn't wait to get changed into something more comfortable. She was marrying the father of her son, the man she loved. It couldn't get any better than this. They would have the rest of their lives to live, love, and learn together while watching Ryan grow.

"Every day is going to be an adventure," he said. "Every night, too," he added with a wink.

She laughed again.

"I'm ready to do this," he said. "Are you?"

"I am."

They turned toward the trellis where Sandy, the maid of honor, stood on one side and Aaron, the best man, stood on the other. Ten minutes later, it was a done deal. The ceremony was short and sweet. Stepping away from tradition, they had written their own vows, both pledging to confide, trust, and love one another until the end of time.

They were officially married.

Derrick and Jill stood hand in hand on the grassy knoll at the Baylor Pony Farm and turned toward the crowd, which had grown to include most of Arcadia.

"Ladies and gentlemen," the priest said, "I present to you, Mr. and Mrs. Baylor."

Everyone stood and cheered while the newlyweds made their way down the aisle.

Jill let her gaze sweep across all of the familiar faces. She looked from Aaron and Maggie. They had married six months ago. They looked happy. Her gaze went from Helen and Phil Baylor, to each of Derrick's brothers and sisters. She felt blessed to be a part of the Baylor family.

Standing side by side, Jill and Derrick talked to the guests as everyone made their way to the area set up for refreshments. A dozen long tables were covered with an assortment of food. Helen Baylor was under strict orders to leave the cooking to everyone else. She was not allowed to set foot in the kitchen, mostly due to the fact that not one Baylor kid wanted to see ham rolls served on such a special day.

Outdoor games such as horseshoes and a bean bag toss had been set up for the kids. Music drifted from inside the barn as the band set up. The pond had been fully stocked and poles and bait were available for anyone interested in doing a little fishing.

A five-tiered cake that included all of Jill and Derrick's favorite flavors sat alone on a special table shaded from the sun. There was also a separate dessert table that would soon be covered with mini chocolate soufflés, carrot cake cupcakes with cream cheese frosting, and homemade vanilla ice cream.

Garrett and his wife, Kris, had kept a close eye on Bailey and Ryan during the ceremony. Bailey was standing in the playpen while Ryan was sitting up, mesmerized by Lexi, who was entertaining them both with a dancing Ken and Barbie.

After everyone congratulated them, Derrick was pulled away by a few of his brothers, leaving Sandy and Jill to themselves.

"I guess congratulations are in order since you can't back out now," Sandy teased.

They hugged and when Jill pulled away she asked, "Where's Connor?"

"I have no idea," Sandy said, her voice tinged with regret. "The last time I saw him was three days ago and I'm pretty sure I scared him off for good."

"He's not coming to his own brother's wedding?"

"Looks that way," Sandy said with a shrug of her shoulders, although Jill could tell she was hiding a mountain of pain behind the gesture.

"What did you do?"

"I made the mistake of telling him how I felt about him. I told him I loved him."

"Oh."

"It's better this way, you know, sooner rather than later," Sandy said, "especially since Lexi was growing attached."

Lexi wasn't the only one, Jill thought.

Jake's date dragged him over to where they stood and offered her hand to Jill. "Hi, my name is Candy. I'm with Jake." She glanced at Sandy and lifted her nose to the air, letting Sandy know that Jake was off limits.

"Nice to meet you," Jill said.

"The ceremony was cute," Candy went on. "I was just telling, Jakey-pooh, that I, personally, would rather have my wedding indoors." She used a hand to fan herself. "I tend to sweat when I get nervous and that could be a disaster, if you know what I mean."

Jill smiled politely while Jake's face turned crimson.

"If it gets any hotter, I'm going to have to strip down to my panties and bra."

"Please don't," Rachel said as she approached, saving them all from an awkward moment. "I have a bathing suit you can borrow."

"Oh, I don't know," Candy said as her eyes roamed over Rachel. "I'm not even a size two. I usually have to shop in the junior's department just to find something that will fit me."

They all looked at Candy's humongous breasts at the same time.

Candy laughed. "I know what you're thinking, but believe you me, these babies are the real deal."

They weren't thinking that at all. They were all wondering how a size two bathing suit would cover it all.

"Would you look at that," Rachel said, saving them all for the second time in less than a minute.

Everyone looked in the direction Rachel was pointing.

Connor had come after all. He looked dead set and determined to get something off of his chest as he looked about until his eyes fell on Sandy. It only took a few long strides to make his way to where they all stood.

"Hi Connor," Candy said, stepping in front of Sandy.

"Hi," he said without looking at her. He only had eyes for one woman. He stepped around Jake's date and handed Sandy the bouquet of red roses he was holding. "I was hoping we could talk."

"It's been three days. I left you two messages. You had your chance."

"I know. I'm sorry. I messed up." He raked a hand through his hair. "I'm an idiot."

"Maybe we should give you guys some alone time," Jill said.

"No," Sandy said. "Nobody move."

Rachel looked at Jill excitedly. Coming from such a large family, Derrick's sister was used to drama, and she was obviously happy to have a front row seat to whatever was about to go down.

Jill didn't like conflict, but she knew that if she took even one step away, her friendship with Sandy would be severely compromised.

Jake, on the other hand, couldn't care less and he walked off, leaving Candy to fend for herself.

"If you want to say something to me," Sandy told Connor, "you're going to have to say it right here in front of everyone."

"I guess I deserve this," Connor said.

Rachel nodded her whole-hearted agreement, while Sandy looked around as if she was bored stiff.

"Can you at least look at me?"

Sandy dragged her eyes upward to meet his, and Jill had to commend her friend's acting skills because she made it look like the worst kind of chore.

"I love you, too," Connor said the moment her eyes met his, which happened to be the same time Cliff and Brad joined their group.

Silence ensued. Even Candy was quiet.

"That's it?" Connor asked. "You have nothing to say?"

"Did he just say what I think he said?" Cliff asked nobody in particular.

"He just told her he loved her," Candy confirmed. "Why haven't you ever looked me in the eyes like that and said you love me?" Candy looked around for Jake and when she realized he was no longer standing nearby, she wandered off in search of him.

As Jill prayed that Sandy wouldn't completely ruin the moment since the man was obviously trying, she felt a hand settle on her shoulder. Jill looked up at Derrick, and despite the tension in the air, she smiled at him.

"What's going on?"

"Connor just told Sandy that he loved her."

Connor took Sandy's free hand in his. "Do you want me to leave?"

Sandy held his gaze, her eyes unblinking. "I want to know why you love me."

His brothers all groaned in unison.

"It's a perfectly reasonable question," Rachel chided.

Connor shifted his weight from one foot to the other and said, "I love your hair and the way it glistens in the sun."

His brothers all looked pleased by that answer.

Sandy frowned.

"What?" Connor asked. "Did I say something wrong?"

"It's not about the hair," Derrick said, hoping to save his brother a little time. "It's about what you're feeling in here." He laid a hand on his chest, over his heart, making Jill love him a little more.

Phil and Helen Baylor were approaching, with half the neighborhood following in their tracks.

"When you step out of the shower," Connor tried again, "and your hair is a mess and you're in a hurry to get somewhere, you make this cute little scowling face and—"

He stopped in mid-sentence when he saw Brad make a slicing motion through his throat.

"Scratch that," Connor said. "When I'm late and you've been waiting for me, your brow puckers just so and—"

More slicing of the throat gestures from the ever-growing crowd.

"Oh, for God's sake," Connor said, clearly frustrated. "I just love you. I like every single one of those silly faces you make when I do something wrong, which I'm realizing is more often than I first realized. Clearly, I don't deserve you. I'm moody and quiet more often than not and yet you never make me feel guilty or less than adequate. You show me nothing but love in everything you do. Go ahead and shoot me down for saying it, but I love your hair: the color, the shine, the way it feels sliding through my fingers. I don't care if that's not something I should tell you. I love the way your eyes light up when I walk into a room, except for today. Today your eyes didn't light up and that makes me sad. When you're annoyed with me and you tap your fingers and make galloping noises, yes, well, I think that's cute. I also like your constant jabber."

That particular statement caused all sorts of mutterings and grumbles, but Connor wasn't paying attention to anyone but Sandy. "I love how you can ignore all of these people staring at us, listening to every word, not because they love me and care about how all of this turns out, but because they are the most meddlesome group of people in the world. Despite the fact that I'm related to many of these people, you still love me - at least you did three days ago - and I can only hope that you will continue to love me because over the past few days, I've been the loneliest, most cantankerous son-of-a-bitch and I can say with absolute sincerity that those three days without you were hell on earth. I want heaven, not hell. I want you, Sandy." He pulled a ring from his pocket and dropped to one knee.

The mob roared with delight, causing Jill to sigh with relief. This was no longer a day about joining Derrick and herself in matrimony, but instead, a day of forgiveness, a day of joy and celebration, a day where everybody and anybody was welcomed to the Baylor farm with open arms.

"Will you marry me?" Connor asked Sandy.

Tears swept down Sandy's cheeks and over her chin, making it impossible for her to find her voice.

"Yes!" Lexi shouted as she ran into Connor's arms, making him drop the ring and causing at least a dozen people to fall to the ground to look for the diamond.

"I LOVE you!" Lexi shouted into Connor's ear. "We will marry you." Lexi looked up at Sandy. "We love him, right, Mom?"

"We do," Sandy said, her voice squeaking with happiness.

"Did you hear that?" Jake asked excitedly from the back of the crowd. "Lexi said LOVE, not WUV!"

For the next few minutes half of the crowd hugged Lexi and made a big to-do over her newfound ability to pronounce the letter L, while the other half continued to scour the lawn for the lost ring.

"Here it is! I found it!" Phil Baylor said, handing the ring to his son.

As Connor slid the ring onto Sandy's finger, one long ponderous sigh of content erupted from the Baylor farm.

"Oh, no!" Derrick cried out.

Everybody's eyes were on the groom as he cut through the crowd and ran after Hank. He almost caught up to the dog, too.

Close but no cigar.

Hank had a sweet tooth and he was on a mission. In one perfect leap, he landed on the table holding the cake that Jill had spent weeks planning and preparing and all day yesterday baking. Derrick had been subjected to dozens of taste tests, and he had watched her closely as she made crystallized edible flowers for the top tier that he knew would be savored on their one-year anniversary, along with the memories of their special day.

Hank was fast and he was hungry, though, and he had a quarter of the bottom layer eaten by the time Derrick caught up to him. Instead of removing the dog, Derrick grabbed the top layer and held it over his head for protection, his eyes beaming with pride that he'd saved the best part.

That one small action might not have meant anything to anyone else, but it meant the world to Jill. His knee had been acting up all week, but Derrick had just run across the yard as if he was a gazelle, as if his life depended on saving the top layer of their wedding cake because he knew it had been made with love for just the two of them.

She loved Derrick Baylor. She loved him more than mere words could ever express.

And if there was one thing she knew in that moment, it was that sometimes actions really did speak louder than words.

♥♥♥

Thank you for reading *Having My Baby!* I grew up with a large family…all sisters, but we always wanted a brother. That's why I love writing about the Baylor family with all of those boys. But the family just wasn't complete without a few sisters to spice things up. I plan to continue writing more books about the Baylor family, so stay tuned.

If you enjoyed the story, I would love it if you would help others enjoy this book, too.

Lend it.

Recommend it to friends, readers' groups and discussion boards.

Review it. Please tell other readers why you liked this book by reviewing it at Amazon or Goodreads.

I also love hearing from readers @ theresaragan@gmail.com or visit my website at http://www.theresaragan.com

~Theresa

OTHER BOOKS BY THERESA RAGAN
TAMING MAD MAX
FINDING KATE HUNTLEY
RETURN OF THE ROSE
A KNIGHT IN CENTRAL PARK

THRILLERS BY T.R. RAGAN
ABDUCTED
DEAD WEIGHT

ABOUT THE AUTHOR

After reading my first romance novel in 1992, I knew what I wanted to do with the rest of my life…write novels…fun, quirky novels that would provide busy women around the world a few hours of entertainment. I knew I was truly a writer when I was working full-time while raising four children and nothing could stop me from getting the words to the page.

Made in the USA
Charleston, SC
13 July 2012